The Boat People

BY

Shiv Sharma

Published by New Generation Publishing in 2020

Copyright © Shiv Sharma 2020

First Edition

The author asserts the moral right under the Copyright, Designs and Patents Act 1988 to be identified as the author of this work.

All Rights reserved. No part of this publication may be reproduced, stored in a retrieval system or transmitted, in any form or by any means without the prior consent of the author, nor be otherwise circulated in any form of binding or cover other than that which it is published and without a similar condition being imposed on the subsequent purchaser.

ISBN
    Paperback   978-1-80031-716-1
    Hardback   978-1-80031-715-4

www.newgeneration-publishing.com

 New Generation Publishing

For my son Sachin

My grateful thanks to Ingrid Cranfield, Melanie Fasciato and Elaine Bishop

Change doth unknit the tranquil strength of men

Mathew Arnold

Chapter 1

JAGGI smiled. Jaggi always smiled.

The telephone rang off the kitchen wall in a soft, subdued tone, like the melodious strain of a songbird on an early spring morning. For a moment he just stared at it with a curious frown on his forehead, as if calling for attention was not one of its mechanical functions. After three or four more rings, wearily, almost reluctantly, he picked up the receiver. It seemed as if he had a premonition that the call was not bearing happy tidings.

Covering his mouth, Jaggi cleared his throat discreetly and spoke into the mouthpiece in a tone that was barely above a whisper, although he knew that he was alone in the house and therefore there was no danger of being overheard by any inquisitive ear.

'Hello,' said Jaggi, pleasantly into the mouthpiece.

'Oh, hi, Jaggi, it's Larry here,' said the voice, quite cheerfully, at the other end.

'Larry who?' Jaggi inquired, his voice going up a notch and trying to sound different and unsure. It used to be a wind-up among friends at the time in parts of the North-West.

'Larry, y' know. Larry Upton.'

'Larry Upton? Sorry, never heard of anybody by that name,' he said, a little dismissively.

'Oh, is that really so?' said the caller.

'Yeah, I'm really sorry I've no idea who he is or what he does or looks like,' insisted Jaggi.

'Hey, c'mon now, Jaggi, don't be like that,' pleaded the caller.

'You're not, by any chance, a salesman trying to sell me double glazing or a new kitchen at a discounted price at this late hour because you have failed to meet your sales target for today ... or anything like that, are you?' There was a peculiar relief in Jaggi's voice, though, because he knew precisely who had his ear.

'Jaggi, I thought you were good at remembering names ... had the memory of an elephant.'

'Sorry, never heard of elephants either,' Jaggi carried on. 'Are they animals of some sort? Don't know which continent they live in or how many you can squeeze into a Mini.'

A longish pause ensued. Cheerful silence on both sides. It was a game they had frequently played with each other and with other friends in the past, sometimes pretending to be an attendant in a Chinese laundry or Turkish takeaway. Each waited expectantly for the other to break the ice and take the conversation beyond the joke stage to a normal, friendly level.

Finally, with an enormous squeal of delight, Jaggi brought the whole episode to a close and bellowed into the mouthpiece, 'A big bloody hello to you, you, old rogue. Where have you been keeping yourself all this time, you ....? You know, I had almost given up on you. Thought you had migrated and it was the end of a beautiful friendship.'

'Oh, no.'

'Anyway, so pleased to hear from you. Just to let you know, I haven't had an intelligent conversation with anyone for weeks and months now... except the odd piece of soliloquy in front of the bathroom mirror.'

'Well, you can add my name to the list now,' chortled Larry. 'Anyway, how are you keeping, man?'

'Fine, just fine. And you?'

'Same here, matey,' offered Larry, in a happy, cheery tone now.

'Good, good. A real pleasure to hear your voice again. I trust the world has been treating you well?'

'The world, Jaggi, keeps going round and round in circles and like an idiot I keep going round and round in circles with it.'

'And which watering hole have the round trips taken you to on a cold and frosty evening like this?' inquired Jaggi, smilingly.

'Only to my local, the Dog and Duck, y'know. Where else do you think, at this late hour on a freezing evening like this?'

'Where else, indeed. I should've guessed. No need to ask, I suppose, what you're doing there, now is there?' said Jaggi, with a knowing tone of voice.

'Not really,' came the short answer.

'Now before you get into a spirited defence of your pub soiree with a pint of beer in each hand as your balanced diet, take a deep breath and listen to what I have to say, are you coming over when they throw you out after closing time?'

'The reply to your simple question in one word is no. Can't, sorry. Some other time, maybe. At the moment I've got company.'

'Well, be a good egg and bring the company with you. The more the merrier, as they say. You know our front door is always open to you and those who keep your company.'

'I know, I know, man,' said Larry.

'Not only are our doors open twenty-four hours a day but also our hearts. What's her name? And what she's like? Good-looking, nicely turned out, eh, you inveterate reprobate? Tell me everything, from alpha to omega, if she's not tightly squeezed in the phone booth with you at the moment. Quick now ... the whole truth.'

'Never mind what she looks like. The reason I'm phoning you at this late hour is . . .'

'Forget the wallet at home again, did you? How much do you need, ten or twenty?' cut in Jaggi, humorously. 'And, another thing, cousin, since when have you started buying rounds?'

'No, no, you daft thing, I'm not trying to tap you up for money or anything of that kind. Listen, I know you've gone off newspapers for quite sometime now. You do not buy them and you do not read them. But did you, by any chance, see last Tuesday's *Guardian*? Business pages, I think. Don't know the page number.'

'What sort of a question is that? If I don't buy newspapers and I don't read them. Also, I don't borrow them from strangers. No, I didn't see it whatever page number it was on. Why, you think I should have?'

'You see, there was an advertisement in it from some Indian big-shot businessman,' explained Larry. 'He seems to have done well, and I mean really well, since coming to this country.'

'Well, if Mr Moneybags has already raked in a fortune and is sitting comfortably on his untold wealth with a huge smile on his face that's fine by me. Okay by you, too, I take it, knowing your feelings in these matters. It's his millions and he can do what he likes with them. If he wants to give part of his loot to charitable causes over here in this country that's equally welcome. A hefty pat on the back for his generosity. On the other hand, if he wants to warehouse his loot in some offshore tax haven that's also okay. Millions of those loaded do it, why not him? Wish him luck from me. Also, the best of British in his future business ventures. And, yes, another thing, Larry, make sure my good wishes are conveyed to him on a Harrods card. I believe that the super-rich, at times, can be a little sensitive about these things.'

'Ha! Ha! Ha! Very funny. It's not that, you silly. The big shot doesn't want your good wishes or your compliments.'

'What then? Is he stuck for ideas on how to spend his gotten gains? Listen, how can a poor wage-slave like me help someone already rolling in millions? asked Jaggi, rather wearily.

'Of course not, you silly. Neither does he want begging letters with heart-wrench, lump-in-the-throat stories.'

'Well, in that case, what can I do for someone who has more money than he knows what to do with? Frankly, off-hand I can't think of anything.'

'Listen to this, Jaggi: in order to celebrate his success, he is planning a celebration for all those who travelled with him on the boat from India to this country way back in the sixties,' Larry said, in a smiling voice.

'Ah, so a jolly bash, a grand do, is that what he has in mind? Well, well, well, why didn't you tell me this earlier?'

'What's the difference, I'm telling you now, a minute or two later.'

'Go on then, shine a bigger light on the subject,' relief was in Jaggi's tone. 'I'm all ears.'

'For the party, he wants to invite all the Indians who were with him on the ship. He would like them to get in touch with him as soon as poss. You get the picture now?'

'Clear as the day. A reunion of some kind.'

'You know ... a sort of class of 1963 or 1966. That sort of thing. And it includes you if you were there on the boat with him,' Larry went on to elaborate.

'I see. Now that puts a new slant on the subject, doesn't it? Makes it a different board game.'

'Good.'

'Well, if he's planning a shindig then I am sure I can definitely be useful to him. No shortage of ideas in that department. Plenty in store and fresh stocks arriving every day.'

'I would've thought so,' a small laugh from Larry.

'You wouldn't know his name, by any chance, not that it matters an awful lot?'

'I'm afraid not,' Larry replied.

'Or the date he arrived in this country? After all, thousands of people must have come here from India by boat in the sixties. That's the time they were heading West in significant numbers.'

'I don't think these things are mentioned in the newspaper ad,' answered Larry.

'They must be, otherwise who his target audience are?'

'I don't know. I just threw a quick glance at it and thought it might be of interest to you. That's all. But I suppose you're right.'

'You got the ad to hand, Lawrence?' demanded Jaggi.

'Course, I have. Cut it out and saved it for you. Unfolded.'

'What a gent you are! Of the highest order, I should say. A scholar and gentleman, twice over. You get five gold stars from me for that.'

'But, I'm afraid, can't read it out to you because I haven't got it on me at the moment,' Larry sounded truly apologetic.

'It doesn't matter as long as you've got it somewhere safe, folded, unfolded or framed.'

'Honestly, Jaggi, the things I do for you.'

'Don't I know it, matey? But then, tell me, what are friends for, eh?'

'Listen, shall I bung it in the post or do you want me to deliver it in person at your residence?' inquired Larry.

'Suit yourself, old bean, whichever is convenient to you. You know the place and you know the people. And, as I said earlier, for you our doors are open twenty-four seven.'

'Oh, I know. You don't have to tell me that.'

'Look, it's been a long time since I raised a glass or two to your health.'

'And I toasted yours.'

'So how about a drink ? Or two … or three? I think home would be an ideal place. Next Thursday suits you?'

'Let me see, next Thursday?'

'Evening, of course.'

'Or Friday if that's more convenient?'

'Sunny boy, nowadays I am at home most days of the week after work, of course, Thursday or Friday it's all the same here,' Jaggi went on to explain. 'So come over whenever you like. Just suit your convenience. Tell you what, it'll be really great to see you. Gosh, it's been a long time since we raised a glass or two to sobriety, hasn't it?'

'Okay, if there's serious imbibing involved, Friday would no doubt be better. No getting up early the next day, you see.'

'Good. Good.'

'So, it's settled then?'

'Well, yeah.'

'And what balm do you take these days to soothe your throat?' inquired Jaggi. 'Our establishment is licensed to serve anything hard, medium or soft, plus a range of in-betweeners – from lager to latte.'

'Oh, nothing special,' answered Larry. 'You know, I'm a man of simple tastes. Something long, cold and wet.'

'Specially wet.'

'Absolutely.'

'Does Bloody Mary with real blood fall in that category?' asked Jaggi, laughing out loud.

'Oh, Jaggi, me ol' mate, just stick a few cans in the fridge, though, as I often say, a beer in hand is better than two in the fridge.'

'About eight, then?'

'Cans?'

'No, the time, you old rogue.'

'Eight o'clock with a few minutes' margin on either side. Listen, shall we say eightish?'

'Eightish, we shall certainly say. In the mean time don't do anything I wouldn't do.'

'Which, in other words, leaves me free to do just about anything. Umm ... well, almost.'

'Indeed, indeed.'

'See you Friday then, Jaggi.'

'See you Friday. Cheery byeeeee.'

'Keep smiling.'

'I will. I will ... as long as they don't put VAT on it.'

Until three years ago they were colleagues, Larry and Jaggi. But for the nine years they worked together as part of a team of scientists, Jaggi as analytical chemist and Larry as formulation chemist, the friendship went well beyond the workplace and spilled into personal lives. They were close confidants and shared each other's secrets, not that there were many to reveal or keep. They were what Jaggi often described to Larry as *"hum piala, hum nivala"* – something along the lines of classmates and glassmates.

Occasionally, when they were together having a pint at one of the real-ale watering holes to "loosen the knots" after a hard day at work, or on Saturday evenings just to make good old-fashioned merry, Larry had heard Jaggi recall, not without a touch of nostalgia, the sea journey he had made from Bombay to Britain in the sixties. So, thought Larry, it was well within the realm of possibility that Jaggi and the Indian big-shot that had put in the advertisement in the newspaper were on the same boat. After all, strange things are known to happen at sea!

He was also aware that Jaggi had begun to show unmistakable symptoms of world-weariness. For example, he had all but given up reading newspapers. That being the case, the chances that he might have known about the celebration that the Indian businessman was planning to hold were between minuscule and non-existent.

So Larry had cut out the advert and saved it for the friend with a genially smiling face.

Smiling was not something for which Jaggi had attended evening classes at the local poly, or taken private lessons. Nor was it a habit he had acquired from self-help books over time and honed into an art form. Good times or bad, flushed or broke, high or down in the dumps, smiling was completely natural to him. He was, you could say, a natural born smiler.

People, we are led to believe, cry at least twice in their lifetime: one, when they make their grand entrance into this world and again as they bid their final farewell to it. But in Jaggi's case, it was difficult – well nigh impossible – to imagine him announcing his arrival kicking and screaming. You bet he wore an enormous smile on his face, genuinely, charmingly and quite disarmingly as he drew his first breath.

It was, in many ways, quite remarkable that he smiled at all, because life had not exactly given him heaps of reasons to put a grin on his face. A marriage to an Englishwoman floundering without hope, the tragic death of their daughter – the only outcome of that union – swept away by an avalanche during a mountain trekking holiday in Nepal along with two of her friends from university, a career that had reached a dead end: these were what he could count among the major landmarks of his life. Hardly the stuff dreams are made of.

Now, at 56 – although his trim, youthful appearance, a mop of dark hair and handsome looks made him look like he had reached middle-age without aging – when most men in his age bracket harbour dreams of settling in climes of sunshine, white beaches and swaying palms and enjoy beach parties, barbecues and do bird-watching, Jaggi, uncomplicated, good-natured and easy-going, was stuck in a cul-de-sac on the road to nowhere, facing serious threats of being thrown on to the jobless scrapheap from his position as a chemist in a chemical plant with little or no prospect of ever finding work again in his field.

This was despite the fact that he had buried his head in books for years, got himself a degree, invested a lot of time and effort on honing his skills and assiduously kept up with the technological advancements in his speciality. On top of that, he had read endless scholarly papers, attended as many conferences and seminars as his work commitments would permit him and had been ultra conscientious whenever and wherever he was employed. In spite of all these feathers in his cap a dark cloud hung over his pension provision and his flaky nest-egg was barely large enough for a few fish and chips suppers.

But the charms of his personality, his fading handsomeness, his core stability and eloquent calm suggested that he had discovered the secret of happiness and hidden it away in a private chamber of his mind. Now he was perfectly at ease with himself, secure in the knowledge that he and he alone possessed it and nobody could take it away from him or even steal a peek at it.

There was something serenely enigmatic about him: kind eyes, pleasing manner, easy grin and a relaxed certainty. Those who knew him found these qualities very reassuring. The overwhelming impression he conveyed was that, a long while ago, the world had made a secret confession to him about some dreadful dark deed it had committed. With great professionalism, he had taken the confessional and put it away in some secret corner of his soul. Now he wanted to show through his demeanour and inner stillness that the secret was perfectly safe with him. He had not divulged it to anyone in the past and had no intention of doing so any time in the future.

Yet, in reality, his relationship with the wider world was just the opposite. He was beginning to feel disconnected with it and ceased to participate in its daily goings-on. He had become a disinterested bystander, a silent, back-row spectator on one side of a giant glass wall, unaffected by the mad happenings on the other side.

Jaggi leaned against the kitchen wall of his home in Heaton Moor, an old, established suburb of Stockport, and peered reflectively at the enormous antique table, which was the pride and joy of the kitchen but groaned under the weight of a million objects on it.

Although the table had not been cleared for quite a while, it still had enough room for him to have his breakfast at it in the morning, lunch at midday, tea in the afternoon, a couple of drinks after sunset and a light supper at night and then put his feet up without shifting a single object of crockery or cutlery from it

And that wasn't the end of the story. The table was a semi-permanent home to several other items – china mugs, coffee beakers, a wicker fruit basket, an aging word processor, letters received and awaiting dispatch, a handful of bank statements, supermarket receipts, small notepads and pencils, postage stamps of first and second class denominations, loose change – enough to fill a supermarket trolley – an assortment of magazines and journals, books, a couple of them open, and various other bits and pieces. Covered by a huge umbrella, it could easily have passed for a stall at a jumble sale.

The amiable disorder of the table was an important part of Jaggi's mindset. He often felt a tinge of sympathy with the poor table, burdened with so much – a sort of wooden Atlas borne down by the immense weight of the world on its shoulders. But for him the clutter did not matter at all as long as it added to the cosiness of the place. His belief was: dust I can't bear, disorder I cannot do without.

Of course the huge table was the idea of his wife Barbara. When it first arrived in the house, Jaggi greeted it with reservation. But slowly as time wore on it found a place in his affection and he began to like it. Barbara was always keen to have a large live-in kitchen. But she also wanted its appeal to be tasteful and personal.

Equipped with an Aga cooker, which kept the place cosy day and night, but especially when she got back home in the evening from the school where she was an arts teacher, it wasn't taken from any television model fitted with all sorts of gadgets and gismos, intended to keep her hands soft and smooth. An artist at heart, she had loftier ideas on her mind.

A hoarder by habit, she hung on to everything that had something memorable about it. Here in the kitchen, every pot and pan and piece of cutlery or china, whether new or going back years and familiar and belonging to her ancestral past, was dear to her and she treated it as valuable. Elsewhere in the house, many items of furniture were a reminder of her childhood.

A real cook's kitchen, it was often fragrant with the delicate aromas of faintly scented candles, herbal floor polish and seasonal fruit and vegetables that were grown organically on farms near by and sold in local corner shops. Anything that came in a tin seldom reached the couple's cooking pans. In the storage units below the sink, there were no chemical cocktails of cleaning products in plastic bottles or air fresheners in aerosol cans.

The well-appointed kitchen also had yards and yards of shelves to store some of the hundreds of books and scores of used sketchpads that Barbara kept adding to her collection. They dealt with an extraordinary range of subjects, mostly art. Passionate about literature, languages, words and their origin, words that had changed their original meanings, she had read most of the books, re-read a few and as for the rest, she simply couldn't bring herself to consign them to the baskets destined for charity shops.

The kitchen was well thought out, planned and put together over years and she was rightfully proud of it. It even boasted a fireplace with a mantelpiece and a large mirror in antique frame hanging over it. The place was in every sense a sanctuary within a sanctuary, a great hideaway from the everyday cares of the world.

For both of them in the morning, it was straight to the kitchen for a hurried, on-the-hoof breakfast. And Barbara, never the one to pass an opportunity to get some fun out of simple, everyday things had become quite a dab hand at catching a toast popping out of the toaster, often successfully grabbing two in both hands. 'Timing is the key,' she would say with a triumphant smile to anyone present in the kitchen and watching her act – occasionally to herself if she was alone.

After the couple had bolted down the breakfast, they planted a kiss on each other's cheek and went their separate way. Jaggi drove to his chemical factory, while Barbara, books in one hand and a large handbag containing a million things slung over her shoulder, made her way to school in her car, normally arriving a few minutes earlier to prepare for the day ahead. This routine included doing display work or dispensing instructions to the art technician or, maybe, attending a staff briefing.

In the evening the pair dived straight back into the welcoming warmth of the kitchen in the large

Victorian terraced house. Here they found joy in the little things of their daily life, preparing the dinner, setting the table, sorting out the drinks. While she washed the plates under the tap and placed them on the drainer, he dried them and put them away. Sometimes, just to change the routine, they would switch roles. As all this went on, they recounted their main happenings of the day to each other, chatting about this and that and every other thing.

They used the kitchen as a living room and spent big chunks of their time there when they were at home. It was also here in the kitchen that they did the entertaining, engaged each other intellectually – both had a good ear for language – generated new ideas about their life and took decisions on matters of importance and those of little significance. They learned new things, tried new things, did new things. In their conversations, there was plenty of laughter, often loud and prolonged, and occasionally until they were gasping for breath. Frequently, they drank wine – he chose red or his favourite scotch, while her favourite was white wine.

If the mood took them, they made love in the caressing warmth of the Aga.

The friends and well-wishers, who came to see them – Larry was among the frequent visitors – often had the feeling that they were in a loving and giving environment. In fact, a number of them had affectionately dubbed it "The Temple of Domesticity." Jaggi had used the description a couple of times and it stuck. It was a house you could walk into any time of night or day without any prior warning and be greeted with cheerful smiles and warm hospitality.

'There's no place like this place,' Jaggi often used to say to Barbara with gesturing hands – and she, in turn, to him.

It was not just newspapers that Jaggi had severed his links with. He rarely listened to the news on the radio and very seldom watched it on television. In fact, he hardly set his eyes on the box and when he did, the viewing was pretty much restricted to documentaries and old, black-and-white film classics.

He took television as no more than an uninvited guest sitting in one corner of the lounge. It was up to him whether to entertain the guest, give him his own time. In an age when life was fast becoming a made-for-TV B-movie and showbiz values were being increasingly imposed on nearly all aspects of life, Jaggi steadfastly refused to be reduced to nothingness.

He did not want to have a tabloid outlook on life, interested only in what the ears heard or the eyes saw – brash front pages, blow-ups of celebrities with synthetic, pasted-on smiles, in-the-face rock stars, grossly overpaid footballers and glamorised women, advertisement billboards, flyers, printed shopping bags, brand logos and their catchlines and other sneaky marketing tricks by big business to scrawl its name on the wall of your mind.

He refused his life to be swallowed up by nothingness by surrendering it to the screaming symbols of hype, wealth, success, power and influence. At times, he seriously wondered why and how it had become accepted practice to associate the word "culture" with blights like drugs, crime and anti-social behaviour. He did not want his life to be turned into a stage show in which others played out their pitiful roles.

He wanted to live at a different level, mentally, emotionally and spiritually. He wanted to think on another plane, be in touch with himself, with his thoughts and feelings. He wanted to be aware of the world he inhabited, retain his keenness and sensitivity to everything that happened around him and his mind registered. He wanted to live a life that had meaning ... experience things for himself and reason them out.

The slow poison of repetition, as he saw it, changed people in ways they did not realise. It blunted every human edge and, in time, rendered it insensitive. When you saw images of unspeakable savagery and scenes of slaughter and suffering or heard soul-scarring tales for the first time it made you feel as if you had been hit in the guts by a horrific punch ... or at least they pin-pricked your conscience. This made you sit up and think. Maybe you waved an angry fist in the air or shouted loudly to express your feeling, but when it was repeated time after time, passive acceptance set in and it all became routine and you got used to it. Repetition, he believed, acted as an anaesthetic on your sensibilities, numbing the edges at first and then spreading to the core, until you lost your capacity to be shocked and the unacceptable was acceptable.

Jaggi did not want this to happen to him. He wanted to keep very much intact his capacity for feeling. If anything, sharpen it further.

He saw no need to upload on his mind failings that were not of his own making. He often recalled how, going to work one dark December morning following a night of heavy downpour, thunder and lightning, he had tuned in to the local radio on his car radio to get an update on the weather and road conditions, only to discover that the entire news bulletin was taken up by two street shootings by warring gangs, a mugging of an elderly woman for a few pennies, a case of arson, another of rape of a teenage girl in a nightclub toilet, and the sexual abuse of a six-year-old child.

He had multiplied the total of these incidents by forty, which he believed was the number of local radio stations in the country and arrived at a figure that was mind-numbing and gut-churning enough to make a motorist with a modicum of sensitivity in their disposition to ram their vehicle into the nearest stonewall.

It was on that morning that he had decided that if this was what they meant by in-car entertainment then that entertainment was not for him. No, definitely not. Why become a part of all that tat when there were millions of other and more interesting things in the world?

From that day on, his entertainment in car came from tapes of Vivaldi's Four Seasons, Mahler's Resurrection Symphony, Ravel's Bolero, folk music, gypsy music and ragas by Ravi Shankar on sitar and Ali Akbar Khan on sarod. Also taking their rightful place alongside these maestros were Bismillah's shenai, Shiv Kumar Sharma's santoor and Hari Prasad Chaurasya's flute.

Between his home in Parsonage Road and his workplace about nine miles away, there were eight traffic lights, two bridges and one aqueduct. To create his own entertainment, he had given each of them an identity, a name.

The first two lights were Caroline and Cornelia. The third, which, for some inexplicable reason, he often found on red as he approached it, he called Natasha. Then there were Claire and Victoria. The sixth, close to a sari shop with the picture of an Indian woman with hand joined together in greeting and sporting a huge vermillion bindi in the middle of her forehead, had been given the name of Sunita, after a girl with a model's looks he knew during his college days in Delhi. Karen and Rosie were the remaining two.

He saluted them as they carried on endlessly their routine of guiding motorists. If, for one reason or another, the car music was not on, he spoke to them and gave them the time of day. When one of them was out of order for maintenance, repair or whatever else, he wished it speedy recovery and on the rare occasion they had fallen victim to mindless vandalism, he expressed his sympathy to them.

One bridge was called Vikram, the other Vincent. The aqueduct was Ol' Man River, and when it came into view, on days when the sky was clear and blue, the sun was gloriously bright and his spirits were on a high, he would croon a few notes from the song, in an imitation of Paul Robeson.

Chapter 2

Jaggi smiled. Jaggi always smiled.

He was swigging J&B scotch from a crystal tumbler while Larry, one of nature's disarmingly affable human being with a chubby, cheerful, pink-cheeked face, drank beer, straight from the can. About the same age as Jaggi but a little taller and a lot heavier in build, he had earlier swilled to his bladder's content from a pewter mug but was now past bothering to shift the contents of one to the other.

'Fancy some Bombay mix or other nuts and bolts to go with your detergent, esquire?' asked Jaggi, with a friendly smirk, thinking all that beer must have made his guest peckish for some refreshment by now.

'No, thank you. You know I don't eat anything on an empty stomach,' Larry replied with a chuckle and patted his tummy proudly.

'God Almighty, all that beer swishing around your belly and you say empty stomach,' Jaggi teased his friend.

'Liquid, my dear sir, liquid. There's a separate section for it in there,' he chortled as he again patted his tummy and picked up the can. Raising it a foot or so high, Larry said to his host, 'Cheers.'

'And to you,' responded Jaggi, raising his tumbler to a similar height in a toast, the seventh or eighth of the evening.

Jaggi called J&B "our own brand". It was the favourite tipple of both Barbara and Jaggi among spirits and they often bragged, in jest of course, that the brand had been named after them.

He held the tumbler against the light and revolved it in his hand, as though trying to figure out the feel-good composition of the light golden elixir. 'So you did come to Britain on the SS Roma?' asked Larry, his eyes pointing to the newspaper advertisement, which had changed hands two or three times and now lay in front of him on the kitchen table, face up.

'O aye, but only up to Genoa,' said Jaggi.

'And after that?'

'Nowhere, really. The journey came to an end there.'

'What about you and the rest of the passengers?'

'Me? Let me think for a moment now,' Jaggi scratched the back of his neck as if the answer lay there and he was trying to coax it out. 'I remember that from there we took a train for some place in France. Where, I can't remember. Paris perhaps, but I'm not one hundred per cent sure.'

'And?' Larry gave Jaggi a quizzical look.

'And then another train from France.'

'So in your case it was boats and trains and ...'

'No planes. Definitely not. Let's not forget that planes weren't that common back in those days. I'm talking history ... old history, my man. As for the train journeys, I'm quite clear, because our passports were checked twice. The first time it was an Italian. He was either the conductor nor an immigration official. Of that I'm sure. He gave each of us highly suspicious looks, a sort of mixture of hard stare and a crooked half-smile as though we were a bunch of naughty boys who were bunking school but, being a man of kind disposition, he was not going to report us to our parents or our headmaster. You know the sort that ...'

'I don't know the sort but I can well imagine,' chuckled Larry, miming a stare and a half-smile.

'The second time our passports were checked by a Frenchman. His every movement was precise and very businesslike. First he said something in French, naturally, and demanded to see our passports and then added *s'il vous plait*.'

'The train must've brought you to Calais. And then you crossed the Channel by ferry to Dover?' Larry attempted a guess.

'Yes, something like that.' Jaggi paused for a moment to give himself time to think and then added, 'God, I don't know, Larry, it was years and years ago … too far back in time. Quite honestly, it's no more than a dim, distant memory now.'

'It's only three or four decades, Jaggi,' Larry cried, incredibly. 'That's only half a lifetime ago, not full. I mean, come on. It's not Stone Age we're talking about here, for pity's sake.'

'Three decades is thirty years and four decades is forty years, my dear sir, as any good mathematician will tell you. That's a long time by anybody's standard. An awful lot of water has flowed under the bridge and through the drains in that time, wouldn't you say?' Again, Jaggi scratched the back of his neck. 'In actual fact, it was much longer than that, come to think of it. The memory … '

'I'm sure there's enough light in the attic to keep the memory going for another three or four decades. The bottom couldn't have dropped off the memory bin so early?'

'Oh, I don't know, Larry. The slow sweep of time takes its toll off every mortal. Besides, remembering things that happened a long time back in time is never easy. Time begins to play tricks after a while. It's years, decades back, man. The power of recall … you know what it's like?'

'Come, come now, Jaggi,' said Larry, waving a hand in the air to brush aside Jaggi's suggestion.

'We were coming to Britain with great expectations. But, of this I'm certain, I never came across anybody on the ocean liner who for a moment thought the streets where we were headed were paved with gold and the roads lined with Rolls and Jags.'

'Streets of England paved with gold? Ha! Don't make me laugh,' sniffed Larry with a throaty chuckle. 'They're not even paved with Wi-Fi.'

'We were all fairly level-headed, down-to-earth, pragmatic sort of people, with our feet firmly on the ground. Knew the score well.'

'I'm sure you did,' Larry nodded.

'Mostly young professionals, you know, an eclectic mix of doctors, dentists and accountants. A variety of engineers, electrical, mechanical. The rest of the cast was made of carpenters and factory workers. We were all setting out to give our lives a fresh start. Some in the professional category, it came to my notice during the voyage, were the first from their family to have obtained university degrees.'

'In other words, the brightest and the best,' said Larry and raised the beer can to his mouth.

'I'd like to think so, Larry. During the fortnight we were together on the boat well nigh every one came to know every one else other to this or that degree.'

'Naturally,' observed Larry, as he set the can down and dragged his chair a couple of feet closer to the Aga for warmth. 'No matter how large in size, a boat is only a boat at the end of the day. Especially in those days.'

'We were the sort of people that every country needs for its long-term prosperity, but, sadly, also the kind of people every country chooses to ignore when they're struggling to earn their corn in their down-at-heel corner of the world. But the minute they decide to up sticks and head for a shiny new life in the richer parts of the world, like the US, Europe and Australia, well, a whole dam-burst of condemnation follows. The moaners and groaners from all sides of the political divide are up in arms against them. They brand them greedy, money-grubbing, self-seeking so-and-sos and the popular press raises accusing fingers at them and hold them responsible for the nation's brain drain and talent exodus.'

'I know,' offered Larry, with a mild grin. 'I know exactly what you mean. That sort of thing happens here, too, from time to time. I'm sure you're familiar with that narrative.'

'Of course, I am,' Jaggi nodded to his guest and took a generous swallow of his drink. He continued, 'In ill-fitting clothes that appeared to have been stitched by upholsterers rather than tailors, most of us may have looked like close cousins of Lowry's matchstick men, but underneath, I tell you, there was no poverty of ambition. Oh no, sir. We had a clear vision for the future … sure of our direction. We were all wannabe somethings.'

'I'm sure,' said Larry, and repeated it, nodding all the time.

'I talked to a number of people on the steamer and the overwhelming impression I got was that we had to do well in the country we were headed for. That was the principal reason the ticket we carried in our pockets was one-way and not return. Successful we had to be, come what may. Failure wasn't an option.

Oh, no. There was no insurance against it and even if there were, we weren't going to make a claim tripping at the first hurdle. So, Larry, you can imagine the strength of our courage and determination. I'd like to think these were our strong points.

'And that, old pal, is what gives staying power to an immigrant community,' Larry gave an endorsement smile.

'To better ourselves we had taken the education route. Believe me, Larry, we were very positive and had a clear sense of purpose as to what we were going to do with our lives. Everyone on the ship, without exception, had the same streak running through them. Well, they openly said so.'

'You mean things like doing something, becoming someone?' inquired Larry.

'Exactly. That was the core. Hard work posed no problem. No problem at all. As India was only into the second decade of its independence, many of us also saw ourselves as representatives of our country, symbols of its aspirations. We were raring to go. All we needed was an opportunity and if it lay a thousands of miles away, we were ready to make the journey, sleeves fully rolled up.'

'And it's amazing what you can do if you try. It's this drive, this get-up-and-go that makes people leave their native soil in the first place.'

'I must admit there were a lot of things we had doubts about. But career was not one of them. On that there was complete single-mindedness of purpose. We were hardwired that way.'

'I'm sure.' Larry acquiesced.

'You see, we'd just come out of colleges and universities. Had all sorts of degrees and diplomas under our belts and yet our thirst for more was not fully quenched. We wanted to top up our Indian qualifications with doctorates and diplomas from universities in Britain ... you know, a sort of cream floating on top, if you like.'

'Whatever for?' demanded Larry, looking a trifle baffled.

'Elementary, my dear Holmes. Some of the degrees from Indian universities were not recognised in this country. So some of us needed to re-educate ourselves in our specialist subjects. Well, you know, that was the case, on paper at least. Get some sort of academic top-up from here to make our CV more attractive. And you know what?' Jaggi went quiet for a moment.

'What?' asked Larry.

'We took damn good care of our degree and diploma certificates. Treated them as our proudest possessions. In many ways, they still are. Wouldn't swap them for anything in the world. But, surprisingly, ever since I came here, no employer, not even a single one for god sake, has bothered to take a peek at them, let alone check them out.'

'Jaggi, my friend, you've got such a trusting personality,' said Larry, with a disarming smile. 'It's so easy to take your word at its face value.'

Jaggi made a delicate bow and smiled in acknowledgement. 'Awfully nice of you to say so. You can quote me as a referee when applying for a loan.'

'Don't tempt me, my friend. I may do just that. In fact, I was recently thinking of buying a brand new top-of-the-range Porsche.' Both laughed simultaneously.

'Going back to where we were, the feeling then was that we will spend some time in Britain, add to our academic qualifications and gain some work experience. Do a few things that we'd be proud to tell our grandchildren when we got to that stage. Many of us also had money on their mind. They wanted to make some before going back home on a high, covered in glory. Now for all that to happen, most of us had a time scale of four to five years on our minds.'

'Why not seven or nine?' asked Larry, out of curiosity.

'You see, Larry, the consensus was,' Jaggi went on to explain, 'that you needed that kind of time if you were working full-time and studying part-time, or studying full-time and working part-time.'

'I see. Makes sense,' Larry nodded, approvingly.

'See, the problem is if you leave it too late, life can slide into a pattern without you noticing it. And once that happens it becomes difficult to tear yourself out of the loop,' said Jaggi.

'Fair enough.'

'One clever chap on the boat summed it up this way: One year, not enough. Two years, fifty, fifty. Three years okay. Four or five years now or never. Six years, forget it.'

Larry gave an amused laugh.

'Hey Larry, you know something? On the ship with us was a darner. He was an expert in what he called *invisible mending* in carpet darning. Spoke no more than a few words of English but, like every Indian on the boat, he was seeking a new start in life. Surprisingly enough, he was the only one out of the whole lot of us who had a job already lined up with a top retailing company in London. Believe me, that man left us all gobsmacked when, ever so coolly, he wished us all good luck for the future and, moving with a bounce in his step, made his way to a spanking new Bentley his employers had sent to collect him from Victoria station.'

'He must have been darned good at his job,' Larry laughed.

'This, remember, was years and years ago, mid-sixties, and the first of the immigration laws had been passed here by parliament to stem the flow of unskilled labour from the sub-continent and elsewhere. So, you can well imagine, the vast majority coming in were professional people and, you know what professional people are like; mainly concerned about getting a job in whatever field they had trained in and getting on with that job. Hardly the marauding beasts of commerce with a calculator for a heart and cash-register eyes.'

'Mind you, Jaggi, who'd say no to making money if money was there to be made? Would you?'

'Oh, I don't know, Larry. I'm a Brahmin, born and raised as one, although by no means a practising one now,' Jaggi went on. 'Brahmins, as I'm sure you know, are top of the heap in the Indian caste system. Well, at any rate, in the eyes of those who believe in these things.'

'I see,' Larry nodded.

'Personally, I would like to think my upbringing was pretty secular. And Brahmins enjoy that exalted position not without reason. It is expected of them not to obsess over material possessions and concern themselves with the higher pursuits of life. You know, matters of the mind. Become priests, teachers and academics. Take up careers in arts, education, spirituality, sciences and so forth. They are not supposed to fritter away their time and energy on the shadow things of life.'

'I see. A million thanks, oh wise one, for that precious piece of information,' Larry gave Jaggi a big, papaya-slice smile. 'One learns something new every day. I never knew that. You didn't throw any light on this topic before. There're many things you haven't told me, you know.'

'Haven't I, really?' Jaggi looked surprised.

'For example, details of your boat trip are news to me. All I knew until eight o'clock this evening was that you came to this country on a ship and the voyage took you over a fortnight to get from there to here ... and that's about the size of it.'

'Oh, glad to have filled a hole in your knowledge pool tonight,' Jaggi said, somewhat grandly.

'Every scrap of information is important, old pal,' said Larry. 'Supposing one of these days some high-flying publisher approaches me and asks to write your biography, and offers a six-figure sum in advance payment, what then, hey?'

'You mean a literary version of my life? Don't hesitate for a moment ... not even a second,' Jaggi said, without a moment's hesitation. 'Get to him as fast as you can and sign the deal. A quick shake of his hand, grab the money and run. As fast as you can. You have my word that the fullest co-operation will be extended to you from the first draft to the final print.'

'Oh, you're such a generous fellow,' declared Larry, with a wink and jerk of the neck.

'Larry, you know when I was knee high to a grasshopper, interested only in spinning tops, flying kites and shooting catapults with my siblings and other whippersnappers in the neighbourhood, one thing was drilled into us by our elders. And it was: in education look up to those who have more and for money look down to those who have less. Although it was an article of faith in our family, to us youngsters it made little sense at that age because it was too highfalutin for our understanding. Still, we accepted it because it came from those we held in high regard and who, we thought, were much wiser than us. Secondly, I thought if it weren't true why would they tell us about it time and again? The exhortation got ingrained in my psyche and has been one of life's important guiding principles.'

'It's bound to be,' Larry said. 'And how utterly sensible your older folks were. Is it any wonder then that Indian children excel in their studies in this country? They're in a class of their own, if you ask me. Year after year, they routinely mop up loads of A-stars in GCSE and A-levels exams.'

'I don't know about children of Indian origin in Britain, Larry. I was talking about what went on in our family and that, too, in India of fifty years ago and not India of today.'

'I'm sure there are many Indian parents here who still try to inculcate that kind of values in their children.'

'I don't know. It isn't like it was then.'

'And here isn't like there,' put in Larry.

'Another thing they drilled into us until it was in our bloodstream was never hold a coin too close to the eye. For if we did that all we'd see would be the coin between our fingers. But if we hold it at a little distance, many other things also come into view.'

'That's good, eh! That really is good. And how very true,' Larry nodded, approvingly.

'These wise words were usually dispensed after the bedtime story and just before we closed our eyes.'

'So you could sleep on them?'

'Absolutely. So you see, having been brought up in that kind of environment, I've come to believe that the best things in life are not things. And here's something else, Larry, I'll tell you for nothing: money will buy you a bed, it can't buy you sleep.'

'Hey, what have you laced your drink with tonight? You're coming out with priceless gems of wisdom.'

'Priceless for others but for you, my dear sir, they're absolutely free of charge … and no VAT either.'

'Mind you, Jaggi, in my top ten values money comes at number eleven.' Larry threw back his head and gave a snort of laughter.

'So, you see, why waste your time, energy and effort on something that the poor don't have any and the rich can never have enough of. Let's face it, Larry, it's not the be-all and end-all of existence unless, of course, you choose to make it so. I must admit, though, there are people in this world for whom it's precisely that … the alpha and omega of life. Their money know-how is so good they can smell it a mile off even if they've got a stinging cold.'

'I know the sort who just can't say yes to money when it is going and no when it's coming. Tell you what, poor old Blighty may not be the land of opportunity it once might have been but fortunes are still being made here every day by those for whom money is the main driving force. Each year, hundreds of millionaires add their names to the UK's rich list and a cursory glance will tell you that not all of them are of the bulldog breed,' Larry said decisively.

Jaggi gave a lukewarm nod.

'In actual fact, the poor rich Brits in the list are there more as an exception than as a rule,' Larry added.

'True. As true as the Olympics have five rings and Audis have four,' Jaggi consented immediately. 'Don't forget, in the case of the people on the Italian steamer with me, we are looking at a journey that took place years and years ago, not last week, last month or last year. More than three decades, Larry, and that is, by any reckoning, a lot of water under the bridge. A whole ocean of it, if you ask me.'

'Oh, I couldn't agree more with you,' said Larry, and took a swallow of his drink. Then, slightly out of breath, added, 'In that period the world must have done what it normally does several times over.'

'Thirty-odd years ago, my dear Lawrence, pubs were pubs and not leisure centres, young men wore hats on their heads and not baseball caps back to front, pocket calculators were a status symbol, Brits drove British cars and curry was only a surname.'

'I know. I know,' Larry added, mimicking an old codger. 'I also know, me young lad, that in them days you got nought for nought but a bagful of everything for a pound.'

'The newspapers had only one section and they didn't drip with leaflets, flyers, catalogues, brochures, pamphlets and what have you.'

'Credit cards were nothing but little lumps of plastic and as far as global warming is concerned it wasn't even on the back burner and environmentalists were scratching their heads over what name to give it.'

'And the M1 was in a quarry?'

'I'm not so sure about the M1 but the M6 definitely was. Jaggi, in those days I had a name given fondly by my parents. Now I'm a computer number given by employers.'

'I bet you know your name, which was given to you years and years ago but can't remember the damned computer number you got when you joined the company not so long ago. Can you, honestly? asked Jaggi.

'You're absolutely right, me old mate. Anyway, who wants to remember a bloody number? Especially on a Friday evening, with drinks and scintillating company.'

'Another thing about those days, Larry,' Jaggi recalled with some relish, 'the airwaves buzzed with the sound of some of the finest music the human ear has had the fortune to hear in the twentieth century.'

'Oh, without a doubt,' nodded Larry. 'Those were the halcyon days of pop music.'

'Whenever you turned on the wireless, any time night or day, you were sure to be treated to the Beatles at their creative best or Stones, Bob Dylan, the Beach Boys, Joan Baez, Manfred Mann, The Seekers and many, many other musically gifted children of the flower generation.'

'Oh, the melodies linger on.' Larry closed his eyes, as if he was astride a big white charger and galloping through time in a landscape of pale, blue mist.

'Remember the beatniks with peace-sloganed T-shirts, flowers in their hair and love on their lips? And, yes, those beautiful, young things in mini skirts, wet-look shoes and black PVC macs?'

'Can I forget those beauties in a million years, even if I tried?' said Larry, rolling his eyes. 'Many of them are still engraved on my heart, just as they were at that time. Must be a Mother Goose now, each one of those young spring chicken of yesteryear, wrinkles in their cheeks where dimples once dwelt.'

Jaggi had a sardonic laugh and added, 'I had come to this country in the sixties and for me, Larry, that decade was special. It was full of first impressions. Each day had its significance. It's a kind of benchmark, if you like. Everything, no matter how trivial or insignificant, that the mind registered got embedded in the consciousness. Now, whenever I recall anything related to that period it is with extreme fondness ... with special affection. The sixties, ahhhhhhh.'

'And the seventies. They were decades like no other.'

'Want to play the sixties?' asked Jaggi.

Larry said nothing. Just scratched his head.

'Tell you what, let's play a few minutes,' begged Jaggi, be nostalgia freaks.

'Go on then ... but, as you said, only for a few minutes and no more, all right?'

'Twiggy,' began Jaggi, without any hesitation at all.

'Monty Python,' countered Larry.

'Common Market.'

'The Pill.'

'The World Cup.'

'Cathy Come Home.'

'Woodstock.'

'Round the Horne.'

'John Peel.'

'Paris student riots.'

'Lunar landing.'

'Dubcek's Prague spring.'

'Enoch Powell.'

'Chinese cultural revolution.'

'Michael Caine.'
'Cash machines.'
'Mississippi Freedom Summer.'
'Ceylon Tea Centre, on Oxford Road, remember?' said Larry.
'Of course, I do. My Lai massacre.'
'Wednesday Play.'
'Che Guevara.'
'Radio Caroline.'
'North Sea Gas.'
'UDI in Rhodesia,' Jaggi carried on.
'The Mini.'
'Sir Francis Chichester.'
'Procol Harum.'
'Inspector Clouseau.'
'Juke Box Jury'
'John Profumo.'
'Ban on hanging.'
'Spend, spend, spend.'
'Abervan disaster.'
'Cuban missile crisis.'
'Richard Dimbleby.'
'Siegfried Sassoon.'
'Stop. Stop. Don't' crank up the nostalgia any further.'
'Why? Giving in? Admit defeat?' asked Jaggi.
'Oh, please let's leave the past alone. End the peek-a-boo. No more flashbacks, please,' pleaded Larry, earnestly.
'Very well, we shall end it forthwith. Memory Lane is shut down to all through traffic for the rest of the night. Goodbye sixties, fare thee well and if forever …'

'No point getting tearfully nostalgic about those decades. Otherwise we'll waste our evening waxing lyrical about times past.'

'Nothing wrong with romanticising the good old days ... and the good old ways that went with them, is there, hey? Simple, harmless fun, don't you think? Oh come on, Larry, don't shake your head like that.'

'Nostalgia is a British disease. Very British disease,' explained Larry, turning a shade serious. 'We can't change a light bulb without getting nostalgic about gaslight and candles and ...'

'Oh, come now, Larry,' said Jaggi, this time he shook his head. 'Opening a small window on the past from time to time is also a way of testing your memory. Keeps it alert and ticking. Basically, it's no more than a pub quiz, if you ask me.'

'No, seriously, Jaggi, first we let new-fangled technology kill off things working in perfectly good order and then, when they are gone forever, we start pining for them ... weave a whole romantic web around them. Since when, old friend, have you developed a fascination for the past, eh?'

'Since I took up British citizenship,' replied Jaggi immediately, and smiled cheerfully into his whisky.

'Fair enough. That explains it. Be British then,' Larry smiled, faintly amused.

'Oh, I don't know, Larry . . .' Jaggi said with something of a sigh and an uncertain shake of the head.

'I do,' Larry nodded, and looked about the kitchen.

'Want something?' asked Jaggi.

'No, nothing really.' He picked up his beer can and took a generous pull at it. 'I'm more of a fan of the memories of the sixties than the sixties itself.'

'Happy and optimistic. We were different then,' Jaggi nodded his agreement. 'And so were the times. But you've got to admit, it was a very special period in our lives.'

'Without a doubt. Very special indeed. These days not even nostalgia is what it used to be.' Larry gave a small laugh.

'For me it was the music that said it all about the decade. It was so splendidly good. But sadly, Larry, as far as people are concerned, I was as bad a judge of them then as I'm now.'

A smirk appeared on Larry's face and he gave Jaggi a look of defiance. 'There's nothing wrong with your judgment about people, man, if you want to know my honest opinion. Nothing, whatsoever, I tell you.'

'Oh, thank you for that resounding endorsement. You are a star, one in a million in my book.'

'Look at me, Jaggi. Just take a bloody good look at me. I've been a friend of yours forever and a day, haven't I?'

'Of course you have. Still are. And a bloody good one at that,' Jaggi assured him, gesturing with a hand in admiration.

'And any person who, sound of mind and body, in full possession of their faculties, completely of his or her own free will, chooses me as a friend for that length of time without falling out once, not even once for god sake, can't be a swimmer at the shallow end of the gene pool. No way, old pal. No bloody way.' Larry shook his head a number of times.

'You are an exception to most rules, my dear sir. Always were and always will be. I can hold up my hand and tell the world that.' Jaggi looked about him.

'Thanks a lot for such a resounding vote of confidence ... I'll drink to that,' Larry raised his beer can to him and took an enormous, shuddering swallow.

Jaggi resumed, 'Now, if my memory serves me right – and memory can be a very tricky business – a total of one hundred and twenty eight Indians got on board the Italian ocean liner in Bombay. Yes, that's right. One hundred and twenty eight.'

'And you were one of them?'

'Sure thing, yours truly Jagmohan Bali was one of them, with two suitcases, one in each hand. Seven in the Indian contingent were women. Although free for the first time from family constraints and sailing freely on the ocean waves, they largely kept themselves to themselves. If they had a mild attack of daring, the seven mingled with each other. Not all seven at the same time, you understand. So, presuming the person behind the newspaper advertisement is a fellow, he could be any one of the one hundred and twenty one fellas. On the other hand, if it's a woman, then anyone of the seven.'

Jaggi's face was a picture of puzzlement as he juggled with possibilities in his mind over the identity of the advertiser.

'There was a serious sort of fellow with a mind-bogglingly long name,' he said to Larry, after a moment of reflection. 'You know the sort of name you have difficulty pronouncing, let alone remembering. Something like Venkatachhatiar or Venkatamudaliar. Doesn't trip off the tongue easily, does it? Clearly from some place in the south of the country. People in that neck of the wood as a rule have longish names. He was a low-key, invisible sort of fellow. But he looked extremely cerebral.'

'You mean someone more likely to make a name for himself in academia than amass a fortune in the cut and thrust of commerce?' suggested Larry.

'Absolutely,' agreed Jaggi, without any hesitation. Then, changing gear, he asked the visitor, 'Hey, Larry, can you pronounce Venkatachhatiar or Venkatamudaliar after six pints of your favourite ale?'

'I won't even venture into that territory, trying to pronounce any of those names you just mentioned without a drink. My friend, the British tongue is not designed to pronounce anything with more than two syllables. And that, too, in a state of complete and total sobriety. I think I shall need at least six pints of good, real ale to have a go at it and the chances are by then I'd be in no fit state vocally to pronounce my own name, let alone those of your countrymen from the south,' Larry said with a wicked chuckle.

'God, what a mouthful, aren't they?'

'More than a mouthful, six pints.' Both laughed at the same time and quite boisterously.

'I remember there was also another man, a small, squishy person with a thin growth of hair on his head and thick glasses in library frame on his face. He was a cheery, enthusiastic sort of fellow, full of pep and dash and a sprightly bounce in his step. Always walked as if he had just won some field competition and was headed for the podium to collect his prize and acknowledge the applause. While we were on the boat Nehru passed away.'

'Who?' Larry looked a trifle baffled.

'Pandit Nehru, you know, India's iconic leader at that point. He was also its first prime minister after we lot sent you lot packing from the country.'

'Oh, I see,' Larry smirked.

'In spite of the busy entertainment schedule on the ship, one person organised a quick whip-round among Indians. Within minutes enough money was raised to send a telegram to the President of India expressing the sadness of the Indian passengers on board the Roma over Nehru's death and offering our condolences to him.'

'A splendid gesture, I'd say,' remarked Larry.

'Now this fellow played an important role in collecting the money. Went from cabin to cabin to meet other Indians and break the news to those who hadn't heard about it. Kept scribbling God knows what in a little notebook about everyone he met and, I presume, what each one contributed towards the cost of the telegram sent from sea. I've to give it to him that he rose to the occasion and did a first-class job with the collection and organising meetings.'

'There you are then, my dear Watson. I think it's fair to assume he's your man, whatever his name was, long, short or somewhere in the middle. Sure sign, collecting money and that sort of business,' suggested Larry.

'But he seemed a nice enough fellow, not the kind to take the cleaners to the dry cleaners. This Mr Clever Clogs Something-or-other was not only a good organiser but also extraordinarily resourceful. So resourceful, in fact, that, right in mid-sea, he conjured up a copy of The Discovery of India which Nehru had authored and, in a very serious and sombre tone, like a veteran of the stage, read three passages to those assembled on the ship's upper deck to pay tribute to the great man. Yes, it could be him. But then, Larry, having the ability to organise a snappy whip-round and possessing that extra special something to rake in millions are two different things ... entirely different, in my opinion. Don't you think so?'

'I'd say so. But they can also be complementary. Can't they?'

'Larry, you know what?' Jaggi asked, with a sudden burst of interest.

'Go on,' answered Larry.

'Did I ever tell you about the Italian crew on the ship?' Jaggi asked in a laughing voice.

'No.'

'Those Italian crew on the boat were a right rum lot ... honestly they were,' Jaggi winked at his guest.

'Mamma mia! What dida they do?' Larry inquired, with a huge, dramatic shrug.

'When dealing with the female passengers, whether European, Australian or Indian, they were all sweetness and light ... would go out of their way to oblige and be helpful to them. Not only that, they would have no difficulty at all making your ordinary, everyday English words sound like pearls of poetry. But the moment any of us chaps asked for a fresh towel or an extra sachet of shampoo, magically their vocabulary would dry up and English become as foreign as Greek or Sanskrit. Shrugging their shoulders like you just did, they would make an operatic gesture and walk away without a glance at us, muttering something to themselves in Italian and then, for our benefit, "No speaka the English" or words to that effect.'

With stagy delight, Larry let out a little scream of laughter, slammed his beer can down on the table, rose to his feet and launched himself into *That's Amore*, showboating his musical flair, swaying from side to side, holding a mock microphone in one hand, an imaginary glass of wine in the other from which he took the occasional sip and generally behaving like a contestant in a talent show.

As the song came to an end, he began to whistle softly, tunefully. Jaggi watched him with a happy expression on his face and then got to his feet, clapped enthusiastically and said, 'Oh, this performance is truly deserving of a standing ovation.'

Larry took a bow but kept going with his singing and his whistling. A few seconds later Jaggi joined him.

'I wonder if anyone's told you, old bean, there are hidden depths to your talents,' said Jaggi to his friend after he had finally brought his act to a close, not without a flourish, of course.

'Thank you, thank you, you sure can spot talent when you see it,' replied Larry, somewhat shyly, looking down and pretending to blush.

'Good pair of lungs, by all accounts ... and quite tuneful, too. I know you've been bit of a crooner in your time, but this is twenty-four carat stuff. Like good wine, your singing has matured with age. I mean it. I truly do. One can detect unmistakable signs of Dean Martin, shades of Sinatra, in the tonal quality of the voice. And then, of course, there's the all-important style, which you have bags and bags of.'

This time Larry made a long and hugely exaggerated sweeping bow, one hand across his tummy, the other firmly behind his back. Slowly, he swung round as if acknowledging a wider audience. Smiling, he picked up his beer can and went back to his drinking, cheeks bulging and shrinking as he took three swallows.

'Listen, Larry, have you ever thought of giving singing a shot professionally? Take it from me, it'll be an excellent career change,' said Jaggi, more in jest than seriousness.

'Oh, it's nothing new, old pal. I've been singing for my supper since I learned to say din-din,' Larry replied in similar vein.

'Well, matey, the way things are going, I, too, will be singing for my supper soon,' Jaggi pursed his lips.

'Welcome to capitalism,' Larry took a big gulp from his can and beamed a big, wet smile.

'It's just a matter of time now, really. That's the way things look at the moment. But the snag is I am not half as good as you and that puts me at a serious disadvantage,' Jaggi shook his head.

'O, O! Something tells me I'd better grab another can. Problems at work, aye chum,' inquired Larry.

'Not problems *at* work, pal, problems *of* work,' answered Jaggi.

'I see,' Larry gave an understanding nod. 'That's worse. Sounds like a two-can job to me.'

'You were with us when new technology first reared its head at the plant. Straightaway, it claimed an appalling number of jobs, didn't it, Larry?'

'Oh, that was a horrid time. Of course I remember it … remember it quite well,' Larry replied.

'More than two hundred people were thrown out in the first round. Ever since that cull – or should I say carnage – there have been cuts without number, one after another. People have been got rid of from every department, the factory floor, sales, admin, you name it. Jobs are being shed like there's no tomorrow.'

'For the poor bastards being chucked on to the scrapheap there's indeed no tomorrow. But why such savage reduction in the workforce?' Larry knitted his brow.

'Badly needed economies, we were told, when round two began. That put paid to another one hundred and twenty six jobs. Nearly fifty workers were thrown out of their posts after that and a further thirty two are currently doing their notice period. Once upon a time, not all those years ago, there were six hundred and ten people at the plant. You know it because you were one of them.'

'Indeed I was. How can I forget? Spent some very happy time working there,' recalled Larry.

'In fact, many still remember you and talk about you fondly. I should add here especially the female of the species,' Jaggi said, with a mischievous smirk.

'Do they, really?' Larry shook his shoulders in a gesture of happy pride. 'Tell me more, tell me more.'

'Seriously, you'll probably find it hard to believe, they have some awfully nice things to say about you.'

'Oh damn, what a pity!' exclaimed Larry.

'And Jane Corby, that heavenly creature from accounts. Does the name ring any romantic bells?' inquired Jaggi.

'Ring any bells? My dear sir, there was a stage in our relationship when she nearly hauled me up before a registrar of marriages, that one. It was her impetuous nature that came in the way and stopped the whole thing going through. Now! Now! Now! Everything now. That was her problem. By the way, how is my body beautiful Jane these days ... bless her delicately-beating heart?'

Suddenly Larry perked up and reached for his beer can and looked at Jaggi, who knew instantly what was expected of him.

'To Jane Corby,' said Larry, raising his can.

'Jane Corby,' responded Jaggi. Both took a mouthful of their drink.

'Drink to her health by all means but as for calling her *My Jane* you can jolly well forget about it,' Jaggi told Larry. 'Sorry to disappoint you, old bean, but your Jane is no longer yours. She's found a new Tarzan and is married to him, quite happily, according to the latest news bulletin on her.'

'Married, did you say?' asked Larry, with more than a hint of disappointment in his voice and threw his hands heavily down on his thighs.

'Very much so.'

'And who is Janey's new Tarzan?'

Jaggi gave a shrug.

'Somebody local … from work?' persisted Larry.

'No, no one from work.'

'Anybody I know then?'

'Don't think so,' Jaggi shook his head.

'Someone dark and handsome, who moved next door, came to borrow a bowl of sugar one morning and stayed for supper at night?'

'Got a kid, Jane has,' offered Jaggi.

'Wasted no time, the sexy beast. Always impatient, always in a hurry, she was. Pushed me towards matrimony at a pace I didn't like,' Larry nodded to himself with a roll of his eyes, drifting back to the past for a moment. 'No patience … no stamina.'

'Brought her little girl to the office recently to show her off to colleagues. A cute little thing, about four months old. Very pretty as babies go. Has her mother's looks. Met Jane for a couple of minutes. Still looks very dishy … still quite slim, Jane the body, as she used to be known. Not an ounce of post-natal meat on her. All her physical attributes well intact. If you want to know my honest opinion, I think you slipped up there, Larry.'

'Ah, well, c'est la vie, as they say on that side of the Channel and that's life, as we say on ours. Still, it was exciting while it lasted,' said Larry who, after a series of relationships that failed to reach the tying-the-knot stage, had settled for a life of happy bachelorhood.

'That was not all that long ago, now was it, Larry?' inquired Jaggi.

'What?' asked Larry who, with eyes more than half shut, was still lost in the memories of the good times he had had with Jane.

'The number of people working at the plant,' Jaggi brought his reverie to an end.

'No, no, it wasn't,' Larry agreed, absent-mindedly.

'And do you know how many are left now? Go on, have a guess?'

'How many guesses am I allowed?' asked Larry, smiling.

'Have as many as you like,' replied Jaggi.

'Three hundred and seventy eight?' Larry made his first guess. 'Two hundred and ninety six? Two hundred and twelve. I don't know, Jaggi, I have no idea. None at all.'

'Brace yourself and hold on to the seat for a shock. You may need some support when you hear the figure I'm going to give you.'

'Obviously bad. I'm ready to be disappointed, go on give it to me straight. To tell you the truth, Jaggi, nothing will surprise me, considering the turbulent times our industry is going through.'

'One hundred and fifty six. And that includes yours truly,' Jaggi said in a low, mournful voice, to put a black border around the figure.

'Hell's bells! Is that all … one hundred and fifty six?' Larry was stunned by the number. The look on his face was of such amazement it looked as though someone had pulled the pin out of a hand grenade and was about to lob it in his direction. 'No kidding. I truly refuse to believe it. You're not having me on, are you?'

'Not at all, my dear sir. It's as true as the pound in your pocket was once a rectangular piece of paper but is a coin now.'

'A clear-out on this large scale seems obscenely excessive to me,' Larry said in disbelief.

'And you know why: because it is excessive. This brutal assault on jobs, which, they tell us, is needed at all cost, is a bit like this terrible weather we're having these days. No sign of a let-up at all. Heaven knows how many more will be shown the exit door before the year is out.'

'This cost-cutting mantra that every firm in the country keeps chanting these days is fast becoming the new religion of the industrial age,' said Larry, with a bitter scowl, 'and wherever you go all companies, whether small, medium or large, are all singing from the same hymn sheet or, to put it more accurately, from the same balance sheet.'

'Every day the company's jack-in-the-box throws up something new, more deadly, more lethal than the previous one … rationalisation, restructuring, revitalisation, streamlining and what have you. The traffic to reduce costs is non-stop and all one way. No pause button. Lots of friends gone. Lots of friends going. First they said the lay-offs were needed to make the firm lean and nimble on the feet … you know, slimmer and fitter.'

'Slimmer and fitter? A load of poppycock! Tell me what kind of apple sauce is that, hey? Words, just empty bloody words.' There was an edge of anger in Larry's voice as he twisted his face.

'If it was the sixties, Larry, they would be writing protest songs about it,' said Jaggi.

'Not only writing, they would be belting them out at every street corner on top of their lungs,' put in Larry.

'Well, any way, the extra fat had a meltdown, as if there was any extra fat in the first place. Then, just as we were trying to catch our breath from the upheaval, certain economies became necessary under what was termed as "the overhead reduction strategy" to put the company in good shape.'

'Again, what a load of humbug! Right-on hogwash of the most stinking kind! What does all this nonsense mean? Please, please will anybody out there on God's green earth tell me that?' Larry looked to his left and then to his right for an answer from his phantom listeners.

'Nobody is going to tell you that, my friend. I'm afraid you've got to figure it out yourself.'

'Don't I know it?' Larry squirmed.

'Increasing the operation's competitiveness which, as we all know, is euphemism for profitability, was the next excuse they threw at us for reducing the staff headcount. Then it was the level of profitability that had to go up and go up pretty quickly. Now we are told that other comparable chemical companies are making more money than us. So the screw is turning again. The squeeze is on although there is no juice. Anyone with only half the brain working and eyes closed can see that.'

'In other words, if it's not one thing it's the other, right?' said Larry, with a wry smile.

'Exactly. All these things are having a terrible effect on the morale of those working there. Right down in the boots, it is. In large measure or small, Larry, employees want to feel valued. In some cases even rewarded for the service they give. Not with gold or silver medals but with a word of appreciation, a pat on the back and, from time to time, a pay rise. Instead, at our place they are being treated with utter disregard. They are ignored, alienated and bullied by management,' Jaggi said, heatedly.

'Jaggi, my friend, these days greed is not only passively tolerated, it's actively encouraged.' Larry added, with a degree of passion. 'It has become something to be cherished. There's an awful lot of money in the world … in an awful lot of wrong hands.'

Jaggi nodded reflectively.

'You know it, everything is cash-computed these days. No regard for those who are willing and industrious and carry out their work diligently and no reward for those who go well beyond the bounds of their duties. As for those who, without asking questions, make bricks without straw for the company …do impossible weeks, sometimes months and even years, helping the firm become efficient, make progress, generate wealth there's nought. Zilch. Grab, grab, grab and keep it all to yourself and then go for more … that seems to me to be the motto now. Human concerns are not allowed to come in the way of profit-making. It's so bloody one-sided. Pure Greed one, Loyalty nil. That's how I read the score.'

'So right you are,' Jaggi nodded.

'I can see it as clearly as writing on the wall the day when life will be all pin codes and passwords. Like common criminals, we'll all have to wear electronic tags and badges on our wrists and other parts of our body so the company bosses can keep tabs on us at workplace, where we are, what we are doing there and, if it is official work, why isn't the level of our activity better, faster and more efficient. And you know what? We'll have no choice, no say, in the matter. None at all.'

'Not only that, my friend, but also how much time we spend having a drink at the water fountain. Our toilet breaks, too, will be monitored ... how long we spend pulling the zip down and back up and keep our hands under the air drier after a wash.'

'I wouldn't be surprised at all if this sort of surveillance goes outside the workplace and becomes a twenty-four seven thing. I believe all this will happen in our lifetime and not in some far-away, Big Brother era,' Larry shook his head, heavy with forebodings.'

'The good old-fashioned virtue of sharing the fruits of progress with those who produce them seems to have been chucked out of the window. It's all Dough-Re-Me, me, me, me.'

'Speculative finance is running the country. Old values no longer have any value, old friend. The human capital counts for nothing. It's money, money, money that matters.'

'Frankly, the cutbacks at work are like the old proverbial lion that keeps coming back for more. The sad thing is it's people, always bloody people, at the end of it who suffer ... people that are prisoner to their house mortgage, their HP agreements ... with responsibilities to take care of their families, send their children to schools for a decent education, pay domestic bills ... they're the ones who become cannon fodder to satisfy the whims and fancies of greed merchants,' Jaggi said, grimacing, serious.

'All this talk of restructuring, increased productivity and better profitability, if you ask me, is nothing but a game industrial empire-builders play to exert control over those who work for them.'

'Judging by what's been going on at the plant these past few months, the widely held view, and I'm talking here of nearly everyone employed there, weather in the offices or factory floor, is that the firm is being primed for takeover by some high priest of free enterprise in manic pursuit of making a lot of money for himself … and fast.'

'So some smash-and-grab opportunist devoid of any moral scruples can move in and start doing his nasty work. Rip the guts out of the company from the top shelf down and sell the pieces bit at a time,' Larry mouthed, sourly.

'Now, for all you know, in these days of globalisation, he may be from London or some other far-flung corner of the world, east, west, north or south,' Jaggi said.

'And, no doubt, make a hefty profit for himself in the process.'

'Naturally, what else? Isn't that, after all, the whole point of the exercise?'

'If you want to know my honest opinion, for what it's worth, half the country has already been handed over in sale to oligarchs, Arabs, international megalomaniacs and conglomerate bullies from outside Britain and the remaining half is being primed for takeover by businesses in ruthless pursuit of profit. For them making a fast buck comes first, second and last. Everything else is of no interest to them at all and so they don't give two hoots and a half about that.'

'My dear sir, you know it as well as anybody else that there's no such thing as shared prosperity in modern capitalism. Never was and never will be. Let market forces go berserk and bump up the returns ... fatten the bottom line, give it a fillip, make it egregious, because in the business world bottom line is the only line that matters, all else is of no importance.'

'And these money-hungry merchants may be from Planet Earth or from outer space,' sneered Larry, with a bitter expression that did not leave his face for quite some time.

'True, but surely no nakedly greedy corporate raider from America, China or Japan in his right mind would be interested in an operation that has been stripped right down to the bone and is bleeding from a thousand cuts. No, in my view, it's not a smash-and-grab capitalist from beyond these shores. More like an internal job,' Jaggi speculated.

'Like you, old pal, I'm a coalface worker. Have been and will be all my life. I'm also a firm believer in an honest day's pay for an honest day's work.'

'I know ... I know. Same here.'

'Jaggi, I see it this way: whether they are burnt at the stake or drowned in the bathtub, it's all the same to the workers.' Larry turned his face away from his host and glued his eyes to some invisible enemy in the room. With a sharp intake of breath he carried on, 'A good workforce increases the productivity of the company. It should mean a lot to the owners, shouldn't it? Instead, the beleaguered workers are made to feel they're not a part of the set-up and therefore have little or no say in how the operation is run or who runs it. And as for having a say in the decision-making process, you can jolly well forget it. It was never in the manifesto and it will never be. And let no one tell you otherwise.'

'The prospect of being thrown out of your job is now a daily possibility,' said Jaggi, gloomily. 'It's hard to get up in the morning knowing your work, your position, may not be there when you turn up at the plant. Quite frankly, Larry, you got out of the place at the right time. Morale is at a very low ebb and wherever you look it's doom and gloom. Anxieties, uncertainties, stress are all there, not to mention the haunting feeling of rejection. Demoralised and dehumanised workmates with worried looks, sweaty palms and chewed finger nails hold secret meetings in the locker room, talking in whispers. Rumour mill working overtime.'

'And rumours gain credibility in no time when you're gripped by feelings of insecurity,' suggested Larry.

'A workplace is where people go to earn their living. Not only for themselves but also for the family. They engage with their colleagues, share their day and experiences, dream their dreams. It's where talent expresses itself, innovates. It is where friendships are forged and bonding takes place.'

'Oh aye,' Larry nodded with great vehemence. 'You spend a big chunk of your life at work, about a third of a day daily, and it should be an enriching experience in every sense of the word, shouldn't it?'

'Sadly now, Larry, each day feels longer than it is. As you are operating in conditions of intense pressure and stress, at the end of the day you feel absolutely knackered physically, mentally and emotionally. It is sad to see best of mates ready to fall out over a wage packet with a few lousy bucks in it after the taxman's grubby fingers have been at it.'

'Oh, come on, Jaggi, you don't expect me to agree with you. It's more than that. Much more than that,' Larry gave his friend a disapproving look. 'You know that work is the natural state of man. I would go so far as to say that a man *is* his job. It defines him and has all sorts of other benefits. Many of our names come from the occupations our forefathers followed. To begin with, there's Smith. Then there is Cook, Baker, Butcher, Butler, Barber, Bishop, Miller, Mason, Taylor, Porter, Parsons, Hayward, Shepherd, Gardener, Weaver and most famously Thatcher. These are just a few that come to mind without any effort. The list is long. Do you want me to keep going?'

Jaggi said nothing.

'I can, you know. But let's leave it there for now.'

'Good, but you see …' Jaggi hesitated a moment.

'The job gives structure to a man's life … a purpose and meaning. It allows him to earn his living, use his initiative and drive to bring out the best in himself. It provides him with opportunities to develop his personality, to pick up new skills, innovate and excel in whatever he is engaged in. A job means stability, security and a whole range of other things. Surely, it's not only about a wage packet with, as you say, a few lousy bucks thrown in?'

Jaggi, deep in thought, gave Larry a look of some intensity but nothing by way of words.

'When you have a job, you have some sense of control over your life. It gives you a reason to get up in the morning … and not overindulge the night before. It makes you brush your teeth, scrub your chin, put on a clean shirt, ironed trousers and a jacket every day … see that the tie-knot is in place, the shoes have a shine and the laces are properly done. You make yourself look your best because you're going to have a productive day, meet your colleagues and, in a way, the world at large ... and you're going to make a contribution to society by what you are going to do.'

All this resonated with Jaggi. The past few months, it had been going to work from home in the morning and coming back home in the evening for him. He quietly reflected on it for a time and then exclaimed ruefully, 'The mortifying thing is all this can be taken away from you in the blink of an eye by some megalomaniac avatar of money culture, dedicated thoroughly to his own cause and ruthlessly pursuing his acquisition agenda.'

'True. Some devoted son of Mama Mammon and Papa More with a big fat wallet and an even bigger and fatter ego, sitting on his fat arse thousands of miles away in a glass and chrome sanctum, deeply immersed in the theology of fattening up the goose that lays the golden egg and then hiding his loot in some offshore account. He thinks it is least of his worries what happens to the foot soldiers that do the digging for him day in, day out, in shifts every day. If their lives are turned upside down by his action, well, so what,' added Larry, sullenly.

'Don't you think it shows how little control we have over our lives now and, as each new day goes by, that control slips further and further away from us? I don't like it at all. In fact, I hate the whole damn thing.'

'In their mad pursuit of profit, the big beasts of business want all the water to run down their own gutter. And money, as conventional wisdom tells us, can be addictive. Enough is never really enough.'

'Their sole purpose for being on earth is to get as much out of you as they can and then toss you aside and move on. Broken-up homes, skilled men and women on the scrapheap, families without hope, all this makes no difference to them. I pray to God wherever He is sitting on His celestial throne and presiding over His monthly meeting of angels and arch-angels, that greed should not be a part of my life for as long as I live and beyond, if the possibility exists,' Jaggi said.

'Oh, the irony of life! Jaggi, you slog your guts out all your working life and when the time comes to put you feet up, you've got severe arthritis in both legs and when you want to let your hair down, you are completely bald.'

'How aptly put.'

'Jaggi, I don't know. All this sometimes brings me to the brink of despair. That's why I say to you, old pal, why worry about something over which you have no control?'

'Except that it happens to be your bloody life,' Jaggi shook his head irately.

'I grant you that but you see …'

'You know, sometimes I wonder whether I've come to the wrong country – or the wrong part of the country? Or maybe the country has gone wrong on me? Wherever you look there's conflict and strife. This addiction pitches North against South, employers against employees, town against gown, old against young, men against women, rich against poor, Tories against Labour, those who can afford the way they live against those who can't . On top of it are divisions of class. That's how brutally split we are. When five hands rise to support something, ten placards go up to oppose it. So fractious, so divided.'

Larry nodded, thoughtfully.

'Sometimes I wish I had wound my life's dial the other way and stayed in London or some other prosperous part of the Southeast instead of moving up North. That way, in material terms at least, I would have been on the winning side.' Jaggi lowered his eyes with the weight of his thoughts, picked up his glass and began to swirl his drink around slowly, peering wistfully into the liquid and listening to the clinking of ice cubes.

'Jaggi, me old mate, it's not only addiction to conflict. In this country, if half a dozen schools, a couple of universities and one city, haven't had their input into your life, your only hope in life is the National Lottery,' offered Larry, reflectively running a finger on the rim of his beer can.

'And, of course, we all know what the odds are against that,' stated Jaggi.

After that both of them were silent for quite a while. Then, with one big tilt, Larry drained the beer down his throat, his prominent Adam's apple moving up and down rhythmically. He sucked in a sharp breath and licked the sides of the can with the tip of his tongue before getting up and setting the can down on the windowsill.

Belching boomingly, Larry smirked from ear to ear at the loudness of the burp. A look of contentment spread across his face, as if he had successfully pushed down something that was bitter and highly unpalatable in taste. Finally he declared, 'Excuse me, a man's got to do what a man's got to do. I'm going to the loo. My back teeth are floating.'

Jaggi, smiling to his guest, got to his feet and decided to go on a little walk in the kitchen, moving with slow, measured steps, one hand in his pocket, the other absently playing with an ear lobe and eyes vaguely scanning the place as if they were searching for something.

All sound died down and a period of silence descended on the place.

Moments later, Larry was back, rubbing his hands vigorously with the twin purpose of drying them out and to generate some warmth. He slouched back into his seat heavily and spread out his legs widely.

Jaggi's walkabout ended near the fireplace where adorning the centre of the mantelpiece was a photograph of Barbara in a broad crystal frame. It instantly drew him in. With a mixture of emotions, he stared at it. It stared back at him. For a second he felt the face leap out of the frame to say something to him. Then it dropped back in.

His eyes lost their blinks and got locked to it. Dreamily, he gazed at it, his head engaged in small nods, lower lip quivering a little, as memories connected with her came rushing from their hiding place in him, filling his mind with the sights, sounds and smells of her.

It was his favourite photograph of her. Although there had been hundreds of them after this, none could dislodge it from its exalted position and it remained his first choice.

In the photograph, Barbara was wearing a ribbed turtleneck jumper, under a waxed Barbour jacket. A lock of her hair peeked out teasingly from underneath the hat that she had knitted herself. She looked quite relaxed and was leaning leisurely against a farm gate, her elbows firmly planted on the wooden rails.

The photograph was taken during a chateau break they had had in France. It was a glorious summer's evening and lances of soft sunlight were slanting on everything in the background.

It was Jaggi himself who had shouted "cheese" or "cheddar" or some other similar instruction as her face came into focus. The idea was to coax a whisper of a smile out of her before pressing the button.

In that era of their relationship, he used to call Barbara "My Northern Light" and judging by the photograph before him, it was not difficult to see why. She looked spellbinding, cool, peaceful.

The holiday was one of a number they had had on mainland Europe before their daughter was born. In fact Barbara was pregnant at the time. Not heavily, but the bump was just beginning to make itself known. Pregnancy had brought a glow to her face and made her look radiant.

At that time of their married life, they had gloriously wonderful times and garnered some of the happiest memories of their life together. With a glint in her eyes and a grin on her face, she would put his hand on her abdomen and give him long and detailed bulletins on the baby's progress, its kicking and wriggling inside her.

For his part, he would nudge her naughtily, gather her in his arms and tell her that when God created pregnancy He had her in mind or definitely someone very much like her. It suited her right down to her tippy toes. If he had his way and her willingness, he would keep her that state all her life.

'Even when I'm old?' she would ask, producing a look of milk-fed innocence and strike a pose, her nose wrinkled and a smile of extraordinary sweetness playing around her lips.

'Time will not affect thee. Nor will age wither thee. In fact, it will add to your charm,' he would rhapsodize, sometimes bending on a knee for dramatic effect. 'Thou shall never be old.'

'Never?' she would ask him, a mixture of amazement and delight on her face.

'Never. Ever.'

'Even when I'm seventy, eighty?'

'You'll still be a vision, turning heads when you're standing in the post office queue to collect your pension. You see, you will mature like a rare wine full of intoxication. And you know why? Because my love will keep you young and breathtaking to watch ... always and for ever. If, by some unfortunate chance, a line or two strayed on to your face, I'd love them like they were your beauty spots, honest.'

During one of their many heart-to-heart talks they shook paws on the deal that if they had a son she would choose the name for him. English or Indian, it didn't matter. If, on the other hand, it was a girl, the choice would be his.

But when the baby did finally arrive, that understanding was pushed aside. He wanted her to have her input into the final decision. So he prepared a list of twelve monikers from which to choose their daughter's name. He gave it to her and she settled on Mandira because, if he so wished, he could use the full first Indian name while she could call her by its anglicised diminution of Mandy or Mandi.

In those days of high passion when they both thought sex was sexy he often thought that when old age did eventually come to her it would take the most scenic route. In any case, things like maturing and growing old were for the future. They lay a long way off, too far away to occupy their young minds now. And who knew, she might be immortal? For him, the sun shone out of her every pore. Her voice was music to his ears and every word that tripped off her tongue sounded like a note from a symphony.

In the photograph, Barbara was neither smiling nor looking serious ... somewhere in between, in a neutral state. But there was no doubting that she looked fabulous. More than fabulous, in fact. Ultra-fabulous.

With extreme care, as if he was handling a piece of china, Jaggi picked up the photograph and polished it on his sleeve in slow, circular motion until the tiniest particle of dust on it had vanished and the glass sparkled brightly. Once again, with the same care, he put it back in its place, not taking his eyes off it for a second.

Floating out of pale, blue mist came her clear blue eyes, shining like tiny meteors, her tumultuous hair, the colour of ripening corn and curling at the edges, taking him back to the Saturday evening years ago when he first set eyes on her. He experienced a sort of inner calm for a time and felt instantly drawn to her.

Then, a moment or two later, his heart leapt in his ribcage like a salmon and did a double somersault. In fact, her beauty held his breath. It was at a student party in Manchester's Withington district, just a few skips and jumps away from Didsbury School of Education where she was training to be a fine arts teacher.

There was something compelling about the way she looked. He had felt a magnetic force in her pose as she sat daintily by herself in an old, ladder-backed chair in a corner of the room away from the door, a model of calm, unbothered by what was going on around her and in the house generally. Jaggi was gripped by it all.

Cleverly, he manoeuvred himself to a spot where he could have a clear view of her – back ramrod-straight, expressive eyebrows, high cheekbones, pearly teeth and a slender nose with a slightly upturned curve.

Her hands, fingers interwoven, were resting peacefully between her thighs and her knees were touching each other in a caress under her dress patterned with small floral decorations. She exuded an air of genteel sexuality.

Her face had a dreamy expression and echoes of a distant smile played round the edges of her mouth, which seemed slightly beseeching.

It appeared to Jaggi that beauty, poise and dignity were blended together and rolled into a human form. She was completely unperturbed by the clatter of Saturday evening goings-on in the neighbouring rooms and by the fragments of conversation that drifted towards her. All this had almost glazed the air around her and it had a mesmeric effect on him.

The room, in keeping with the prevalent custom at party venues in those days, was in semi-darkness. But her corner was fully alight – by her presence.

Jaggi was a little surprised that in such friendly atmosphere of happy, care-free laughter, non-stop music and the presence of so many young and carefree male students, she sat alone. A few did pepper her with glances and made comments about her, but only from a distance. Perhaps, speculated Jaggi, she was new to the scene or they were in awe of her beauty to strike up a conversation with her. Another possibility was that they were quite content to remain on the sidelines until drink had made them bolder and her, mellower and more approachable. They would then make a pitch for her.

As for Jaggi, he was completely swept off his feet. The harder his eyes tried to part company with her, the more they kept coming back to her. What a treat it was for them to feast on.

It was quite a while before the spell broke and, with great reluctance, he moved from there to mix and mingle with other students who were engaged in conversations about the activities on the campus and, of course, were busy drinking – mostly beer straight from cans and bottles stacked close to the sink by those who had brought them.

But Jaggi's thoughts kept racing back to her as he played guessing games with himself as to what she was doing at the party, why was she alone, if she had come by herself, with a partner, or had found someone there who was temporarily engaged somewhere else in the house. But most important of all he wondered if he had found his way into her consciousness and, if he had, how had he fared in her estimation on a scale of one to ten – four, six, eight or what?

As he stood no more than a few yards from her, Jaggi had the feeling she was the one for him. He was desperate to get himself noticed by her and wished there was somebody there who knew her and would introduce him to her. He wanted her attention, wanted her to be aware of his presence.

But from her there was no response of any kind whatsoever; not even the slightest hint of a desire to want to know him, or anyone else at the party for that matter. But there was no sign of rejection either and that, felt Jaggi, was something positive and he would hold on to it. It augured well for him. He had been at the party only minutes and there was plenty of time to go because he knew sometimes these student parties went on until the early hours.

A few suspenseful moments passed, each tightening her hold on him. With a steely determination, Jaggi turned his face to her chair and focused his eyes firmly on her. He wanted to gain her attention. Summoning all the conviction at his disposal, he willed her to look at him, muttering his mantra and urging her, 'Come on, girl, turn your head this way. Go on, look this way and notice me. Make contact with me. Give me some sign. Send some signal.'

He said this in his mind as well as mouth over and over again with intense feeling, like a mantra, believing that these things sometimes really worked mysteriously. With hope in his heart, he waited with bated breath to see if the message had got to her. He was confident in himself that something important was about to happen any second. And so right he was. What happened next was something extraordinary, something magical out of a fairytale.

Moving slowly, serenely, she swivelled her head in his direction and, responding to his silent call, looked straight at him. It was as though some invisible cord had linked them together. Then, equally slowly, equally serenely, she rewarded him with a smile that was like the sun coming out from behind the clouds. She followed it up with a slight tilt of the head and a small wave, the slender, tapering fingers of her half-raised hand moving no more than minimally.

Had the gesture come from someone else, it would have been insignificant, signifying no more than a flicker of recognition. But coming from her, it was full of meaning. It stopped his world in its track. The moment was indeed momentous, one of pure joy. It immobilised him, pinned him to the spot for a bit. He was utterly convinced that behind hand was another hand – that of fate.

That delicate hand-wave had made him the happiest man in the world. He wanted to leap into the air for joy and touch the ceiling. He wanted to slide down the banister rail of the house, yodelling at the top of his voice. He wanted to do backward rolls. His pulse was a runaway train. It was pure fairytale stuff he was experiencing.

A feeling took hold of him that he was about to meet someone special. Very, very special indeed, who would change his life for ever and he would gladly, quite willingly, let her do so.

A tingling shiver raced down his spine at the speed of lightning. It was a happening and it had happened, releasing hundreds of symphonic fountains inside him.

It was a truly magical moment in his life. Jaggi ran a hand through his hair to steady his nerves and told his heart to get a grip on itself. A voice inside him whispered that this was the girl for him. He yearned to meet her, get to know her, be close to her. He wanted to share the little and big experiences of life with her, grow old in slow motion with her and spend his life with her. All these feeling hit him in the space of a few moments.

While these thoughts whirled in his head, Jaggi, more confident now, responded to her smile with one more than matching hers in sweetness and, coolly ambling up to her, offered his hand to her with his name 'Jaggi, Jaggi Bali.' She, in turn, responded in similar fashion, 'Barbara, Barbara Harris,' and confidently accepted the outstretched hand. Her well-modulated voice was deep and seductive. On the twenty-fourth beat of his pounding heart after their first bodily contact with each other, he was in love with her and she had become the most important person in his life.

Soon they connected and it was a two-way thing. The days that followed marked the start of a romantic merry-go-round of the most incredible kind. She was the first big love of his life and he had surrendered to her charms totally and utterly. On her part, she saw him as her knight in shining armour on a white charger. She radiated with happiness when he was with her, holding her hand, fingers intertwined, or had his arm around her waist. Love was just lovely.

The sparks they struck off each other were bright and plentiful. Giddy with glee in each other's company, they considered themselves the happiest pair on God's green earth. They had put rationality on a dinghy and sent on a sea voyage China-way with a broken oar and no compass. Their life had no routine. Most of what they did was what they thought on the spur of the moment. Nothing was planned, worked out days and weeks in advance.

It was open season on love as their bodies fizzed with excitement and they did hundreds of little things to strengthen the bonds their romantic relationship. They were living in a happy bubble in which only two were allowed, him and her. For anybody else there was no room. The whole world remained outside.

Often, when they were together and whether the eyes of the world were looking or not, he would gather her in his arms and hold her as close to his body as possible. The two would close their eyes like a pair of yogis in a deep meditative trance and enjoy the delicious sensation of togetherness. The timetable for love was wide open and as such followed no pattern, no routine.

He had turned her world into one of wonderful madness and she had made him madly wonderful. They made commitments to each other and poured out their feelings in endless conversations on the phone at all hours, first thing in the morning, at lunch, in the evening, at night after dinner and the last thing before bedtime, all about love and romance.

Then dawned the era when telephone calls that began in early evening went on late into the night and each call got longer and more romantic than the one before. Every word was charged with magic, with possibilities, meanings and shades of meanings.

Next was the turn of funny cards and funny gifts, funny balloons, funny toys and funny chocolates. They started to arrive with increasing frequency. This was followed by gushing letters. Every day the two of them invented new excuses to do heart-warming things for each other. They were a pair of lovebirds, floating wingless in their own private firmament, their secret wilderness on an unnumbered cloud.

When they were together, they breathily murmured words of cloying sentimentality into one another's ears while their hearts beat with happiness and contentment. Their eyes were for each other only and love's flame burned brightly in them. At the slightest excuse – and often with no excuse at all – they would touch each other. Both made a list of each other's good points and it got longer and longer as they kept adding to them every day.

In those days of heady romance, Jaggi often used to think that, with the sun shining above him, the wind behind and Barbara by his side, nothing could ever possibly go wrong. In the new land, life was coming swimmingly together. If loving and being loved in return was sheer heaven, he was in it good and proper.

It was, therefore, only a matter of time that their romance began to move in the direction of marriage and hopes of years of contended family life.

With a wry smile, he recalled the cold winter Sundays when, exhaling great white clouds of frozen breath, the two used to race each other in Didsbury Park. The wind carried snow into their faces and, squealing and screaming with delight, they had long snowball fights before seeking shelter in the Red Lion for a drink and a bite to eat.

On clear days, when the sky was blue and the sun shining, they would just sit around on a park bench and munch, quite contentedly, whatever they had brought with them in a basket. Barbara was quite a dab hand at organising impromptu picnics. It was a hugely enjoyable time of their life. A vast chunk of his past was linked to her.

There were a whole host of other things connected with her whose memory he cherished and carried fondly in his heart – the soft, indefinable force of her personality, her natural elegance, the delicate perfume her presence brought to the air, the perfect symmetry of her face, her live, observant eyes, her relaxed manner of speaking, the way she curled her lips and beamed a smile when she was truly happy, the manner in which her cheeks pinked when she blushed, the lines of concentration that cut into her forehead when she was deep in thought, the way she wrapped confused spaghetti round her fork, impersonated Joyce Grenfell or expressed surprise over something, by softly sucking in her breath, tilting her head a little to one side and, drawing back a little, exclaimed, *Is that so?* The list went on and on.

There were also things of an intimate nature, like her special way of coming from behind on tiptoe and touching him, the way she shuddered on cold winter nights in bed and clung to him for warmth, the manner in which she dropped into his arms laughing uproariously, affectionately hit him in the ribs with her elbow when he nudged her and told her he found her sexual magnetism virtually impossible to resist and then, when he pretended to be hurt, pushed her head into his shoulder and rubbed her nose against his chin to make him better.

Then there were his mad, mid-winter dashes to Manchester from his digs in Eaton Drive, Slough, where he worked full-time for a pharmaceutical company and studied chemical engineering on day release in London.

At the end of his long journey on freezing trains from London to Manchester, she would be there waiting for him on the concourse of the dreary, wind-blown Piccadilly station, tremulous with cold despite the protection of a hand-woven hat, a long, thick scarf swaddling her neck from the cold and layers of clothing under an ankle-length overcoat, pinching the side of her nose with a knuckle to stifle a sneeze. She would look artistically untidy and to do that she did not need to make much, or any, effort. It somehow came to her naturally.

Although both of them had their bodies protected by heavy clothing, they would try to banish the chill from each other's bones with long, warm embraces and breathy endearments. These would be accompanied by plans that, the day their guardian angel smiled on them and sent a windfall or, more realistically, they had saved up enough money from their salaries, they would buy their idyllic haven – a white-washed, sun-drenched, palm-fringed cottage with filigreed balconies, unbarred windows and gently swaying hammocks in the garden on an island far, far away from everywhere and in the middle of nowhere. There, each new day would be sunny, the nights dark and mysterious, the people warm and friendly.

Back then, many parts up and down Britain were exposed to the full force of xenophobia, ethnicity and racism. The all-embracing term for it was known as "colour bar". In the affected areas, public houses, restaurants and cafes refused to serve blacks and Asians. Hotels and guest houses with rooms to let openly displayed notices of "Whites Only" at the entrance of their premises.

A white girl hugging or kissing a black or coffee-coloured Johnny in public places provoked strong reaction from those who happened to witness it. In extreme cases even holding hands raised hackles. It was taken as letting the side down. Although acts of intimate nature seldom provoked violence, they were greeted with snide remarks to the effect that the girl could have done better by finding someone of her own race and colour.

For the two of them there were also great times for partying at the weekends when Jaggi, carrying a four or seven-pint can of Watneys Ale, and Barbara, clutching a four-bottle pack of Babycham or a bottle of whichever wine was the flavour of the month, would visit their friends in the student-belt of Whalley Range, Fallowfield, Withington and Didsbury districts of the city.

In those days, newly-arrived migrants from the Indian sub-continent enjoyed a virtual monopoly of jobs in the public transport sector, especially driving and conducting trolley buses.

Whenever they saw Jaggi and Barbara strolling happily towards the bus stop with arms around each other or holding hand, they would exchange meaningful glances with each other and then, with a slightly mischievous smirk, transfer those looks to Jaggi, without uttering a single word. He knew exactly what those looks meant.

The photograph had also spooled back the years to the days when he bought his first woollen suit in Britain from Jackson the Tailor, his first tweed jacket with leather patches at the elbows from Dunn and Co. and his first flat cap from Lewis's store in Manchester city centre. Whenever in town, Jaggi wore the cap with immense pride – to the point of showing-off, in fact – to prove that he was a northern lad through and through – from the north of Hindustan to the north of Englistan.

What enormous pleasure Barbara received from running her fingers through his dark, thick hair, brushing it aside so it did not fall into his eyes and also in making adjustments to the cap on his head, taking a lot of time and trouble to give it a jaunty angle, sometimes tilting it to one side, sometimes the other to get it perfectly right.

Life was one huge ball of fun then, rolling along merrily. They were absorbed, totally and completely, in their own bliss and eschewed any outside intrusion in the intimate world of their togetherness. Deliriously happy in each other's company, all they wanted was hours and hours of togetherness, of chatting and of silence, of romance, of touching each other at the flimsiest excuse – not that they needed any excuse to do that. He loved her mind, body and soul from the bottom of his heart and she loved him from the core of hers.

Their marriage at Manchester Register Office was one of the earliest inter-racial weddings the city had witnessed. It was a picture-postcard event. She wore pinkish white, the sun blazed down gloriously and friends sang. Media made it a big occasion. Especially, local weeklies went overboard to cover the occasion and devoted acres of words under bold headlines like "East Meets West". There were also images galore.

Some of them even gave it a double-page spread. In the photographs, Barbara looked beautiful – stunning, alluring, entrancing. As for Jaggi, he just smiled all the time, with all the ease. It came naturally to him.

They saw their marriage as a challenge not only for themselves but also for those that were to follow their path. Hence they were determined to make it a model marriage and confound sceptics and doomsters and deny them the satisfaction of seeing it end up as yet another example of East is East … and all that.

They had bought several copies of each newspaper, plus many of the photographs they had published of the wedding, and posted them to friends and relatives and other loved ones wherever they lived in the world and that included Jaggi's parents in India.

He was sure some of the newspapers were still in the house, almost certainly in the attic, their pages dog-eared and yellowed with age, covered in dust and awaiting a clear-out. As were dozens of wedding cards and scores of photographs, now without any relevance to their lives.

In the early stages of their marriage, the only thing that mattered to them was love. Love and more love. In ever increasing circles. Every hour spent together was a happy hour. In those days, she used to get gloriously merry on a couple of glasses of her favourite white wine and become quite insatiable in bed, often collapsing after sex into the sort of giggles that is hard to come back from.

Now, the house was just an unhappy arrangement of bricks, mortar, paint and bits and pieces of furniture. The ceiling dripped gloom and the walls were cold with memories of times past.

Larry uncrossed his legs and leaned backwards. The body movement made the chair squeak faintly and jolted Jaggi out of his reverie. He was back to the present and the warm kitchen.

'Good old days,' he sighed. There was an ache in his voice and his head was lowered by the weight of his thoughts.

'You mean when you were in India ... blue skies without a speck anywhere in sight, wall-to-wall sunshine all day, mum's wholesome home cooking and the family cow tethered to a tree in the yard?' inquired Larry, eyes on Jaggi, aware that his friend's mind had been away from the cosy surroundings of the kitchen.

'No, with the old girl,' Jaggi said, eyes turning glumly to the photograph. 'Oh, she was some woman.'

'Kind, gentle and generous, all that's good in human nature, she possessed in abundance. On top of all that she had a lively mind and was excellent company and a superb hostess,' Larry said, almost reflexively. 'So artistic, she could make table-setting a thing of beauty.'

'We had such a fabulous time when she was here with me. I miss terribly her comforting presence. I do. She was the sort of person who could change the atmosphere of a room by just making her way into it. Without her, the house doesn't feel the same. It's a lonely house and a lonely house is a sad house.'

Larry nodded a small agreement.

'Gone is the rustling sound of clothes she produced when moving about the place with purposeful aimlessness, or just shifted her posture on the sofa watching TV or reading a book.' As he delved into the past, his voice went weak, almost whispery, and his eyes became slightly misty. Pensively, he began to gaze across the room.

Larry said nothing. He just shifted a little in his chair and looked about the place which had been so familiar to him once and where he had spent many a happy hour eating, drinking, chatting in the company of the couple, and occasionally, of all three, including their daughter.

'Had the parting been bitter and acrimonious,' resumed Jaggi, 'I would have erased her from my mind without thinking twice about it …if such a thing is possible with someone so close as she was to me. But it's this niceness about the whole thing that I find so hurtful and hard to understand. She was good to me. I was good to her. She was everything I could have wanted in a partner and I never hesitated to tell her that. She was no different. She was equally forthcoming.'

Larry, sitting with his eyes to the ground, looked up and moved his head with mixed feelings.

'Whenever I rang my folks in India, everyone there wanted to talk to her. In fact, more to her than to me. The phone went around from person to person and a three-minute sprint became a thirty-minute marathon.'

Larry choked on his beer.

'And you know what? Each one said more or less the same thing, mostly asking about her health, her work and when she would come to India to visit them. They all expressed their desire to meet her. Although she hadn't met any of them, she was liked by one and all.'

Larry nodded in approval.

'Sometimes she used to get really overwhelmed by the affection she was shown by my people on the phone. Then suddenly, in one single stroke, we lost it all and now ... now I fear, we're losing each other, if we have not done so already. At times, Larry, it makes me wonder was all that love and affection not real? Was it just pretence ... some sort of game we were playing with each other?'

'Of course not. How could it be so? It's silly of you to think so. Just plain silly, if you ask me, Jaggi.'

'I don't know, Larry. When things go as badly wrong as they have with us, doubts are bound to creep into your head. No?'

'I suppose so, but ...' Larry shifted in his chair noisily and did not complete the sentence.

'Stop,' suddenly Jaggi raised an instructive hand. 'Silence please. I'm thinking.'

'Thinking? About what?' demanded a puzzled Larry.

'Aren't you peckish or something, man?' inquired Jaggi, with a hand to mouth gesture. 'Want a bite to eat?'

Larry hesitated and shook his head uncertainly.

'Hey, listen, if you think you're going to get a full-on sumptuous treat with all the trimmings, the doo-dahs and the blah-blahs you're badly mistaken. No fancy stuff after eight o'clock in this establishment. The kitchen staff have shut shop and gone home. Only titbits are on offer ... crisps, peanuts, olives, cheese bites, etcetera, etcetera. However, that said, if you are feeling really, really ravenous, a culinary feast can be lushed up in absolutely no time at all.'

'I know. And I also know that it will be presented like a painting on a plate.'

'I'm not sure of that now. The supreme authority of this kitchen is presently on sabbatical leave.'

'No, I'm not thinking of that. I'm thinking of the pressures of making decisions ... the tyranny of choice, man,' said Larry, smiling, gratefully.

'You're sitting in the Bali kitchen. Here, me old bean, you can get served a decent meal inside fifteen minutes, twenty at the outside,' Jaggi assured the visitor. 'Not quite Michelin Star but not without star quality of a different kind. No problem at all, as I said.'

'Oh, please don't put temptation in my way. You know how low my resistance is. I'm seriously watching my weight,' Larry said, running a hand over his tummy.

'Let others do the watching for you. You just keep going your own merry way.'

'All right, you sweet-talking charmer, you've talked me into it. Go on then, lead us into temptation.'

'And what temptation is it on your mind that you'd like to see on a plate, hey, organic peanuts or gourmet popcorns?'

'Tell you what, some of your cashews from Goa or a bit of your special Bombay mix would be just fine,' said Larry. 'Something to munch, as you just said. Let the body sort out its mineral imbalance.'

'Tell you what, Solomon couldn't have made a better choice. Good. That's what I wanted to hear.' Jaggi looked pleased with Larry's response, He rose to his feet smartly, fiddled with a couple of jars in one of the drawers, poured their contents into two bowls of Rajasthani pottery inlaid with figures of elephants and trotted back to his seat.

'Tell me, do you see much of her these days?' Larry looked Jaggi in the eye, as if he wanted the answer in a simple yes or no, as they do in melodramatic court scenes in films.

'Who?'

'Barbara, of course, who else do you think?'

Larry gave Jaggi a look of polite concentration.

'Haven't seen her for what seems like an age and, to be quite honest with you, I don't know when, if ever, I'll see her again … unless it's by chance. Really I don't know.' Jaggi's voice went pensive and buckled a little. His head dipped.

'Oh c'mon, Jaggi, there's no need to feel that way, like a gloomy philosopher,' said Larry, before picking up a couple of cashews from the bowl and popping them into his mouth.

'Can't help it. That's exactly how I see it and that's exactly how I feel. I'm not going to pretend otherwise You wanted to know the truth and that's what I've given you,' explained Jaggi.

'Very well then, take this bit of advice from your uncle Larry and snap out of such a pessimistic frame of mind.' Once again Larry looked straight into Jaggi's face as he spoke. 'The sooner you do that the better it is. Such negative attitude is not you, Jaggi. No, not really.'

'You know so well ours was an equal marriage … there were no leadership roles and we didn't impose our codes on each other. Neither our values. It was the same track and we went parallel on it, like two people on a joint trail. I always treated her as an equal partner and, credit where credit is due, she likewise. You know it, Larry, with equals you can only reason things out in a cool, calm, grown-up way. Unfortunately, reasoning doesn't work on a person who's just turned into an enormous knot of perplexity. At least not my reasoning with her, I tell you.'

'Oh come, come, now, Jaggi, you know I won't buy it,' Larry said, a dismissive wave of his hand.

'I know. I'm not trying to sell it. Merely giving my opinion on the subject,' offered Jaggi.

'You know what I mean, for god sake. Barbara was a little mixed-up, I'd say. That's all.'

'A little mixed-up, did you say?' Jaggi threw a glance of total disbelief at his friend.

'All right, a lot mixed-up, then. Happy now? But, mind you, that was only later on. Much later. After the tragedy in the family.'

'It hastened the end that much quicker. My only fault in all this was – and I'll be the first to put up my hand – that, from the moment Mandi brought up the subject of going mountain trekking in Nepal, I was opposed to the idea. Barbara, on the other hand, gave it her unqualified support. Even actively encouraged her to go …'

'Well, you know what she was like. She knew and understood her daughter's love of the great outdoor, her independent spirit … her zest for life and adventure.'

'As I had a number of work-related commitments, I couldn't drive Mandi to the airport. She did. Heaven knows what last-minute words of encouragement or advice she offered her on the way,' said Jaggi.

'A dozen pieces of motherly advice. What else?' Larry speculated. 'Barbara talked in all seriousness and Mandi listened with half an ear. That's what happened, as far as I can imagine. Jaggi, let's be absolutely honest about it, you can't have a meaningful discussion on any subject with anybody during a short journey from your house to Ringway airport. There are a million and one things milling around your head at that time.'

'If she had the slightest idea that events would take such a tragic turn, I'm sure she would have opposed the trip as much as I did.' Jaggi spoke in a pained, haltingly voice, one word at a time, as though words were brittle objects and needed to be handled with extreme care.

'I've no doubt about it,' consoled Larry.

'Mandi was our only child and the most precious person in our lives. You could say the nucleus of our universe. We both doted on her. I wouldn't be far wrong if I said our lives revolved around that bright pole star. We were incredibly proud of her. More than any parent could be.' And Jaggi began to mist up, his voice barely audible.

For a time the conversation got muted. There were long pauses between words and even longer ones between sentences. 'With her death everything changed. Our world fell apart. A tragedy in the family of this magnitude can affect your life at every level.'

Larry gave a sympathetic nod.

'We cherished every minute Mandi was with us. Made her life full of love and affection. And I will say this, without any feeling of guilt or shame, that, at times, we felt we were pampering her and yet we willingly continued to do what we were doing. As parents, we wanted to see our daughter happy, enjoying her life to the full.'

'As it's meant to be enjoyed,' intercepted Larry.

'But, apart from being indulgent, I was also protective towards her. Maybe over-protective at times. All I wanted was that no harm should come to her.'

'Don't I know it, Jaggi?' Larry reassured his host. 'Parents all over the world are the same. They want the best for their offspring whatever state of development they are in. Whether they have the means or not is a different matter. You had.'

Jaggi nodded with something of a sigh and lowered his eyes. Although the tragic incident had taken place over three years ago, time had failed to undim its memory. It was as if it had happened just a few days back … such was its impact. 'These past few months have been really hard for us, both Barbara and me,' Jaggi's voice choked with emotion. 'We've been swamped by the loss of the most important person in our lives.'

'I can well imagine,' Larry said quietly and nodded again.

A long breath eased out of Jaggi as he said, 'We handled our grief differently, Barbara and me, and that caused a lot of strain on our relationship. But just because we are different on one level, doesn't mean it has to tear us apart, does it? We shouldn't find ourselves at opposite ends? We have millions of other things in common. What about those? I don't know, Larry, I have heard people say that couples who lose a child often feel that way.'

Larry paused for reflection, delicately balancing the beer can on his thigh, near the knee, and then gave another nod.

'Quite honestly, I thought the old girl was made of sterner stuff. She was my ideal of the English woman – good looks, a flagship of beauty one could say without fear of contradiction, super sharp brain, well informed, possessed a liberal attitude towards life and ... and pure class.'

'I know, I know – and much more besides,' Larry agreed, readily. 'She oozed personality, that girl. Calm, thoughtful, lucid, she had great human qualities and a glow about her. A delightful human being ... a real one-off, someone to marvel at, if you ask me.'

'She was never afraid to speak her mind in a firm and fair-minded way. Larry, she could think originally and argue compellingly if she believed herself to be right, which, I must admit in all honesty, nine times out of ten she was. Also, very articulate ... always could produce the right word at the right moment. In spite of all this, she never made a show of her abilities and her talents.'

'A great girl, as I always say. In a class of her own,' Larry picked up his beer and, pointing it in the direction of the photograph, raised it in a gesture of toasting. 'Anyone who met her for five minutes felt drawn to her. There's certainly a depth to her that is hard to find. The last time I saw her she was at a petrol station on Wellington Road.'

'In Stockport?'

'Yes. I didn't get a chance to talk to her as she was coming out of the kiosk after making payment while I was still struggling on the forecourt to fill up because it was pouring down and I had the car a yard or so away from the pump. Not only that, silly me, the car was also pointing the wrong way. So, it was just a cheerful wave to each other. As usual, she looked in fine form. Never saw her better before.'

'So why did she' – Jaggi threw a baffled glance in the direction of the framed photograph – 'fold up so quickly? Why, why?'

Larry declined to speculate. He offered no explanation. He had none. Just glanced at his friend in a helpless sort of way.

'Our whole world came to a stop when Mandi was so cruelly taken away from us. Barbara cut herself off from the world ... from her colleagues, from her friends, everyone. She put herself in seclusion. Went into a shell and was quite content to remain there. Always looked caught up in emotional criss-crosses.'

Larry shook his head in sympathy with her at the enormity of the loss.

'Brooding at deep level became routine with her. Always in silence, always alone. She never let her feelings show ... kept them inside. And as time went on, she turned more and more inwards, torturing herself, seeking from herself answers that weren't there. Now, surely, shutting yourself down like this isn't a mature way of dealing with life's gloomier realities? Is it, Larry, tell me, is it?'

'I don't know,' Larry shook his head sadly, then, 'People deal with their grief differently. You were dealing with it in your way, she in hers. You see, pain can so easily seep into your soul and, let's face it, Jaggi, a mother's pain is always deep.'

'Very deep indeed, no denying. I know with Mandi no longer with us we couldn't live our lives as before. It just wasn't possible. Everything had changed, our perception of life, our values, our faith, proportions, everything. We were no longer the ideal family we once were. And Barbara just put herself into social isolation.'

'Probably she saw it as her way of dealing with her grief,' suggested Larry.

'But surely with time the ability to deal with grief grows although the pain never goes away? Larry, there must come a point when you let go off your shattered dream … stop crying over what's happened. You can't allow the rest of your life to be ruled by it. You pick yourself up from the ground and, however reluctantly, however painfully, begin to rebuild it. At least make some kind of start, don't you?'

'Of course you do. You've got to move on with your life. Force yourself to it,' returned Larry. 'You have to place your love, affection and your emotional energy in those who are with you and around you. Ask yourself some hard questions and try to find the answers. If you feel you can't do that, get the help of those who can … those who are close to you and you can trust and rely on for emotional succour.'

'I would've thought that I was the person closest to her … and also the dearest,' put in Jaggi quietly.

'You were. Undoubtedly you were. I can think of no one else. There's only her mother besides you for her to turn to and she …' Larry bit off the sentence because, not knowing her well enough, he wanted to say nothing against her … or in her favour.

'I'm trying to come to terms with the new reality. Believe me, I am. It wasn't in our fate to have our daughter any longer than we did. I realise I can't go on punishing myself by refusing to accept what's happened. But Barbara, oh no, sir, she just would not let go. She wouldn't even let the healing process begin. The past, I believe, has to be the past some time, like it or not. Why did she then just fold up at the first major crisis of our married life?' lamented Jaggi, as a crease of puzzlement cut into his forehead.

'You know the answer very well, my friend. She wanted Mandi to go to Nepal. You didn't. The tragic consequence of the trip proved you right and her wrong. This has created a conflict in her mind. That's what has happened, that's what I'd like to think.'

'But Barbara and me, we were both on the same side ... traumatised by the same tragic event, going through the same grief, enduring the same agony. She should have been by my side every step of the way, not at the opposite end, surely? By being together, we would have healed each other, brought some emotional stability into our lives.'

'Of course she should have been with you in this all the time and all the way. You know it and I know it. But she doesn't. Her mind saw things differently,' explained Larry.

'I tried to make her see sense in what I was telling her. Not once or twice but a number of times ... countless times. Tried to reason with her that she wasn't guilty of anything. There was nothing she could or should have done in the circumstances. Nothing at all. What had happened wasn't her fault, nor was it mine. We were its victims, not its perpetrators.'

'Oh, absolutely,' Larry nodded.

'Mandi had made up her mind to go trekking in the Himalayas and, given her independent nature, a bit like her mother's, really, she would have gone anyway. That's the way the young are these days.'

'That's the way the young have always been and that's the way they will always be,' offered Larry.

'You're right. Absolutely right. We were no different when we were at that stage of our lives and that's how the generations that follow us will be. But, sadly, all my attempts to make Barbara see sense in all this came to nothing. I'd thought she knew the world, understood life, its ups and downs it puts in your way.'

'Oh, the mysterious ways in which the human mind works!' said Larry, heaving a slow and longish sigh. 'Mind is a funny thing, Jaggi. Very funny, indeed. You don't know what's going on inside the great ivory dome from one minute to the next.'

For a time Jaggi was still, almost motionless and deep in thought. Then he resumed, 'Maybe you're right. What's going on in some people's head can never be known by others. Sometimes you can live with a person all your life and then wake up one morning and discover that you don't know the first thing about that person. After our daughter's death, we were two broken people. While I was coping with my grief in my own silent way, she was dealing with her torment in hers. Inside her there were no words for anyone. Not only that, she had also lost her capacity to listen to others.'

Larry nodded, more to himself than to Jaggi because he knew his friend's attention had drifted off somewhere else and he was not looking at him. 'Barbara had such a good presence. She was so easy to talk to, listen to and spend time with.'

Jaggi looked about him a trifle absent-mindedly. When he spoke his voice was ground down to a low, melancholic whisper. 'There was a dreadful ache in her heart. The look she wore on her face told me that every single day. Smile from her face had disappeared, replaced by a thoughtful frown. Her eyes had a ten-yard stare in them, as though they were not interested in what was close at hand. How deep the pain inside her was, I could only guess at. She wouldn't talk about it with me. Perhaps she believed doing so would show her feelings. Sharing them with me was out of the question.'

'Jaggi, my friend, you can talk and talk to Barbara till you are blue in the face, but you cannot change the way she feels. It's quite possible that, on the odd occasion, she may come round to your point of view, but that change will be only temporary. Guilt knows its way back so well.'

Jaggi nodded, wistfully.

'Excessive grief can block out rationality,' argued Larry. 'Your tragedy was of such magnitude, it's hardly surprising that …' again Larry left the sentence in mid-air.

Another nod. Jaggi closed his eyes and breathed in deeply.

'Hindsight can be a very cruel thing, Jaggi,' continued Larry. 'Barbara blames herself for letting Mandi go. It's not easy to have your only child taken away from you. So brutally and so far from home. I know Mandi was *your* daughter, too, but, terribly hard though it has been, you've come to accept what has happened, or at least are trying to accept it. You see, you can bear it much better, my friend. You have this something extra in you. You are cast in a unique mould.'

'Oh, I don't know about that, Larry,' declared Jaggi, eyes now open. 'I may be cast in a different mould, as you so kindly say, but, believe me, that doesn't make it any easier for me.'

'Mandi and Barbara were so close to each other … more like sisters than mother and daughter. In fact like mates. Good, fast friends. I knew them both and I can say with full confidence I knew them well. The special mother and daughter thing between them exceeded all boundaries. They used to enjoy doing things together, didn't they? The affectionate hugs, the high-fives, laughter …and that sort of things.'

'Oh, like friends they certainly were … no question about that,' agreed Jaggi, with a faint smile. 'Went shopping together … to films and plays together when I couldn't join them for one reason or another. Even wore each other's jewellery and clothes. Used each other's handbags, although dictates of fashion kept some exchanges to a minimum.'

'See. You can only do these things if your understanding with each other other is deep and strong.'

'True,' nodded Jaggi, reflecting. 'Mandi loved posing with her mother's things. I have a large collection of photographs in which she had her things on.'

'And then it was Barbara who, hoping desperately against hope, endured all those tearful journeys to Nepal,' recalled Larry, sadly.

'I don't deny that for a moment, Larry. But it wasn't for lack of intention on my part. It's simply because she was working in a school and, being a teacher, she had more time off than I could ever have. On top of that her headmistress and other colleagues understood her situation very well. All of them, without exception, I can say. Each one of them went out of their way for her. She was so liked at work.'

'Everyone's favourite. Top notch.'

'Anyone who came into contact with her, even for the briefest of moments, just couldn't help being impressed by her. I shouldn't be telling and retelling you all this because you know it all so well already. She was also one of your favourite persons.'

'Still is, Jaggi, always will be. She is that kind of person. She draws people to her.'

'I work in industry and you know the sort of pressures we're under, more so lately. I don't think there is any need for me to dwell on that. You're in the same boat yourself. But, in spite of all that, I did accompany her whenever I could. However, there comes a time when you accept it as your karma and move on ... in your own sad, wounded way. You don't stand in front of the world's highest mountain range in the forlorn hope that, by some miracle, your missing child will come back to you.'

Larry nodded in acquiescence, without saying anything.

'You can't will your daughter to wade out of an ocean of snow, taking slow, faltering steps and embrace you, comfort you, seek your forgiveness for her absence. You ... you do not look for the help of Hindu holy men in the hope that, in some spiritually-inspired moment, they'll make contact with some higher power and tell you everything that happened to your child, where she is and how she is. Barbara sought answers where there were no answers, from people who didn't know. If we could have got Mandi back that way, believe me, I would have gone there a thousand times.'

A hush descended on the room. All sound died. Thoughts on the egg-shell fragility of life took over Jaggi's mind. He wondered about the futility of life's daily struggles, all the pushing and prodding, the desire to get ahead and stay ahead. Slowly his mind began to drift away from the room.

He remembered, with crystal clarity, the fateful evening the news of Mandi's disappearance in an avalanche was broken to them on a crackly, echoy phone line from India.

The call was from Jaggi's father in Lajpat Nagar, New Delhi, and it turned an ordinary day of their orderly life into one of pain, agony and devastation. Three days had already passed when they got the news themselves from Nepal. This lapse of time had left Jaggi and Barbara numb to the core. It was the bleakest day of their married life. Their cosy world was torn asunder and in their heart there was darkness, dread and despair. They thought the sun would never shine again in their life. The two of them were like lost souls, unable to deal with the severity of the shock and the manic speed with which it had struck them.

Barbara's shell-shocked face, pale and vulnerable, all colour drained from it, swam into Jaggi's mind's eye and then, like part of a dream, it was gone.

He remembered how, at the end of that evening, after they had consoled each other with every means they had at their disposal – words, looks, touches, gestures – they retired for the night. Unwillingly, Jaggi turned off the light and lay in bed on his side, his eyes wide open and hopelessly moored to her.

Barbara was facing him without seeing him. She was all curled up with the chill inside her. Her lips were still, her shoulders motionless and her hands at her side in an unconditional surrender to hopelessness. In the scowling silence of the night he could hear her breathing, slow, rhythmic, full of pain.

For a long time he brooded on her face, thinking maybe they would have coped better with their grief if they had another child, or children. It would certainly have taken some of the pain away. He recalled how, in the early days of their marriage, he used to tease her and say that he would keep her with a child always because the radiance it brought to her face made her look even lovelier than she was. The thought added to his anguish. It was dark in the room, but in their lives there was greater darkness.

He felt a strong impulse to take her in his arms and offer her every comforting word he could think of. A desire to pull her close to his heart and make passionate love to her seized him. He wanted to rip out all the pain she was hiding inside her and put another child into her belly, a bright, beautiful child who, like Mandi, would have its mother's nose, her lips and her mouth and his forehead and chin and the mixed complexion of both. It was his way to console her, heal her. He wanted their union that night to be one of shared grief. If it resulted in a baby, it would be a baby made with extraordinary love.

But he didn't know how her English sensibilities would take it – accept it as a part of their vow to share with each other good times and bad, or repel him as though he had only one thing on his mind, even at the darkest time of their lives.

In his heart he was fearful of being turned down outright. He had his own Indian sensibilities to think of. And, for the first time since they had come to know each other at that students' party a couple of decades ago, he felt there were strands in their lives that did not come together, a path they had not trodden before.

Then he turned on his back and lay there a long time, thinking about her, occasionally looking at her but not touching her. That night he did not sleep a wink. Neither did she. He knew this because her breathing, her sniffles, the low sounds she made as well as those she did not make told him so.

In his reverie, Jaggi took a deep breath. The kitchen tap released a few drops of water into the sink, derailing Jaggi's train of thoughts. It brought him back to the here and now and once again he was in the cosy warmth of the kitchen, facing his long-time friend who looked quite relaxed as he silently nursed his drink.

'You know what she was like,' Jaggi picked up where he had left off. 'The prettiest thing in the world. And you know why? Because of the light that shone inside her. Besides that, she was a brilliant mother to a chirpy, cheerful daughter, full of life, full of fun. And then, because of the tragedy, she decided to withdraw from everything.'

'A temporary retreat into one's self is inevitable, I suppose, under the circumstances,' offered Larry. 'It takes time to come to terms with new realities, especially considering the enormity of the loss.'

'A temporary retreat, yes, I'd be the last person to deny that,' continued Jaggi. 'But she shut everyone out of her life and stubbornly refused to come out of it herself.'

He got to his feet and went for a little walk in the kitchen, silently recalling how, in those dark days of despair he used to wander aimlessly from room to room himself, wondering what a cruel blow life had dealt on them.

'For a long time I avoided meeting people. I used to feel like that myself,' he admitted to Larry.

'That's what I mean,' replied Larry, sympathetically.

'But with her it seemed to have no end. Time had lost its identity. Tuesday or Thursday, it was all the same with her. Her brow was always lined with thought, her inner anguish undiminished. In her everyday conversation she had gone monosyllabic. And when she spoke her voice was toneless and seldom above a whisper. Gloomily, obstinately she fought with herself, as if the tragedy was of her making. Here at home, she would often lean on furniture, looking like she was about to cave in. She was never like that before, Larry. Never.'

'Poor Barbara,' said Larry, even more sympathetically. 'She must've been going through hell.'

'She was lost in her own world and a very sad and gloomy world it was. At times she would pick up a book, any book really, open it at random and start reading aloud, as though trying to stop herself thinking or expel something that was already there in her mind.'

'Now isn't that a shame?' declared Larry, shaking his head, 'such a thing happening to one of the nicest people in the world. She had a warm core.'

'And, as for looking good, well, she had all but given up on that. Didn't care one bit what she looked like, or what others thought of her appearance. Sometimes she wouldn't iron her clothes … sometimes her hair looked a right mess. Her smile, which once could brighten up anybody's day, was forced and fleeting.'

'Clearly, she had decided to turn off the charm,' Larry added, his face turned away from Jaggi, who was pressing the corners of his eyes to relieve some kind of strain that was building up there. 'And this is the woman who used to be always well groomed, always well turned out. So soignée, so classy.'

'The most hurtful thing in this soul-searching of hers was that there was no place for me … no participating role of any kind. She wouldn't face me, let alone share her innermost thoughts and feelings with me. Often, she would suddenly get up in the middle of a conversation and walk away. Then, after a few minutes, she would reappear, wiping her eyes and dabbing her nose with a paper hanky.'

'I see nothing wrong with shedding a few tears in front of your husband if that's what you feel like doing. A perfectly normal thing, I would've thought. A lot of wives do it when they get upset over some family matter or are undergoing an emotional crisis.'

'Other wives, yes, but not Barbara. Oh, no sir, not her. She had received special training in not showing her emotions. She kept them bottled up tightly. She wouldn't open her heart to anyone, not even to her husband. No, I wasn't allowed a peek into her unquiet soul. She was married more to her grief than to me. And I used to think we were together in it, the two of us. Isn't that what marriage is about, Larry?'

He turned an understanding face to Jaggi and nodded.

'Sometimes she'd just stand here in the kitchen, close to the sink over there or near the Aga, silently twisting the ring around her finger in slow, distressed movements. Call it superstition or what you like, but I saw it as a bad omen, symbolic of our marriage breaking up. I'd ask her not to do that and, to be fair to her, she would stop immediately without saying anything. But a few minutes later she would start it all over again. It gave me the horrible feeling that I was losing her.'

Larry appeared to reflect on this for a moment and then said, 'Poor Barbara. Didn't know what to do. A real nightmare she must have been through, the seven months it took them to find Mandi's body and then fly it back to this country and the rest of it.'

'Deep inside she was full of turmoil and unspoken anguish. And you know it well, Larry, the cry that's unuttered is the loudest.'

'Oh, absolutely, my friend. Deep grief has dry eyes, as they say,' agreed Larry.

'I've lost count of how many times I tried to get her out of herself. Not once or twice but multiple times, thousands of times, and not only with words but with whatever else was at my disposal. My heart, my will, my soul. Time and again but it all came to nothing. I just failed to penetrate the carapace to reach her inner self. Not only that, she started saying hurtful things, like, "*You're right. You're always right. Of course, you know best. You're a better judge of these things.*" This went on for a while, I tell you. I persevered with it believing that it couldn't possibly last forever and a stage was bound to come when she'd snap out of it. But how wrong I was! That stage never came. And you know why? Because she made no effort. In the end, I had to throw up my hands and admit defeat.'

'I'm sure it wasn't easy for either of you.'

'No, it wasn't. Neither of us had experience of emotional trauma on this scale. It was a situation with which we were not familiar in our life together. We were novices, Larry, in coping with our grief. And when it struck, it struck with the force of several thunderbolts and we found ourselves hopelessly unequipped to deal with it. And to add to our bad luck, we did not have any support group or the benefit of counsel from someone closer, older and more experienced than us in these matters. It was the worst crisis of our lives. Before the tragedy, our home was a piece of heaven on earth and our lives were filled with happiness. Everyone who knew us thought of us as the happiest couple around and held the three of us as an idyllic family.'

'You're telling me, Jaggi? I was one of them,' Larry said, smilingly for once. 'Saw everything with my own eyes. Felt it. Experienced it so many times.'

'Whenever Barbara was well turned out and someone complimented her on her appearance …'

'And I bet there was no shortage of those,' cut in Larry.

'You're so damn right. If I was there I used to tell them she was the family's Dorian Gray … and I was the portrait in the attic.'

Larry allowed himself a small chuckle.

Jaggi fell into silent thought momentarily and then, 'You know, Larry, in spite of being a career woman, she considered being a mother as the greatest achievement of her life. She had charted Mandi's growth from a tiny, week-old thing to a full-grown, twenty-something university-going student in hundreds of pencil sketches, sometimes drawing only her hands or her eyes or her feet, hair, but mainly portraits and profiles. On numerous occasions I noticed her gazing at Mandi with deep concentration and later doing her pencil sketch from memory. When Mandi was no longer with us, she used to go through those sketches quietly on her own. I know this because I found the sketches in different parts of the house at different times.'

'She obviously wanted to grieve in private,' offered Larry.

'Just one look and anyone could see that she was bleeding inside. Whenever I tried to address the problem I came up against a brick wall. Anger, as I understand, is a phase in the process of grieving. I wanted her to get mad – shout, scream, yell, rage around the house, throw things, smash up crockery, tear up everything in the kitchen, or indeed the house, if she felt like doing that. I wanted her to do anything to free herself from her torment, the hurt, the feeling of being cheated ... the negative energy or whatever it was she had stored inside her. But would she do it? No, sir, she just wouldn't show any sign of moving on with her life. And when these things are inside you, going round and round in your head, they begin to choke you with their poison after a while, don't they?'

'Oh, I'm sure they do,' agreed Larry.

He had to wait a while for Jaggi to pick up the thread because he had risen to his feet and, although his whisky tumbler did not need replenishment, he poured a measure as a sort of complaint. Then, silently, he weaved his way to the fridge, spiked his drink with ice, throwing in three or four cubes into the glass with calculated carelessness and added a titchy amount of water. Grabbing a can of beer for the guest, he walked back and set the drinks on the table. As he sank back into his chair, he made a murmuring noise in his mouth, arguing with himself whether to say what he had on his mind or stay silent.

Finally, changing gear and moving from the particular to the general, he said with philosophic weariness, 'You are born one day and from that day on you begin to die, a little each day. Monday, Tuesday, Wednesday. Three days gone out of your life. Gone for ever.'

'But, Jaggi, you're not talking about some old woman who had had a long and fulfilled life. Mandi was young, barely out of her teens, lovely, lively, outgoing. She was highly intelligent and had her whole life ahead of her. She had so much to look forward to.'

'You're telling me, Larry?' Jaggi cried bitterly. 'She was my daughter, my only child. How do you think I feel knowing I'll never see her again? The day she opened her eyes to this world I was there. Her first burp, her first step, her first tooth, her first word, I was there. I was there when she uttered her first full sentence. Her first day at school, her first birthday party, her long drive to university, I was there when all these things happened. And I remember them like they happened yesterday … or a few days ago.'

'I'm sure ,' nodded Larry.

'Most nights, I tucked her into bed, got a book out to read bedtime stories to her about fairies, angels and ballerinas before I kissed her goodnight. I carried her on my shoulders at village fairs, took her to the park to feed the ducks, wiped the food from her face, played endless rounds of scissors, paper and rock with her. When Barbara was not at home, for whatever reason, I got her ready for school and drove her there. Took her for private Hindi lessons on Sundays and ballet lessons on Tuesdays. I was as attached to her as her mother. More than her mother, in many ways.' There was an edge to Jaggi's voice as though he was defending himself against some unspoken accusation, but Larry knew that his anger, if anger it could be called, was not directed against him but at life itself and its injustices.

'God knows how sorely I miss that woman, Barbara' Jaggi continued, after a meditative pause.

'Maybe acceptance comes to you more easily than to her. Who knows, it may have something to do with your past karma, your previous-life deeds, religious beliefs, whatever you want to call it. I don't know. I'm no authority on these things ... I'm just a simple lad from Lancashire, man and boy. They didn't teach these things in the schools I attended.'

'They don't teach these things in schools, Lancashire or Sri Lankashire. There are no self-help books on the subject. No instruction manuals. No guides. It's life that teaches these things and, boy, it does exact its price for doing that. The lessons are hard ... painfully hard.'

'I couldn't agree more with you,' Larry said. 'The school of hard knocks, they call it.'

'Hard knocks, indeed, from the school of life. Believe me, Larry, nothing comes easy, especially the acceptance of pain. Other things if life may come and go but pain can take forever to pass. Sadly, however, it's a term we all have to serve. Some do it with a smile on their face, others bear it in silence. Some just moan and groan all the time.'

'Wounds to the body may heal with time but scars to the soul remain, for ever. I know that for certain,' Larry put in to support Jaggi.

'I still tend to keep things to myself because, let's face it, at the end of the day, Mandi was my daughter and I was her father and I am the one who has to live with the memories,' Jaggi said.

'Of course it's you. That's what I mean by acceptance,' Larry added.

'But smiles only conceal the pain. They have no healing properties. The hurt is there inside you all the time, clinging to your soul.'

'It is. Undoubtedly it is.'

'Barbara put distance between us and then, knowingly or unknowingly, allowed it to grow.'

'And it grew and continued to grow,' said Larry.

'Once we were inseparable, like two peas in a pod. She loved me … and being with me. Then she couldn't bear being near me. During conversations, she would turn her back to me and keep it turned, as if I wasn't there with her. Even such a severe blow couldn't pierce the protective armour of her English reserve.'

'Jaggi, in my opinion, other cultures are better equipped to deal with grief than our own,' Larry said, thoughtfully. 'In many countries, when the initial shock has ended and all the breast-beating is done, people begin to come to terms with their loss and put it down to the will of God or someone else in charge of their destiny. Then they move on. We, on the other hand, rather than confront it full face, tend to look the other way in the hope that sooner or later the grief will somehow go away. But it doesn't.'

'I tried to bring Barbara back into the real world. At every opportunity that I got. Wanted to give our lives a new start.'

'But there was no encouragement from her?' asked Larry.

'Encouragement? Larry, she wouldn't budge an inch from the position she had taken. At such a mutually stressful time, we should have pulled together as a couple, husband and wife, partners, mates. We should have healed each other. Instead, we could find no words to say to each other. Completely shut out of everything.'

'Mandi's death had doubtless left an enormous hole in her life.'

'It left a huge hole in our lives, both hers and mine. But in her case it also rang the daughter bells. It reawakened in her the feeling that she, too, was someone's daughter and now that she was no longer a mother herself, she decided to resume her daughterly role ... go back to the mother who, she thought, must have been missing her the time she was away from her. The emptiness that she feels in her life and her way of dealing with it are now tearing our marriage apart.'

Once again, Larry shook his head wordlessly, as a way to offer comfort to Jaggi.

'There was a time I had two women in my life – Barbara and Mandira – my wife and my daughter and they brought so much joy and happiness into my life. They were my family. I thought the world of them and loved them from the bottom of my heart. Now they are both gone and I feel alone. There's no family.'

'I know there are thousands of women in this country who make tremendous sacrifices and go to extraordinary lengths to care for their elderly parents in their old age or when they are bedridden or infirm,' said Larry. 'But they are largely spinsters. Barbara was married, had a home and husband. A marvellous home and a splendid husband.'

'I suggested that, if she wanted, she could have her mother come over and live with us.'

'Yes, that's a simple solution to the problem,' remarked Larry.

'God knows this house is large enough' – and he gestured to indicate the size of kitchen and the upper part of the dwelling. 'We've more rooms than we know what to do with. I'm sure the weight of one additional person wouldn't have made the floorboards creak.'

Larry acquiesced with his eyes.

'In India, Larry, parents are an integral part of one's family – well, at least the India that I knew and grew up in. So when one talks of the family one also includes the parents and their parents and all the uncles and aunties and cousins. All right, I'll be the first to admit that living in large, extended families can throw up lots of problems.'

'Jaggi, don't you think it can be quite stifling for people of independent disposition to find themselves in that kind of environment?'

'Oh sure. But that's a separate issue altogether and it can be resolved with a modicum of common sense and understanding on all sides. Barbara's mother is a woman of fiercely independent nature. I've absolutely no doubt she would have rejected off-hand the idea of living with her daughter and son-in-law in their house. So, forsaking all others, her dutiful daughter decides to go and live with her in her house instead.'

'And how are the two of them are doing?' demanded Larry.

'Fine, just fine, as far as I know,' Jaggi said with a resigned air. 'I'm presuming here, of course. We've not been in touch, oh, for …' and he fell thinking.

'When did you last speak to her, Jaggi?' Larry inquired, tentatively.

'I don't know, maybe four months ago, more like six. Even longer perhaps, who knows? I've no idea. I've lost track, Larry. She wanted to know a mutual friend's address. She went to live in Australia a couple of years ago and now lives somewhere near Melbourne. Barbara didn't say whether she was planning to go there herself or wanted to invite her to come over here for a break.'

'And how did she sound on the phone?' he asked.

'Very business-like, as only she can when she chooses to do so. Brief and to the point. Not a word more, not a word less. And this after we had known each other for more than twenty five years, most of it as husband and wife. We'd shared an interest in so many things – art, music, food, our beliefs, a delight in origins of words, phrases, languages and a host of other things. You know it.'

'Yes, I know. I was lucky enough to be a part of all that many a time,' Larry gave Jaggi a look of understanding.

'This house was once filled with love. It was full of fun,' recalled Jaggi, three curvy lines appearing in his forehead as he delved into the past. 'Laughter bounced off its walls. I used to look forward to coming to this den of happiness after work because I knew the light would be on and there would be someone with a warm and friendly smile on the face to welcome me.'

'I bet the welcome was no less warm for Barbara and Mandi when they got back from their outings and you were home,' put in Larry.

'We were all attached to each other as well as to this house ... had some great times together here. Now all that is gone. As I leave for home after work I know it will be bleak because there's no one to go home to. An empty house is a lonely house. No one there to say hello to you, greet you with a smile and ask how your day had been. She was the heart of this house. Now I just rattle alone in this big place. Silence in every room ... in each corner. No one to share meal with. I eat alone. Sometimes it feels the walls are closing in and I want to scream at the top of my voice.'

'I can well imagine. It must be terrible,' Larry shook his head.

'Hardly a minute passes without something or the other reminding me of her. Every evening, a part of me expects her to walk into the house like she used to, looking a little worn-out after a busy time at school, her bag on her shoulder, car keys in one hand, maybe a book or two in the other. Whenever I feel I heard fabric rustling or chair creaking I think it's her. The curtains stir in the wind and I get the feeling that she's behind them, making adjustments to the folds, putting things right as she always did.'

Larry took all this in and gave Jaggi a look of profound sympathy.

'Every part of the house reminds me of her. There's not a corner that hasn't got an association with her reassuring presence, the right side of the sofa where she always sat and lingered over one thing or another. I always felt it was a real house because she was there. Now, coming home from work, I sometimes ring the doorbell and wait because I think maybe, just maybe, she's back and will answer and, as if by magic, lights will come on, the door open wide and everything will be like old times. But when nothing happens, I start to look for the keys in my pocket. It hurts, hurts real bad, when someone so close takes that attitude.'

'You wouldn't be human not to feel that way,' Larry pursed his lips. 'Tell me, Jaggi, on a scale of one to ten, how do you rate the chances of you two getting back together again?'

Jaggi appeared to think for a moment, then, 'The answer to your question lies with her, not me,' he said somewhat, somewhat bitterly.

'But I'm asking you,' persisted Larry. 'This evening clearly shows that it's affecting you.'

Jaggi was silent, thinking, sorting things out in his mind. Then bit his lower lip doubtfully and said, 'I don't know. Honestly, I don't. My hopes are dangling by a thread. Getting together again seems a dream, a distant one now. The oneness we shared with each other is no longer there. The glow has gone, definitely for now and probably for ever. Believe me I feel a physical pain when I say this but that's the honest truth. The marriage is nothing more than an empty shell now ... the relationship is over. I think only a miracle can bring her back to me.'

'And never forget miracles do happen. And they happen when you least expect them. So wait for it. Trust me, I'm not saying this to console you or cheer you up. Jaggi, my friend, maybe one day you will wake up in the morning, pull back the curtain of the bedroom window and find her walking up the drive, towards the front door ... like you said, bag on her shoulder, maybe a book or two in hand.'

'I don't know, Larry,' Jaggi shook his head and rolled his eyes to the ceiling as if the answer lay there. 'I wish we would get together again but, frankly, that's wishing in the wind.'

'Don't talk like that, old pal. And there's no need to get your hopes down,' said Larry with a swift turn of the head, his voice soft, genuine. 'I hope to God it happens and happens soon.'

'But it's hoping against hope.'

'Listen to me a sec,' said Larry solemnly, raising a hand in warning, 'Look, I'm going to say things that you may not like. You know it, I'm not in the business of giving advice. Hate it ... I really, really mean it. But, old friend, in your case I will make an exception: No more doom and gloom from you. Deep down, I'm absolutely certain, Barbara still loves you, thinks highly of you. There're places in the human heart where these feelings lie dormant for years until something triggers them and they come racing to the surface. You understand what I'm saying?'

Jaggi gave a nod.

'I'm sure the flame that brought you two together in the first place is still flickering somewhere in her heart and, Jaggi, this is your old pal Lawrence Upton talking to you and not just any Thomas, Richard and Harold. So, whatever happens, if you think there's a chance, however slim, however remote, do give the wheel another spin. Chin up, man. Things are going to be all right … and, for heaven's sake, don't slam the door shut on any possibility. Seriously, you don't need me to tell you that an ajar door is an invitation to enter and a closed door says go somewhere else.'

Jaggi gave another nod.

Chapter 3

Jaggi smiled. Jaggi always smiled.

He was looking reflexively at the tick-tocking wall clock. The hands of the clock showed that the time was ten minutes past two, just under six hours since Larry had come to visit him. But it mattered not a bit to him or to his guest. Time had flown on supersonic wings while they got whittled on a fair amount of alcohol. Jaggi had shaken out the last drop from his bottle of scotch and there were no beer cans left in the refrigerator for Larry. The ones on the table were empty.

They had chatted and put the world to rights, taken account of their own lives, the big and important things as well as those small and insignificant, the serious and the not-so-serious ones. Memories going back years had been dredged up, coated in new gloss and tossed to and fro.

During that period, Larry had got to his feet at least four times, somewhat uncertainly – the last time also unsteadily – to take leave of his host, but each time Jaggi had pushed him back into his seat for "old times' sake", telling him the night was young, that he had come after a long time and as the next day was a Saturday, neither of them had to get up early and go to work. Larry had succumbed to his friend's power of persuasion without offering any resistance at all.

It was not until the early hours that he finally heaved himself up with something resembling resolve and, brushing a few crumbs, more imaginary than real, from his trousers, gave notice of his intention to call it a day, both literally and metaphorically, and take his leave. Jaggi would have insisted on his friend staying on a few minutes more but by this time his own eyes were getting drowsily shut and the heavy drinking session was beginning to show its effect on him.

'Wait a minute, shall I phone for a taxi?' Jaggi spluttered while his mouth split open in a huge yawn. 'If my guess is right, it's sheeting down outside. Bloody rain.'

Larry shrugged his shoulders dismissively, 'I've got my coat and my brolly. Rain has never stopped play on my pitch … not in the past and it won't stop now, I can tell you. Horse to the stable must go.'

'Listen, listen, all it takes is one phone call and the taxi will be here in a couple of minutes, right on the doorstep for you,' Jaggi assured Larry, a hand gripping his shoulder.

'Nothing of the sort. Sod the rain and sod the taxi,' replied Larry, with drink-induced daring. 'You'll do no such thing. I shall leave the car here on your drive and take a taxi from round the corner. Collect the car tomorrow evening. Is that all right with you?'

'Of course it is, man. You know it. No need to ask.'

'So, if you don't see my car on the drive tomorrow, don't call the police. It would mean I've taken it. Right?'

'Right,' nodded Jaggi. 'But don't be an ass. Ring the bell or knock on the door. When the door opens walk right in and pull out a can from the frig. We shall take up tomorrow from where we leave off tonight and have a drink or two. I'll make sure the frig has been restocked.'

'And leave the car again for some other time?'

'Sunday. Send your chauffeur to pick it up.'

'My chauffeur, my dear sir, is on holiday in the Bahamas with his wife and three children,' Larry said loftily, with a laugh. 'Like every hard working citizen of this country, he deserves a break from time to time to recharge his batteries. It looks like I will have to collect it myself.'

With a loud noise, Jaggi sucked the last remaining drops from his glass, rose to his feet and padded behind Larry.

'I'd better see you to the front door, old chum,' he muttered, more to himself than to his departing guest.

'To make sure I'm gone?' chuckled Larry.

'No, no, don't be a silly ass,' he waved his hand about in denial. 'To make sure you don't swing from the lamp-posts and start your Fred Astaire routine of "I'm Singin' in the Rain".'

'Fred Astaire?'

'Yeah.'

'No, no. I think it was the other fellow.'

'What other fellow?'

'Oh, umm ... his name is hanging at the edge of my mind but I can't get it out for all the boozing that's been going on. Tell you what? I'll give you a ring when it comes back to me, no matter what time it is ... even five in the morning.'

'Hey, listen, old pal, if you do that, make sure the phone is at least a yard from your ear because I don't think, you will like one word of the blast you will hear, I can tell you that.'

Both began to laugh simultaneously, throwing friendly punches on each other's arms.

When the jesting was finally over they shambled to the front door. Jaggi put a hand on Larry's shoulder and told him that he must come again soon and more often in the future. All he needed was to make sure that Jaggi was at home and the easiest way to do that was to give him a tinkle and if, for some reason, he was unavailable leave a message on the phone.

He reminded Larry of the good old days when they had a lot of fun "tasting the waters" in real ale pubs, eating in ethnic restaurants known for their authentic cuisine and having big nights out on the town at weekends.

'You remember the club where we used to dive in for after-hour supping with all those journalists and other newspaper people from Thomson House?' asked Jaggi, smiling profusely, as he shifted his hand from Larry's shoulder to the front-door knob but gave it no twist because he wanted the conversation to carry on.

'I know the one you mean,' replied Larry, and appeared to fall into thinking. 'It was the same as the pub in the film Hobson's Choice. You know, Jaggi, where Charles Laughton and his drinking pals used to sort out the problems of Salford over a pint.'

It made Jaggi fall into thinking.

'I got it. I got it. It was Moonraker.'

'You're so right, eh man. You remember the Moonraker Club.'

'Clear as the day, sunshine, both the club and its Greek owner, such a friendly fellow. Always had a smile on his face,' replied Larry. 'Oh, it was such fun, wasn't it?'

'Yeah, those were the days. Manchester was our town … Manchester was our city,' lisped Jaggi and, taking his hand off the door knob, raised a wrist in a gesture of celebration.

'And look what has happened to it now. Half of it is owned by half the world.'

'Be grateful it's not London. Half the world owns whole of it now.'

With an unsteady hand, Jaggi finally gave the knob a turn and stepped back to enable his friend to proceed. The lights were shining brightly outside in the street. A gust of wintry wind, laden with moisture, greeted them and sent a shiver down their spines. The chill was sharp and stabbing. Rain had scrubbed the road clean while they were busy knocking back their drink in the warmth of the Aga kitchen. Jaggi remained rooted to the spot holding the door open just a slit to watch his friend.

Vigorously, Larry rubbed his hands together to generate some heat, then hunched instinctively into his coat, his eyes closed momentarily as if they didn't like to see what was before them, not that there was much in the street at that late hour except drizzly rain, light mist and near-freezing temperature. Taking a deep breath, he put his head down, opened his umbrella and dived into the darkness.

A little unsteady on his feet, Larry had barely gone a few yards down the street when he suddenly stopped and glanced back. Jaggi was still there, holding on to the door and waving cheerily to him. He returned the wave and howled, 'The other fellow was Gene Kelly.' Then he gave a short demonstration of the Hollywood star's dance routine for Jaggi's benefit before melting into the night.

It had been a busy boozy session and as soon as Jaggi closed the front door, he began to think of turning in for the night. Drink had taken its inevitable toll and he felt worn out although he, like Larry, did not get sozzled easily. His eyes were heavy-lidded and it was a struggle to keep them open.

But in his mind a new dawn was breaking. Hours of dredging up memories had rolled back the years. So far into the distance in fact that, in the haziness and confusion of his thoughts, the present had been reduced to a blur. Only the past was relevant. It had become the present.

With so much going on in his head, Jaggi saw no point in going to bed because he knew he would not be able to go to sleep. Although physically he felt tired, his mind was quite active. With a bit of struggle, he made himself coffee in a large mug and, turning off the lights, slumped into a rocking chair. The first sip of the dark, sugarless brew tasted bitter but he did nothing to change that.

As the chair rocked, he drifted into a state where he was neither fully awake nor fully asleep. Cosily somewhere in between. The memory of his final, slow-slipping days in India began to tap against his head, like waves lapping a seawall.

It was the last week of May in 1964 and he was just hours from sailing for Europe from Ballard Pier in Bombay, a city with which his past association was no more than a nodding one.

The sky was an uninterrupted blue, not a speck of cloud in sight anywhere. But the day was blisteringly hot and the temperature swung between that of a hothouse and a Turkish bath. The unrelenting, midday sun was sending blinding rays of light on the city. They stung the eyes. As if that was not enough, there was also plenty of cloying humidity in the atmosphere. The clothes stuck to the body like second skin.

With his employment voucher, passport and other travel documents tucked safely away in his pocket, Jaggi had only one thing on his mind: a fresh start in new surroundings, full of possibilities in a land of magnificent countryside, rolling green hills, verdant meadows, hedgerows, hawthorn bushes, rows of quaint cottages with flowers bursting out of hanging baskets.

Although he knew quite a lot about the country he was going to and had recently added to that store of knowledge by reading every book about it that he could lay his hands on, there was still a lot of mystery in the adventure.

Jaggi was not a person to be unnerved by thoughts of any last-minute hiccups, hitches or glitches. So, he decided to treat himself to a sumptuous meal and blow the last remaining rupee notes in his pocket. He knew they would have no value once he set foot on the ship.

For the meal he chose Persian Dairy, a popular restaurant with plenty of ambience and within whispering distance of the sea at Marine Drive. Carefully, he went through the tasselled menu, taking his time over every dish and its price. He ordered whatever took his fancy – butter-fried silver pomfret, garlic prawns, meatballs in Malabari sauce, mutton biryani, Goan fish curry, ice-cream, coffee, far more than he could possibly eat. But it did not matter because the idea was to indulge himself rotten on his last day in India.

Jaggi had a long, lingering lunch, savouring every bite, each morsel of the rich, spicy preparations, aware that these treats would not be available for quite a time where he was headed. He felt hugely relaxed under the restaurant's open-air roof, from which pink, violet and brilliant white bougainvillea cascaded down.

Smiling to himself from time to time, he felt he was in love with the world and everything and everyone in it.

A young couple at the neighbouring table was engaged in the hushed tete-a-tete of lovers, giving each other melting glances and murmuring in honeyed tones promises of eternal love to each other. If they felt that no one was looking, both squeezed hands gently, affectionately.

The sea breeze came in gentle caresses to cool Jaggi and the gloriously bright colours of the flowers dangling above him added to his cheerful state of mind. He glanced around the surroundings and felt happy in himself.

Jaggi was buoyed up by the feeling that in a matter of hours he would be leaving the heat and humidity of India behind him. A thing of the past it would soon be ... and of the distant past a few years later. Who knew? But this he did know that the climatic changes that many countries went through in a year, Britain experienced in a day. However, such thoughts were not allowed to interfere with his joyous state of the moment. On the contrary, they filled him with a delicious thrill of anticipation because in just over a fortnight, he would be a part of that scene.

Whereas tipping in restaurants in the past had brought tears to his eyes, the amount of money he left on the table that day brought tears – of joy – to the eyes of the waiter. It wasn't calculated in percentage terms. By his standards, it amounted to a small fortune.

Jaggi wasn't making amends for his past parsimony; it was just that he had money to blow like a sailor on shore leave and what better way to dispose part of it than by being over-generous to the Goanese waiter who had served him with a huge smile on his face and made the meal a truly memorable experience?

The crowded excitement of a mega city was right before his eyes. The teeming streets buzzed with people going about their everyday business in a quiet, understated way, unbowed by the baking heat.

To all the gorgeous women who caught his attention, Jaggi, feeling full of food, bid his silent farewell. The marvellous music of their movements, the delicious rustle of their dresses, the rich colours of what they wore on their person, he was storing up all these impressions in his mind to take with him to England as his last-minute souvenirs from India.

Although he was sorry to be leaving them behind, the prospect of wandering leisurely in green, rolling hills speckled with "meadow ladies" and rain-lashed barns, he felt, would more than compensate for that.

The SS *Roma* was berthed on the quayside at Ballard Pier. It was coming from Australia and was headed for the Italian port of Genoa, its final destination.

Besides Jaggi, there were another 127 Indians who boarded the ship in Bombay. Bound for different destinations in Europe, they included men and women, Hindus, Muslims, Christians, Sikhs, Parsis, Buddhists, you name it. They had come from many corners of the richly diverse sub-continent.

The quayside, festooned with bunting, streamers and balloons, was bursting with people. For each departing passenger, there were at least a dozen relatives, friends and other well-wishers, who had travelled some distance to bid final farewell to them. Wherever the eye went there were people, milling around, hugging, hand-shaking, kissing in never-ending, tearful farewells, constantly shifting their weight from one leg to the other, talking animatedly, gesticulating excitedly, mothers fanning themselves with the corners of their saris and dhotis, fathers, uncles and brothers wiping sweaty faces with cotton handkerchiefs.

Reminders on the good, old-fashioned virtue of regular letter-writing and keeping in touch with friends and family back home were rammed by the elders into excited, preoccupied minds of those departing, as was counsel on the benefits of taking good care of oneself, staying on the straight and narrow, eating healthy, wholesome food and staying out of trouble of any kind. But these vibrant urgings fell flat on deaf ears.

The atmosphere was almost festive. Buskers, jugglers, acrobats and other street artists, including some with animals such as snakes, monkeys and bears were putting on their shows for the benefit of Australian tourists on their way to Europe for holidays and Europeans returning home from their holidays in Australia. Everyone watched the performances with great interest from the ship's decks and, from time to time, threw money to reward the entertainers.

A young Muslim, choking under the weight of garlands in which marigolds, roses and jasmines mingled with tinsel and crisp banknotes of both big and small denominations, was engaged in a foamy farewell with his family and relatives. They must have numbered around a hundred if not more, most of them wizened old men with faces wrinkled like unmade beds and sad, rheumy eyes. Their tired, worn-out faces clearly indicated that they had travelled from far and wide to witness one of their progeny, probably the first in the clan, embark on a journey across the seven seas to give his life a new start in a distant land.

Dressed in black, knee-length coats, white trousers and flat skull caps, these white-bearded elders looked visibly curious about the surroundings they found themselves in. With raised hands and pointing fingers, they kept drawing each other's attention to one thing or another.

A worried, harassed photographer with patchy hair, bushy brows and protruding teeth, who seemed to have been hired to record the occasion for the family album, was trying his desperate best to herd them together, using all the social skills at his disposal, shouting a stream of instructions, begging and beseeching them to take their place and hold still while he got his camera to work. But as soon as he managed to bring some of them together, others would break loose and stroll out of his frame.

Just one niggly little problem was preying on Jaggi's mind. India at that time was woefully short of foreign exchange and those leaving the country were allowed to take with them no more than three pound sterling in cash. However, he had an extra ten shillings on him.

A long time ago, when he was a student in Delhi University, Jaggi had bought a copy of the book *The Body's Rapture* from a local second-hand shop and found a ten shilling note tucked away behind the brown paper cover its owner had put on the dust jacket. Many students and other reading public used this method to protect their books from dust and grime. He had put the ten shilling note away in a safe place with other important papers and forgotten all about it. Now it was inside his wallet which was in his trouser pocket.

Ten shillings was hardly a significant amount of money over the permitted limit. Besides, since he had already cleared all the official formalities, there was no danger of being stopped from leaving, unless officials decided to conduct a thorough body search or something of that nature. So, in reality, it was no more than a mild prick of conscience and nothing more than that.

A giant roar of excited cheering went up when the ocean liner sounded its horn to announce it was time to depart. Those lining the decks began to blow enthusiastic kisses first with one hand and then with the other – in many cases with both hands. Those on the ground responded in similar fashion with caps, white handkerchiefs, folded newspapers or anything they could lay their hands on in the mounting excitement.

Finally, amid a great fanfare of hooting horns, thumb-ups, waving and whistling, exploding firecrackers, ticker tape and tears, the ship set sail for Europe.

The sea was calm and slowly India began to slip behind under a pink and gold-streaked sky.

With a faint smile on his face, Jaggi slowly fell asleep.

****

Back at work on Monday, Jaggi rang the number given in the advertisement during his lunch break. Twice he found the line engaged, but got through the third time.

'Sagar Enterprises, good afternoon,' answered a woman's voice in a plummy, southern accent.

'Good afternoon to you,' Jaggi answered back, in his most courteous voice. 'I'm phoning in connection with the advertisement that appeared in the *Guardian* newspaper a few days back.'

'Just a moment please, I'll transfer you to the person who is dealing with it,' replied the woman, even more pleasantly. 'It's Margaret Brown ... you will be speaking to her. She handles the inquiries about the ad.' There was a pause and for a moment everything went quiet. Then another woman came on the line. 'Margaret Brown. How can I help you?'

'Oh, hi there, good afternoon to you,' Jaggi began, in a smiling voice. 'I'm ringing about the advertisement that appeared in the *Guardian* newspaper recently. 'I believe someone at your end wants to get in touch with the people who travelled on board the Italian ship, the SS Roma, from Bombay to Britain, oh, a few decades ago ... '

'That's right,' replied the woman. 'It's Mr Ravinder Sagar.'

'Does he work there?'

'Yes, you could say that,' she answered, with a small laugh. 'He is the managing director of the company.'

'Oh, is he?' Jaggi said, exaggerating his surprise.

'He certainly is. He owns the company.'

'Another one of those who liked the company so much he bought it? Sounds like a real big timer.'

'No question about that.'

Ah, well. Jaggi had a feeling that it had to be someone fairly higher up in the pecking order in the organisation. You can't go any higher than owning the company, can you?

'And who is it I'm talking to?' the woman inquired.

'Jagmohan Bali. That's my name. I'm a chemical engineer by profession and I work for a company in Stockport, which, I'm sure you know, is around one hundred and sixty miles north of Watford.'

If it was his intention to inject a modicum of humour into the conversation, Jaggi more than succeeded. There was a sound of a small laugh, politely stifled, followed by a brief pause.

'Could you please spell out your name for me? I'm going to add it to the list we're preparing at the moment.'

'Sure. But before I do that, may I ask how many have responded so far to go on your list?' demanded Jaggi.

'I'm sorry I can't tell you off-hand,' she replied, a little apologetically. 'But if you bear with me for a moment I can find it out for you.'

'Oh, please don't bother. It's not that important. Just my idle curiosity to find out what sort of response you've had so far.'

'Actually, the replies to the advertisement have just started coming in. So, as you can imagine, the list is not very long at the moment,' the woman added as Jaggi heard some fiddly sounds in the background.

He spelt out his name, speaking slowly and clearly, and the woman, suspending whatever it was she was doing, took it down in her notepad in capital letters.

Then, asked Jaggi, 'I shall be grateful if you could give me some idea what the whole thing is about?'

'Oh sure, sure. It's Mr Sagar's idea. He came to this country from India on this ship named SS *Roma*. There were along with him many of his countrymen. After some protracted exchange of correspondence with the shipping line in Italy, who owned the ocean liner at the time, we have managed to obtain a list of their names.'

'Well done,' Jaggi said. 'I'm surprised the shipping company had kept it for that length of time. I was under the impression that once the journey was over …'

'Oh, they did, believe it or not,' she answered, with an amused laugh. 'Coming back to your question, as Mr Sagar has been successful in his business ventures in Britain, he wants to celebrate his success with, among others, the people who travelled with him on that journey.'

'What a splendid idea!' exclaimed Jaggi, enthusiastically. 'He has my whole-hearted support.'

'He would, therefore, like to meet as many of them as possible. It's all in the spirit of having some good old-fashioned fun. Like a get-together of old students from a school or college, if you will. But it will be on a much bigger scale than that.'

'But of course,' offered Jaggi. 'Like I said, it's a splendid idea and has my one hundred per cent support. Is it Miss Brown or Mrs Brown I'm talking to, if you don't mind my asking?'

'Not at all. It's Mrs Brown, but Margaret will do fine.'

'Good, Margaret.'

'Wait a minute, I've found the list you were asking about. So far nineteen people have been in touch with us. Of course, it's early days, you understand. We'll see how it pans out in the next few days and weeks.'

'Oh, I'm sure it'll go well.'

'Good. I'm pleased you see it that way. The advertisement has appeared twice in the past fortnight and we may repeat it … possibly also put it in other newspapers. The idea is to reach as many of those who were on that ship as possible.'

'Great. A total of 128 Indians boarded the ship in Bombay. Of that I am absolutely sure. The list was posted on the ship's notice board. I saw it with my own eyes.'

'Many, I believe, are no longer in this country. A few might have gone back to India and others moved on to mainland Europe, America and Canada. Who knows? In fact, the other day we received a telephone call from a gentleman in Germany. He's working in Munich on some research project. His family is here in the United Kingdom. Obviously, someone from here must have told him about the ad.' Her voice had an element of surprise in it.

'Oh, it's bound to take time to reach everyone, but nineteen in two weeks is not bad. Not bad at all, according to my reckoning. That's more than one a day. Besides, as you just said, it's early days,' said Jaggi. 'Incidentally, where does Mr Sagar plan to hold the get-together?'

'In London,' she answered. 'Everyone is familiar with London. Even those who have never been to this country know where it is. According to plans, as they stand at the moment, the venue will be in London.'

'Not some exotic, faraway location, such as Hawaii or the Seychelles, Bahamas, with blue skies and swaying palms … with total disregard of the expense?' asked Jaggi, light-heartedly.

The sound of a cackle poured into Jaggi's ear and it acted as an incentive for him to have a laugh himself.

'I'm afraid not,' went on Margaret Brown, after a moment's pause. 'I'm sure those living outside find London quite exotic, don't they?'

'I suppose so. It is south of Watford.'

'Anyway, Mr Sagar plans to invite his guests for a weekend get-together whenever the whole thing is finalized. And that, I'm afraid, is all I know and all I can tell you at this stage of the proceedings. But then, it will also be determined by what sort of response we get in the coming days,' she added.

'I have no doubt at all that the response will be good. But tell you what, Margaret, you can put a large tick against my name on your list,' said Jaggi. 'No 20, Jagmohan Bali. Anyway, Bali should be somewhere at the top the list if it is in alphabetical order.'

'You can rest assured it will be done. I'm glad to hear you'll be coming to the function, Mr Bali.'

'Rain or shine ... hell or high water, and whatever else they say.'

****

Jaggi peered out of the kitchen window gingerly as he made last-minute preparations to catch an early Inter-City train to London. The weather was at its worst, the day was dull, drab and dreary. The morning sky was dark, the light outside the kitchen no better than the darkness inside. It seemed the night had decided to extend its duration an hour or two.

Rain was slanting down out of a low, black cloud, pelting the window with the force of air-gun pellets. Whipped up by a blustery wind, it did a rain dance before sliding down and disappearing into corners of the woodwork. As it was cold outside, his breath made the window fog up as soon as it touched the glass and he had to wipe it with his shirt-sleeve. The glass was cold to touch.

Jesus Christ, Jaggi said to himself with a feeling of exasperation, there must be an end to it somewhere. Rain, rain and more rain. Nothing but rain. Nine days of it. It waxed and it waned but never completely stopped. It came down in torrents one moment and was relentless and loud the next. But there was no let-up of any kind.

Living in the city was like living in a rainforest. Not only did it drench your clothes, it doused your spirits too. Also, it soaked everything it touched and there was nothing it did not touch. Manchester seemed determined to put Cherrapunjee in the shade. The butt of a thousand jokes over the vagaries of its weather, the city was well and truly living up to its reputation of being wet, wet and wet.

Jaggi looked up at the low clouds. Raindrops, hanging on rusty barbed-wire fences – the garden of nearly every other house seemed to have one – were pitilessly blown away by the wind, which hissed and howled like a wounded hyena. The year, thought Jaggi, was certain to go down as one of the wettest on record when the figures were released. The only question was how far back? Twenty years? Fifty years? Since records began?

Carrying in one hand a suitcase containing the essentials for a weekend away, and holding an umbrella in the other, Jaggi stepped out of the house to face the elements. A gust of chilly wind smacked him in the face with the wrath of an angry god. He said something under his breath and shuddered in the numbing cold as he got into his Honda Accord parked on the drive.

Children, squeezed into one-size-too-tight waterproofs from last year, picked their way to school, their eyes, filled with tears from the wind, stepping carefully over every shallow pool of water that every dip and depression in the pavement had become.

Matronly housemothers, bronchial-breathed and old-fashioned in their plastic macs and hoods, went about their early morning business with sullen, deep-creased faces. They coughed and they wheezed and trapped sneezes in paper handkerchiefs while they poured scorn on the weather and muttered things to each other, or just to themselves. Shopkeepers, opening up for the day, rolled their eyes at the dark clouds hanging above them and grumpily wished each other good day with special imprecations reserved for the day.

Oh, it does get to you, the weather, Jaggi thought to himself. Can drag the spirits right down into your boots, this never-ending torture of drip, drip, drip, plop, plop, plop of rain on car windscreens, rooftops and windows. It certainly flattens in a single swipe any reason you might have to get up in the morning and face the day with a smile. The city must have immensely powerful absorbers in its foundations, he thought, otherwise it would be floating by now, or turned into another Venice – the poor man's Venice in the north of England.

Birds had deserted the area and those that did remain made a sorry spectacle as, whipped and lashed by the wind, half-blinded by rain and reduced to no more than little bundles of sodden rags, they staggered aimlessly in all directions or struggled to hold on to their perch on leafless branches, folding and unfolding their wings to shake off the water trapped in them. Over a period of nine days, this ritual had become something of a habit with them.

Public parks were devoid of any human presence and leaves lay rotting everywhere on the ground. Fungi sprouted from tree trunks. Bronze statues of great inventors and war braves gazed sorrowfully into puddles of rainwater that lay around them.

Shops had their awnings tilted at angles to protect wares put on the pavement for sale, but rain somehow managed to get at them. The whole dismal scene seemed as unreal as a cheery grin on Monday morning.

Jaggi left his Honda in the car park at Stockport station and made his way to the platforms to catch the train. An elderly individual, badly asthmatic, following a few paces behind him, was coughing and wheezing noisily. In the subway leading to the platforms, water dripped from the ceiling in a number of places and also from the noses of many people passing through it.

The travellers, largely commuters by appearance and muffled up in overcoats and scarves, pushed past Jaggi with impatient strides. He took no notice of them and carried on at his usual serene pace. At the back of his mind, he knew there was plenty of time to get to the platform, so he saw no need to rush now and wait longer there for the arrival of the train.

A little boy, drowsy with sleep and yawning uncontrollably, was being dragged by his mother against his will. She kept up a non-stop chant of exhortations in a husky, chain-smoker's voice to inject some urgency into the youngster's steps, but he showed no inclination to respond, looking like he would rather be at home tucked up in bed with his beloved cuddly toy than being pushed against his will towards a railway platform.

As Jaggi and other passengers waited on the platform, an antiquated public address system crackled into life with an announcement by a woman who, it seemed, had taken special lessons to sound unintelligible and had, as a favour to the passengers on that day, slipped a plum into her mouth, which she had then covered with her hand or a cotton handkerchief.

The train roared in at speed, covering the track like a bandage covers a wound. It scraped on the track, groaned, lurched and finally came to a halt with a high-pitched whine. Hurriedly, the passengers opened the carriage doors and charged in, eyes looking hungrily for seats.

Without losing any time at all, a few of them buried themselves into newspapers, books and magazines. Others quickly spread out their laptops on the tables and glued themselves to their devices.

Among the people who entered Jaggi's compartment was a woman who reminded him of his wife. For a moment, she stopped near him to shift her suitcase from her right hand to the left. Memories of Barbara suddenly flared up in Jaggi's mind.

He felt an urge to help her with her luggage but suppressed the temptation in case she turned out to be a feminist and took offence at Jaggi's friendly gesture. For her part, the woman gave him a furtive look and moved further down the carriage where seats were available.

Jaggi gazed out at the scenery although the window was badly streaked and stained by raindrops on the outside and covered with a film of condensation inside. It was a long time since he had last made this journey. On that occasion he had travelled to London with Barbara. They had taken a package deal, a birthday treat from him to her, to see "Les Misérables" in the West End, have a Thai dinner and stay in a hotel at South Kensington.

Jaggi had done this route many times in the past. The difference was in those distant days the journey began where it was now going to end. He had grown so used to the travel that he knew every bend, each curve, in the track, where the train tilted, as well as all the straight stretches where one could go to the dining car, grab hold of a cup of tea or coffee, bring it safely back to one's seat and drink it in peace without spilling a drop or scalding one's mouth.

Announcements by the senior conductor welcomed the new passengers on board, told them about the location of the various carriages, the validity of their tickets and wished them a pleasant journey.

They were quickly followed by further announcements, this time by the chief steward of the buffet car. He reeled out details of catering arrangements and items of food and drinks available that day.

Further announcements about maintenance work being carried out on the track were accompanied by apologies to the passengers for the possibility of delay by a few minutes in their journey.

People read and did crossword puzzles. Others played with their electronic devices. Those who got tired quickly yawned, stretched and rubbed their eyes with their knuckles. A twentysomething miss seated within Jaggi's view watched her face in a small hand mirror and curled and uncurled her lips like a mime artist as she applied lip gloss layers to them. From time to time someone's mobile telephone would ring and provoke hostile reaction from those rudely awakened from their asleep.

An hour later, the click-a-clack rhythm of the train made Jaggi drowsy. He leaned against the headrest and closed his eyes. In no time, memories moved into gear and the years that had vanished were back. Fragments from the past, like feathers floating in autumnal mist, began to drift to and fro, reminding him of the days when, almost without fail, he used to head north every week or every other Friday, weaving romantic fantasies in his head.

Through the mist of time, he remembered his very first visit to Manchester when he spent a weekend with a friend, Subhash Anand, whom he knew from his university days in India and who was now doing his doctorate in textiles at the University of Manchester Institute of Science and Technology. It was this fateful trip that had brought Barbara into his life.

It was also his first trip out of London by train, apart from a few excursions to places close to the capital, Maidenhead, Windsor, Slough and such. The day was no different from any other and the train, punctual to the minute, left Euston station for Manchester from platform 14.

Surprisingly, it was not crowded at all, considering it was Friday evening when thousands of people headed North for the weekend. Eagerly, he looked out of the widow to catch his first glimpse of the English countryside, but by the time the train got to the Midlands and came into the open country it was already dark.

At Manchester, Jaggi was met at Piccadilly station by his friend. Next day, they went to the party, which was given by one of Subhash's friends from the university. As Jaggi was the guest of a guest and knew not a soul there, he stayed with his friend for large part of the early evening, until he clamped eyes on Barbara and their chance encounter changed the course of their lives.

The journey out of London was so different from the myriad of train trips he had made in India. There, as soon as you deposited your bag on the luggage rack and took your seat, often with a huge sigh of relief because of the problems you encountered getting to the station, someone sitting opposite you or within talking distance would strike up a conversation on any topic under the sun and open up his life to you, spilling out details of where and under which astrological sign he was born, the name and description of the street where he spent the early part of his childhood, the town where he went to school and the place he was headed that day and, of course, the purpose of the visit.

The talkative stranger would then swap family stories with you, unleash anecdotes, such as the train journey he had made three and a half years ago when the waist measurement of his trousers was thirty-four inches, and since then it had gone up by more than three inches, mainly because of his love of good food, or any food. Finally he would reveal with enormous delight what his mother, wife or sister had cooked for him for that journey and which he was carrying with him in a tiffin box and would invite you to break bread with him, thus setting the scene that you met someone as a stranger and parted as friend.

But here in Britain, no one took any notice of the person sitting on their left, right or opposite and no one offered to share their newspaper or magazine, let alone food or refreshments. You bought your own from the dining car and quietly ate it without making any fuss at all.

Back in the present, the train slowed down to a gentle roll and a sign along the track gave notice that London Euston was one mile away. The voice of the senior conductor reminded passengers to take their personal belongings with them. That marked the end of the journey.

Once again Jaggi found himself in the city where he had spent many long struggling years at the time he was trying to get a foothold in the new country. Now full of confidence, he proceeded to the taxi rank, got inside one, slammed the door shut and gave the driver his destination as the Churchill Hotel.

Chapter 4

Jaggi smiled. Jaggi always smiled.

He was stepping out of a black limousine at Westminster Pier. It was here that the business baron's yacht, The Indian Princess, was berthed to await the arrival of his guests. Fleets of other limousines were bringing invitees from their hotels in different parts of the capital.

The driver held the car door open for Jaggi with a gloved hand and with the other pointed in the direction of the yacht. Flashing a huge smile, he said courteously, 'Over there, sir, that way,' and wished Jaggi a splendidly good time aboard the vessel.

A reception party comprising three people, two bubbly, vivacious young women in their late twenties and a man at least ten years their senior, stood at the entrance of the yacht in a neat formation, within nudging distance of each other, to welcome the guests as they came on board.

To Jaggi it was clear that Sagar was not the man squeezed between the two beauties. This man was white, not Indian. Also, he was a lot younger for someone who had travelled as a fully grown adult from Bombay to Britain in the sixties. The man had a high-crowned forehead which was etched with wavy lines that emphasised his somewhat beaky nose and slightly jutting chin.

The women were exquisitely turned out in identical two-piece, light brown, woollen suits and sported matching lipstick. They had the stunning good looks of magazine beauties – pale blue eyes twinkling, white teeth gleaming, bodies alluringly well-proportioned, hair the colour of runny honey.

Both radiated a glow that suggested they had either spent the last couple of weeks sprawled on a sunny beach in an exclusive Caribbean resort or had spent a large amount of money in some swanky tanning salon in London's West End. One of them proudly displayed a huge whirlpool of a dimple slap bang in the middle of her right cheek.

A short distance from the trio stood a host of svelte young waitresses in black and white outfits, razor-starched white caps and aprons, holding silver trays with chilled champagne in fluted glasses and finger food of both English and Indian variety – delicate canapés, prawns in spicy sauce, miniature Kathi kebabs, cocktail samosas, small, almond-sized idlis with greenish-white coconut chutney to go with them as dip and other bite-size goodies on sticks.

It was evident that the waitresses had come from a top event management agency, because the rocking-chair ease with which they dispensed the mouth-watering comestibles – and their own luscious grins – indicated that it was all part of a good day's work for a good day's money.

Scented candles flickered in frosted glass holders and gave out a wonderfully enticing, sandalwoody smell, which is always a hit with Indians the world over and is guaranteed to warm the cockles of their hearts.

'Welcome to Mr Sagar's evening,' trilled the woman closest to the entrance as she greeted the arriving guests enthusiastically with a nod and the suggestion of a bow. Now and then she would extend her slender hand that had exquisitely tapering fingers and freshly painted pale-brown nails to them. But it was largely restricted to those who made a good impression on her, or took her fancy. A stretch-limo smile made frequent, albeit fleeting, appearance on her face.

'Welcome aboard The Indian Princess,' gushed the man with infectious smiles. 'Hope you have an enjoyable time with us tonight.'

'Good to have you with us this evening,' warbled the second woman in a softly caressing voice, as she beamed a sparkly white grin, 'Hope you have a good time.' She made a small, courteous bow to the guests and offered her hand to those who made a good impression on her.

In spite of faces wreathed in melon-slice smiles and eyes shining brightly with anticipation, the guests looked a trifle uneasy. There had been no contact of any kind between them since they wished each other good luck, good health and good fortune as they bid their final farewell amid engulfing embraces and crushing handshakes at Victoria station in London more than thirty-odd years ago and dispersed in different directions to carve out a future for themselves, each in their own way and on their own term.

Here on the yacht, all that seemed, as it really was, years and years ago, almost something that belonged to a different time in a different era. No one had any idea how changed their one-time fellow-travellers would look like, or whether they would be able to recognise each other. This was all too clearly reflected by the somewhat anxious expression some of them wore on their faces.

However, they were cushioned by the knowledge that once upon a time, for over two weeks, they shared with each other a sea journey from India to

Europe. Fragments of what took place during that voyage still lingered in their heads and it was sufficient to give them courage to make their own reintroductions, shake hands, exchange friendly greetings and reconnect with each other.

And so, amid cheerful smiles and polite nods, the game of face spotting got under way in the sumptuous surroundings of the millionaire's yacht.

Scores of middle-class, middle-aged, middle-income sub-continentals under one roof. Spread out waists, overweight bodies, grey hair or balding domes everywhere.

A motley mix of medics, dentists, accountants, engineers, architects, factory hands, a handful of them were retired, the rest were winding down their careers. They were all nattily dressed in penguin outfits, three-piece, pin-striped suits and had matching ties around white collars, as they peered into each other's face apprehensively, doing their best to pierce through the haze of more than three decades for the vaguest clue, the faintest hint of recognition.

Gushy greetings punctuated by shrieks of delight and squeals of incredulity went up in the air as somebody managed to recognise someone – a teller of tall tales, amusing anecdotes and an interesting turn of phrase strolling on the sun deck of the Italian ocean liner or a habitual early riser, going through the routine of light exercises or power-walking round the deck with long, impatient strides.

There were also prolonged, bone-crushing embraces from those who, familiar or not, were eager to demonstrate their fellow-feelings towards their countrymen. Hands were pumped with gusto, backs slapped enthusiastically and friendly punches thrown on the shoulder, arm and chest. Strangers clinked glasses to drink each other's health.

Compliments flew in the air like confetti at a wedding on a windy day, and the guests lavished the party host with gold-plated praise for organising a get-together of such an unusual nature and on so grand a scale.

'It's ten out of ten plus one to the man today or on any other day for his initiative and generosity as far as I'm concerned,' enthused a distinguished-looking man, cutting a dash in a jacket of raw Assam silk, a matching tie and black trousers. Of average build, he had a bulge tumbling over his belt. His head was capped by battleship-grey hair that was neatly pasted to his skull.

Ostensibly he was addressing the person standing next to him but it was also meant for all those within hearing range of him in the reception hall of the yacht that had been tastefully decorated for the occasion.

'Let me say this: It takes guts by the bellyful and dosh by the bucketful, to throw a party of such high standard. Goodness me! It's truly fabulous, on any feel-good scale … and that, too, for virtual strangers. Let's face it, Bhai Sahib, it's not a reunion in the traditional sense of the word, now is it? Just take a good look around you,' he said.

'Of course, of course,' came the swift answer. 'One looks from Punjab, the other from Gujarat, the third from Bengal or maybe from Maharashtra or Himachal … who knows? We were complete strangers to each other – weren't we? – when we boarded the Roma in Bombay all those years ago and we weren't exactly close friends or bosom buddies when we got off it in Italy, now were we?'

The listener hastily shook his head.

'The man obviously possesses a large heart. There's no question about that.'

'None at all. Such a grand party and let me tell you this: all it cost me is the Tube fare from my house to the hotel I have been put up. And, you know what? I live in Harrow.'

'An excellent and rare combination this: to have untold wealth and be generous with it. My kind of man through and through. Three rousing cheers to him. Bravo! Hurrah! Hip, hip hooray! Long may his tribe increase!'

'You know what my ambition is?' he asked his fellow guest.

A shake of the head in reply prompted him to explain, 'It is to have a wallet bulging with notes – fifty notes of fifty pounds, twenty notes of twenty pound, ten notes of ten and five of five – all told a grand total of over three thousand pounds in my pocket. All the time, mind you, not just for a few minutes. Take out a fistful from the wallet to spend and replace them in the next few minutes. Not much to ask for, now is it?' he demanded, and broke into a smile and a huge shrug.

'No, not at all.' Another shake of the head. 'You know what? I have something similar on my mind.'

'Don't tell me that?'

'Oh, yes. I'll tell you about it in a moment. Let's first lubricate our throats and raise a glass to the host of this social whirl.'

'Of course, of course, my thoughts, too. Which part of India are you from?'

With great enthusiasm, he raised his champagne glass as high as it would go towards the crystal chandelier – spilling a few drops in the process – in a toast to the high-living, free-spending, money-no-object host. Two other guests standing close by, who found the reunion at the upper end of their expectation, decided to join in, raising their glasses with matching gusto.

Bowing low to the wealthy, well-connected and powerful is stitched into the fabric of Indian society and it was all too evident in the high-octane praise garlanded on the mega-rich financial wizard.

'Well deserved cheers, to be absolutely honest,' observed a tall, pin-striped Sikh with a sturdy frame, bright red turban sitting on his head like an enormous crown, a waxed twirling moustache and an impressive beard on a cheerful, half-smiling face and bright eyes under bushy brows.

He swirled his scotch three or four times with a somewhat careless abandon, the ice cubes clinking in the glass, before he rinsed his mouth merrily with a generous quantity of the liquid. Then he proceeded, 'The kind of hectic lives we lead in this country, whether out of choice or due to circumstances beyond our control, what chance do we have of being able to organise an awesome affair like this in order to reconnect with people from days long gone by?'

Happily munching canapés and other goodies, the guests moved about freely in the large reception hall, relishing every minute of being aboard the sumptuously appointed vessel. They had never been inside one of these before in their life. The fact that it was a unique experience for them showed in the looks of joyous wonderment that shone on their faces.

All of them also seemed somewhat overwhelmed by everything around them and their eyes kept darting from object to object and from one direction to the other, consumed by curiosity as to what these expensive sea-going toys looked like from the inside.

Most of them were only aware of the royal yacht Britannia, which had taken the Queen round the world and aboard which two of her sons had sailed on their honeymoon. But they had glimpsed it only in news coverage on television from the outside and had little idea about its interior.

A few of them had also seen, again on their television screens, Robert Maxwell's yacht, Lady Ghislane, from which the pension-plundering media mogul had mysteriously disappeared off the Canary Islands in 1991.

One theme resonated throughout the Indian Princess: that Sagar was a man of immense wealth and generous heart. But they found it hard to believe that someone who had travelled with them as an economy-class, fare-paying passenger on a ship from Bombay to Genoa, in circumstances not much different from their own, had pulled off the masterly feat of owning a luxury yacht with all the lavish trappings that went with it.

In their collective view, a vessel like the one on which they found themselves having the time of their life was the ultimate status symbol of wealth. That he should be magnanimous enough to host a party on it and invite them to experience the delights of its ambience was something that had never occurred to them in their wildest dreams. For them it was the stuff of fairytales.

With breathless admiration for their host Sagar, the guests, who had invested their working life into Britain and had, in the process, notched up stellar successes in their own fields of activity, marvelled at the size and opulence of the Indian Princess. What they found was vastly different and enormously superior to what they had envisaged. It was luxury at the highest level. So, in thrall to his wealth and success, they wondered how one of their country cousins had carved up such an impressive patch in Britain's financial turf.

In their eyes, Sagar was an alchemist straight out of the top drawer. Certainly knew the magic ingredients of success. Riches of such staggering proportions that most ordinary mortals could only dream of could not be conjured up by keeping your hands in the pockets. Oh no, sir, you had to strain every sinew in your body for each shining penny.

Money, by all accounts, was no object to him. He had it in heaps and piles, tens of millions. It was taken for granted that his business dealings ran into telephone numbers – not from national but international section of the directory. Millions were small change and four-figure sums something he casually put in his pocket while changing from one Savile Row suit to another and forgot all about it in the next few seconds.

Also convinced were they that he had a staff of servants and they waited on him hand and foot twenty-four hours a day – secretaries, butlers, chauffeurs, chefs, the whole lot – and when one added to that number the live-in housekeepers, maids and nannies for the other members of the household, the household workers probably outnumbered the family three or four to one. Some suggestions went so outrageously far as to proclaim that those who polished his shoes had a Rolex dangling from their wrist.

In the most modest of their estimates, he had a string of luxury homes dotted around the Home Counties. On top of that he had several other places overseas, sunny penthouses, holiday villas, luxurious retreats.

The palatial mansion which was his principal residence in the United Kingdom was probably in Surrey or Hertfordshire or Buckinghamshire with a long, tree-lined drive leading to it. It was lavish and aristocratic, hung with original masterpieces and had a garden stretching across acres and acres of land. It had stunning views with woodland on three sides and boasted its own private lake in which scores of swans glided gracefully.

Deer frolicked freely in the garden and on its manicured lawns with fountains and cascading waterfalls, peacocks from India strutted their stuff without a care in the western or eastern world. And, yes, it had fruit-laden orchards, a mini golf range, tennis court, helicopter pad, garages for at least a dozen luxury cars, all of them, it went without saying, gleaming and top-of-the-range. Rolls, Mercs, Jags, a Porsche and a Lamborghini plus "Ferrari on Friday", each personalised to meet the needs of the individual using it.

Was it any wonder then that the super-rich boy had got himself a super-luxury yacht to spend his spare time on? Oh, it really was a blissful state to be in when you could live your life to the full at such rarefied level, be in a position to clear your bills with a scratch of pen on a cheque and indulge your every whim and fancy! Some wondered which Hindu god he worshipped in his prayers to have his wishes granted for a multi-storeyed fortune.

And what's more, in spite of his phenomenal wealth and high-rolling lifestyle, the money mogul had not succumbed to the temptation of being a pukka gorah toff. Steadfastly, they speculated, he had stuck to his Indian roots and was close to the core values acquired in the old country. So much so he had even named his yacht *The Indian Princess*. It showed the good side of Indian influences at the highest level.

Well, for goodness sake, you can't ask for more than that from a man of his standing, can you? It was quite possible, some guests took the view, that he was closely connected to royalty back home. Probably a fair-to-middling, second-eleven royal himself … or a close cousin of some maharajah? Anyway, royal connection or not, there was scarcely any doubt that he was a gentleman of the highest order.

Plenty of hearts were also a-flutter in anticipation over what was to follow on the yacht later. If the hospitality that lay ahead was half as good as they had experienced in the first few minutes, they were sure when the party was finally over and all the foamy farewells said they would go back to their homes with a huge grin on their faces and gladness in their heart that they took up the invitation and that the excursion was worth every penny spent by the host.

The visitors to the yacht were not wealthy, but neither were they poor. They were comfortably off, some even borderline rich, certainly affluent enough to pick up the tab of a good lifestyle, including a sprinkling of luxuries, like a portfolio of shares in blue-chip companies, private medical insurance for themselves and their family plus sufficient means to send their offspring to elite universities and other prestigious institutions of learning.

Their marriages were enduring and they had done well in their professional life. Many of their sons and daughters were doing even better, pursuing careers in top professions, as doctors, lawyers, dentists, pharmacists, architects and they were proud of their achievements, feeling doubly successful because their offspring were high achievers.

English wasn't their cradle-tongue but their command of it was impressive, considering they had not made any wilful effort to improve it. As a consequence, their accent had a heavy Indian inflection.

Their outlook on life was quite positive. They were not insular at all and made every attempt to integrate with the local community and had, by and large, assimilated well into British society. They considered themselves an integral part of their adopted homeland and their complete loyalty was to it. They thought they contributed richly not only to the economy of the country but to its social fabric as well.

Many of them played important roles in public life and actively discharged their community duties. Some had become magistrates to dispense justice in smaller courts while others had gone on to be presidents, secretaries or treasurers of their local Rotary clubs. There were also those who had set up their own charities and staged local events for funds.

All this was in addition to rattling charity cans at street corners or pounding the pavements of their towns and cities in sponsored marathons, full or half, to raise money for all sorts of causes, national as well as international. The more adventurous journeyed as far away as Mount Kilimanjaro in Kenya, and the Himalayan region on sponsored cycling and trekking trips. It gave them the feeling that they were winning their way in Britain and making useful contributions to the society of which they were an important part.

In their favourite sport of cricket, they supported England, home and away, except when England were playing against India. Their loyalty came into conflict then and homeland's gravitational pull kicked in and they rooted for India.

But in spite of their total commitment to their adopted country and the fact that they had lived in Britain most of their working life and given it their best, they sometimes felt they were considered by a large section of the population as no more than guest workers whose stay in the country was temporary and one day they would pack up their bags and go back to where they came from.

The general feeling among them was that good-news stories about Indians that reflected their traditional values of treating people with respect and kindness, commitment to the job in hand and working hard for a better future were either spiked or not given the positive coverage they deserved. Also, their contribution, collective or individual, to the country's social and economic advancement was wilfully pushed to the back pages by sections of the media, especially the right-wing rags, and political parties of similar persuasion.

They resented being lumped together with other migrant groups from the sub-continent, branded as "Asians" and portrayed in negative light when the only thing they had in common with them was the region they had come from and nothing else. In attitude and outlook they were worlds apart and as far as ideology and core values were concerned they might have been from different planets millions of miles apart.

Their bonds with the land of their birth remained strong. India continued to be close to their hearts and kept cropping up in their conversation every few minutes. They kept in touch with their aged parents, getting-on brothers and sisters and close friends in the old country and shared with them news of major events in their own lives and that of those close to them.

Every so often they felt an ache for the old homeland and returned to it, in their heads and in their conversation with others. There was another alternative – hop on the first flight bound for Delhi or Bombay and be there in a matter of hours. In their experience, it was easier to travel by air from Britain to India than by rail or road from one part of India to another, a fraction of the distance.

With age bearing down on them, they feared that their family's close connections with the mother country would weaken when they were gone. And it caused them a degree of anxiety. Their offspring were born in Britain, grew up there and as such, rightfully, considered themselves British. The outlook the youngsters had on life was different, vastly different, from their own. This forced them to think of themselves as the last generation with close links with India.

Most of them believed that the country you were born in and your upbringing in it, good, bad or indifferent, democratic or ruled by an autocratic dictator, was like a parent to you. It was the land of your forebears and the forebears of their forebears. On its soil you first opened your eyes to the world and its soothing cradle songs brought the first sweet sound of music to your ears.

It was on its ground you learned to crawl on your hands and knees and take your first faltering steps. It was here children were nurtured and grasped the basics of life. Its tales were part of your folklore and its streets the classrooms of life where you spent an important part of your adolescence, learned what friendship and loyalty were all about and how to deal with moral and ethical dilemmas. With its books, music and films you grew up and its social influences played a pivotal role in shaping the person you became in life and the worldview you formed and kept.

Its temples, mosques, churches and other places of worship taught you the difference between good and bad and how to untangle yourself from the bad should you, by any misfortune, find yourself in it. Its institutions of learning prepared you with knowledge and wisdom to navigate your way through the complexities of life. The country also prepared you with the tips and tricks of survival and imparted valuable life skills and lessons on how to engage with the world around you.

All of them were weaned on the Indian way of life and they had never lost connection with their roots. The old links still played a significant role in their daily dealings.

Often they went down to the local cinema complex with their family to see Bollywood blockbusters, subscribed to Indian television channels, listened to Indian film songs at home and in their cars. Whenever the demands of their busy professional and equally busy social life allowed, they read books in Hindi, Gujarati, Bengali and scores of other Indian languages.

The spiritual side of life, too, was not neglected. The vast majority of them, if not all, refrained from eating beef, the cow being considered holy. Once a week, mostly on Tuesdays or Thursdays, they had purely vegetarian food and also abstained from drinking alcohol.

Religion played a small but fairly important role in their life. Every home had its family shrine, usually the smallest room in the house. In the case of those whose commitment was not so strong, it was just a corner of the smallest room. Many had personalised their religion and it was here they worshipped their favourite deity from the pantheon of gods and goddesses that their henotheistic Hindu faith allowed.

Apart from dresses bought on the high street, their womenfolk wore traditional saris, dhotis and shalwar-kamiz suits, sprinkled the parting of their hair with vermilion powder to symbolise their marital status and, once a year on the festive occasion of *Karva Chauth,* observed a dawn-to-moonrise fast for the wellbeing of their husbands.

With cheerful faces, receding hairlines and expanding waistlines, the suited and booted silvery sub-continentals stood within nudging distance of each other in knots of threes or fours, happily lapping up Sagar's hospitality.

Holding a drink in one hand and a little party treat in the other, they chattered freely and gesticulated animatedly, between bites and swallows, about their memories of the sea voyage, about the highs and lows, the twists and turns of their life in Britain as well as about anything and nothing, flitting from one topic to another, taking in a whole range of subjects – politics, their profession, their holiday excursions, their families and the everyday events of their busy and flourishing lives.

With more than three decades gone since their sea journey, they doubtless had plenty of ground to cover.

The overwhelming impression this eclectic bunch of mature years gave was that they were quite well-adjusted, orderly and upright citizens of the land they had chosen as their new home.

Jaggi spent a short time in the company of four men whose working life had only a short time to run and, therefore, their attention was focused – with mounting concern – on pensions, annuities and, above all, the state of their health. Matters of wellbeing included physical fitness as well as ailments – who suffered from what disease – and which stage it now was in.

'I live in Pinner,' said a heavy, plumpish, diminutive man with a balding dome. He was wearing a dark brown suit and a lipstick-red tie. He had a jovial, lived-in face, a grey head balding at the front and small gaps in his teeth. 'In our close friendship group there are fourteen people. All of them from India and, as you must have guessed, seven men and their spouse girls.'

It raised a smile from those listening to him.

'Now would you believe it if I told you that five out of the magnificent seven men have been under a doctor's knife for operation of one kind or another – angioplasty, stent, bypass, valve replacement, hip replacement, knee surgery, you name it, we've had it. One even had a triple heart bypass. Yours truly, needless to say, enjoys the privilege of belonging to that exclusive group.' A wide, gummy smile spread across his face and he ran a hand over his heart in a highly theatrical manner, as if it was a highly desirable feat to achieve, some sort of badge of honour to be worn on the chest with pride.

The three looked on rather sympathetically, doubtless remembering some parallel experience of their own or that of their friend or close relative. 'We're now thinking of forming an exclusive club. Of the five, one has had so many heart bypasses that after the last round of surgery on him the transport ministry wanted to put up road signs.' The man let out a high, discordant, woodpecker laugh, his head cocked to one side, pleased with his attempt at humouring his listeners who, after a little hesitation, joined in.

'I take it he will be the president of the club?' asked one of them, with something of a cackle.

'Sure ... until someone with a quadruple bypass comes along to take the crown from him,' replied the man and gave a squealing laugh. 'Or maybe next time the biggest scar on the body will determine who becomes the new chief.'

Jaggi detached himself from this group and strolled over to the next one where a man with a gleaming head, fringed with a border of silver hair and wearing glasses in a rectangular frame, was propounding, somewhat grandly, on differences in everyday life between India and Britain.

'Even after spending a huge chunk of their life in this country, some people still behave as if they are in the back streets of Batala or Baroda. Array bhai, try to get this into your head that you are in England. Things are different here. Have been for centuries and will always be so in the years to come. Therefore, it is entirely your responsibility to retune your own mindset. Nobody else is going to do it for you. Anyway, if the Indian way of life was so dear to you, you shouldn't have left your rural backwater in the first place. Should have stayed put where you were. Right?' He waited for a moment for response from any of his listeners.

Two of them nodded, giving their somewhat lukewarm response. The third, with curly black hair going grey at the temples, just looked on sceptically, without saying anything.

'There is no point carrying little Punjabs and little Gujarats on your back wherever you go in the world, be it London, Leeds or Lancaster. You can't live with India forever in your head. You have to open up to new thinking, new experiences, new influences ... and, in my opinion, the sooner you do that the better it is.'

He stretched out his hand and set his drink down on a table nearest to him. Carefully wiping a bit of grease from his fingers with a napkin, he looked around for a waste bin to dispose of the paper but unable to find one, the man neatly folded it and put it into his pocket in a display of good manners and sense of decorum.

'Wait a minute, that's nothing new. Every migrant community does that,' said the sceptic at last, an amiable, homely sort of individual, with well-brushed hair, the colour of sardine paste, and dark brown eyes behind scholarly bifocals. 'Take it from me Indians do not have the monopoly on that.'

He stabbed a finger into the air forcefully to underline the point. It was evident he had heard this argument before, many times perhaps, and found it easy to deal with it. On each previous occasion he had probably put forward the same argument that he was doing now.

'Look, more than five million Britons have settled in other countries. What do you think they do when they go to live in Spain, France or Australia or wherever else? Now don't tell me they don't create little Englands, mini Scotlands and little Wales there? Of course they do. The values we acquire from the family and the society we live in largely determine what we are. These values shouldn't be thrown out of the window simply because you have decided to give up one country and take up another. You should value them, cherish them, no matter where you are.'

For a few seconds, he looked around expectantly for someone to get involved in the discussion, support him, refute him or just state their opinion, whatever it was. But when response failed to materialise from any of the listeners, he went on to elaborate his view, 'I'll tell you what they do. They do exactly what other migrant communities do in this country or in any other country for that matter. Bhai Sahib, it is human nature we're talking about here and as such, it applies to all humans, be they English, Indian, Chinese or Eskimos. Let's face it, most of us are creatures of habit. It has to do with our upbringing, our lifestyle, what we're used to and what we're comfortable with. Right? Am I making sense?'

A nod, albeit an uncertain one, from one of the men in the group, an elderly gent with a snowy white goatee, the only bearded guest on board the yacht – apart from the Sikh gentleman – gave him encouragement to expand upon what he said was his theory.

'A man creates a lifestyle for himself, whatever it may be … a pint in the evening with friends in the local, football on Saturday afternoons with the lads, big nights out later, church on Sunday with the family, roast dinner with two vegetables in the evenings and so on. Over a period of time, this routine makes its way into the bloodstream and becomes his lifestyle. Now when it's taken away from him, for whatever reason, like change of scenery, migration and what have you, he misses it, pines for it and, naturally, tries to recreate it. Believe me, it makes perfect sense to me. Being out of one's comfort zone is not a good place to be, is it?'

The line of reasoning and the way he coolly built the case brought a nod of understanding from others.

'And let me make it clear to you that as far as I'm concerned, I see nothing, repeat nothing, wrong with holding on to core values and traditions from your own culture, or your lifestyle for that matter, provided you don't become dogmatic about it. Never close yourself off to the good aspects of other cultures. You see, other cultures also have good things to offer that can enrich your life. You have to be ready to integrate them into the fabric of your own culture. I admit all influences are not necessarily good but nor are they all bad. So exercise your judgement. Simple. Now do you think there is anything wrong with that? I don't think so. Oh no, sir.'

'You're right. Perfectly right. On this point I will agree with you ten times out of ten,' said one of his listeners, nodding vehemently.

'According to my way of thinking, we should be ready to take on board anything from other cultures that helps us become better human beings and better citizens of the country we live in, whether it's the land of our birth or of domicile. We Indians living in Britain have dual culture and need to carve out our own identities … immigrant mentality has to give up its hold on us.' The man took a sharp intake of breath and glanced around for confirmation of his views, his eye flitting from face to face. Everyone duly obliged, nodding their understanding almost simultaneously.

'When America farts, Britain says "pardon me" and that's what, I seriously believe, is the problem with this country.' This observation came from a rotund man with a full-moon face, luxurious white hair and slightly protruding teeth. He was having his say in a group that was engrossed in a debate on present-day politics.

'Britain can't make up its mind whether it's an independent sovereign state, a member of the European Union or the fifty-first state of America. Now, honestly, if you have one foot in Brussels, the other in Washington and still want to hold on the belief that London is the world's centre of gravity, you're bound to end up with a sore arse, aren't you?' and he looked up at his audience, his smiling eyes seeking endorsement. If the remark was intended to inject a little humour into the discussion, it more than achieved its purpose. Everyone within earshot chuckled.

'When I was coming to Britain – goes without saying with you good people on the Roma boat – I strongly believed that I was going to a free country. But, frankly, now I'm not so sure,' added the man. 'If I knew then that we'd be just an outpost of America I would have gone straight there. Look at it this way: if you have to ride an animal, why not choose an elephant?'

Every listening head nodded. It gave him encouragement to continue. 'Britain follows America like Mary's little lamb. What happens there today is sure to happen here tomorrow. This principle applies to you and me and millions like us. But when it comes to power at the top level, they march to a tune that's completely different.'

'Absolutely right,' a voice went up.

'Take, for example, the presidency of America. The president has to give up the job after two terms. No more than that. Not so here. Oh no, sir. Our prime minister can go on till he or she has one foot in the grave and the other is suffering from severe rheumatoid arthritis.'

'That's what power does to you,' his listener concurred. 'Once you've developed a taste for it, it's hell-hard to give it up. And for career politicians, like we have many of them in Britain, it's just a job, and they are in it for themselves, first and foremost. Naturally, it is in their interest to hang on to power for as long as they can.'

'Craving for power is nothing new, you know,' a third intervened. 'It's been going on since time immemorial. It was the same story with ancient empires, Rome, Greece, Egypt … you name it.'

'Okay, that maybe so, but just because it has been going on for thousands of years doesn't make it right for it to go on for another thousand years, now does it, tell me?'

'I don't know about you but I feel the two biggest threats to mankind are Americanisation of the world and Radical Islam. Mark my words, friends, if we are not careful all the males of this world will end up with a back-to-front baseball cap on their heads and a circumcised dick in their pants, if pants indeed they would be wearing.' This brought a chorus of amused laughter.

'No, I'm not kidding,' returned the man, with a thin smile. 'I'm deadly serious. From where we are at present, it's not going to happen next week or next year. But then nor am I thinking of centuries away. More like middle distance. You get it?'

'You mean somewhere in between?' he was asked.

The man offered a slow, thoughtful nod in reply.

Jaggi moved on and next encountered a three-strong group whose topic of conversation was films, of the Bollywood variety.

'From the very outset let me make it absolutely clear that I'm not a lover of Indian films. Never was, never will be. So when my family – mainly ladies – pays one of its periodic visits to the local multiplex to see a Hindi film, I tell them to switch off their brain as soon as they enter the cinema.' This opinion was voiced by a tall, angular man with an elongated face.

With the tip of his moist tongue he licked his lower lip, perhaps out of habit, smiled a set smile and continued, 'Bollywood largely churns out mind-numbing dross. Its films, as I see it, are like a meat burger: you eat one and find it so distasteful you resolve never to go within an arm's reach of another again. But, as it happens, time passes and the shock wears off. So you put the awful experience behind you.'

'I know, I know,' said the man listening to him. 'A few months down the road you say to yourself, well, what the heck, let's have another one, this time without cheese and the vinegar-dripping slice of cucumber. Maybe the experience won't be that bad after all.'

'Yeah, yeah, yeah, so you stop by a burger joint and order this soft-meat, fast-food thingy glistening with grease, slathered with some white stuff and slapped between two halves of a bun with a sliver of gherkin and a dash of tomato ketchup. One bite and your worst fears are immediately confirmed. Sure as hell, it is as bad as the last one. Probably worse. It's the same with films.'

'I don't know about burgers, but I can tell you this: chicken drums taste a lot better on a yacht than in a fast-food joint,' offered the guest listening to him and holding a piece of chicken in his hand.

'If Indian boys keep marrying English girls at the rate they are doing at the moment, what chance do we as parents have of finding suitable boys for our daughters?' lamented a shy, low-key fellow. Full of jerky movements, he had deep lines of anxiety etched on his kind, plain face. Anchored in the middle of a loose circle of five men, he let everyone around him ponder the point, anxious eyes scanning each face for reaction.

One grimaced and shook his head in a show of disappointment. Another behaved in a somewhat similar fashion but to indicate that, in his opinion, the chances were somewhere between minuscule and non-existent. The remaining two nodded in varying degrees of agreement with him.

'I have two daughters,' he proceeded to explain. 'The older one is thirty-three and the younger will be 29 next June. Believe me, friends, my wife is sick with worry over the prospects of their marriage. Can't sleep at night for thinking what will become of them, when they will see the colour of henna on their hands. She wants to see them settled in loving relationships with their husbands, planning a family and making her a grandmother. It is her passionate belief that marriage is part of a girl's destiny. It makes her complete and fulfilled. Lies awake at night, she does, troubled by all sorts of negative thoughts. Wants to see the girls nicely settled down with Indian husbands.'

'As any good Indian mother would,' reacted one.

'You see the problem is that our boys are brilliant academically. They put their heart and soul into their education. The upshot of which is they do well both at school and college level. Naturally, all this comes in useful when they are looking for a job. Sadly, there's a downside to this high achieving: it makes them what they call these days *a catch* and, as we all know so well, a catch gets caught sooner or later,' put in another.

'Now, although they are my daughters,' returned the father, a shade proudly, 'and, I'll be the first to admit that all daughters are pretty in the eyes of their parents, I can tell you this in all honesty – hand on my heart – that both my girls are good-looking. We have brought them up well ... given them the best education that we could afford with the means at our disposal. Both are bright and have social skills. No shortage of pluses, I tell you.'

'One question, I hope you don't mind me asking you. Are the two young ladies working ... I mean employed full time?' inquired another, showing keen interest in the father's problem.

'Working? Oh, surely they are. In fact, both are professionals and in well-paid jobs. The older is a barrister at King's Bench Walk at Temple, here in London. The younger one works as a pharmacist in Maidenhead. So you can imagine they have a lot going for them. And yet, in spite of all their good points and our untiring efforts to see them settled, they are still unmarried. No sign on the horizon of life partners for them. We simply cannot find any Indian boys. You tell me, what is one to do under these circumstances?' With a morose expression, he looked around for an answer from those listening to his tale of woe.

'With the sort of good jobs they have, you think they are willing to accept marriages arranged by parents?' the father was asked.

'I feel confident they will have no objection when we show them the boys we think are suitable for them,' came the reply.

'There's a flipside to everything, isn't there? I guess this is the price we have to pay for coming to this country. Have you thought of using one of those marriage agencies?' asked the first one. 'I believe they are quite good at this sort of thing, you know, introducing people, matching their tastes, their likes and dislikes on computer and all that sort. Hardly surprising, therefore, that so many of these outfits are springing up everywhere in the country.'

'We have, believe me, we have,' nodded the anxious father and clicked his tongue regretfully. 'We're doing everything we can … leaving absolutely no stone unturned. Unfortunately, there's a problem with these agencies. The male clients they have on their books are largely – how shall I put it? – not exactly the type that would suit our girls. They are mainly from working class, I mean, not professionals as such, you know, doctors, dentists, architects, accountants and that kind of people.'

'Well, you know what they say: marriages are made in heaven,' sympathised the second one, with a heavily creased face.

'I don't know about heaven,' returned the father, 'but I can tell you this: they are definitely not made in Britain. No, not if our experience is anything to go by.'

As he laid bare his heart to his patient listeners, his troubled face twitched and he ground his teeth, producing a sound at the back of his throat that everyone could hear. He then shuffled somewhat uneasily from side to side. The hand holding his drink went up a little, in a gesture of seeking succour from some heavenly power that would put an end to his paternal problems and restore his wife's night sleep.

'If any of you gentlemen have someone in mind, in the family or know of anyone who, in your opinion, will be suitable for my girls, I shall be only too pleased to hear from you ... you know family background of the boys, their education, profession, star sign and things of that kind. Well, you know the score now.'

'We understand. Of course we fully understand,' replied the one standing closest to him and patted the man's back to give his morale a boost and also to express his sympathy.

'I'm sorry for going on like this. Truly I am. I should've realised that we are meeting after over thirty years and instead of talking with you gentlemen about the time we were coming to this country from India, I started prattling on about my problems. Not only that, I tried to enlist your help in dealing with them. I suppose, in a way, it shows how seriously concerned my wife and me are about our daughters' marriage prospects. As you just said if we were in India these problems would probably not have arisen.'

'But then there may have been a whole host of other problems,' suggested the sympathiser. 'Anyway, since we are not in India, there's no point talking about it, is there?'

Jaggi, who was standing not far from the anxious father and watching him sympathetically, took all this in and his mind was filled with the images of the cheeky charms of his daughter, first as an energetic, full-of-fun youngster and then as a sober grown-up with mind on books and sporting adventures.

His eyes closed dreamily and with wry affection he began to imagine what she would have been like now if she was there. Certainly of marriageable age. Probably a lot wiser after her time at the university. Possibly a high-flyer with a career full of glittering possibilities and determined to carve a name for herself in her chosen field of endeavour, medicine, media, finance. But most definitely she would have been lovelier, livelier and more vibrant.

How he wished he had the problems that were gnawing at the heart of this simple, loving father. But then, having known Mandi's fiercely independent nature, he wondered if the question of an arranged marriage to a Indian boy would have ever arisen in her case. She was no sheltered child, Mandi. Very much her own woman, she would have exercised her own choices in life.

And, as far as he was concerned, he would have fully respected her decision. Since he had chosen his life partner himself, how could he have denied her the right to do that?

He remembered something about Mandi and smiled wryly to himself. Among the lasting memories of Mandi in his mind was of her as an eight-year-old girl, using her mother's magnifying mirror in the garden on a bright summer evening, the look on her face of intense concentration, counting the sixty-two or sixty-three light freckles that had appeared on her face after spending a couple of hours out playing in the sun. The other was of her as a teenager wearing ripped jeans, a light grey T-shirt with *Free Tibet* emblazoned on it in large letters and hair tied in a ponytail, frolicking about the house, tossing peanuts into the air, one at a time, and catching them in her wide open mouth.

Many times he had joined her in what she called "peanut basketball". It had taken her just a few hours

– and a handful of dropped peanuts – to master the technique. He, on the other hand, kept bumping into furniture and often had to cheat to beat her. The memory of those happy times brought a bitter-sweet smile to his lips.

Jaggi's routine on the yacht was simple. He would introduce himself to other guests, briefly exchange pleasantries with them, engage in small talk for a few minutes and then quietly move on.

His next social ramble took him to a group of men who were standing in a broken circle and were engaged in a well-lubricated discussion on the state of television in Britain. Loudly off-loading their opinions, they were mainly critical in their pronouncements. Especially one of them, a man of average build looking dapper in a three-piece pinstripe suit and wearing a hearing aid neatly concealed behind his right ear, was scathing. 'Honestly, I tell you if there was no adultery in the world there'd be no television in Britain,' he pronounced in a rather high-pitched tone and followed it up with a brief hiss of laughter. 'No, I'm not joking … quite serious about it, I am. Marital infidelity has become a TV staple. The programmes are up to their neck in adulterous behaviour. Take extra-marital sex out of telly and what's left? Well, you can work that one out for yourself. In my opinion nothing … nothing at all.'

'Of course not,' reacted one of the listeners. 'You have cookery contests, chat shows, game shows, quiz shows, panel shows, talent shows and … and … well, what more do you want? Is that not enough to turn you into a first-rate, mindless dummy?'

'We are all contemporaries and came to this country on the same boat at the same time, didn't we?

Therefore I'm sure everyone here remembers what television used to be like at the time?'

'Oh, clear as the day, I remember a lot of the programmes, if not all,' spoke one while others signalled their agreement in emphatic nods and smiles. 'In fact, it was the first time in my life I had clamped eyes on television screen and the memory of what I saw that time is fresh in my mind to this day.'

'There were only two channels and programmes began in the evening. Sex was completely off the menu … virtually banned, you could say. It was like it didn't exist or, if it did, its place was in the bedroom. As for adulterous behaviour, well, you know it as well as I do, there was absolutely no place for it on the small black-and-white screen. Totally taboo they were, sexual encounters. Weren't they? Even your low-key hanky-panky between a man and a woman was kept to a minimum. Of course with lights off and clothes on.'

'Yeah, yeah a tender peck on the cheek, a gentle embrace and a gush of wind would slam the bedroom door shut with a few bars of suggestive music. The camera would move on, either to flames roaring in the fireplace or straight out of the window to waves tumbling insanely on each other in the sea, even though the nearest beach was a good two hundred miles away,' agreed one. 'That the couple had inevitably moved on from kissing to stronger stuff was left to the imagination. It was your mind that had to fill in the blanks.But now, just one kiss and they start banging each other like a pair of stoats. Every drop of sex is squeezed out of the act. The whole thing grinds on and on endlessly. Ad nauseam, at times, I'd say. Far longer than sex in real life.'

'Absolutely right. I'm glad you remember all that. Must have a good memory. Then, within the space of a few years, ever so surreptitiously, almost on tiptoe, when the world's attention was directed somewhere else, some Artful Dodger sneaked the contraband of simulated sex and marital infidelity into TV programmes. Mind you, it must have been done very cleverly ... in the name of freedom of expression or some highfalutin reason like that because there were several committed watchdogs with a bark as well as bite keeping their beady eye on what was being shown on the box.'

'Mary Whitehouse – I'm sure you remember the white-haired former school teacher that BBC banned from entering their premises? – to name just one,' chipped in the second man.

'That's right. Slowly these programmes became what some people would call *advanced*. They kept taking liberty with what they produced, branding it as freedom of expression. That freedom of expression soon changed to greater freedom, full of challenging material ... or some such ruse. Still, programmes showing this so-called challenging material' – and he waved two fingers of each hand to indicate inverted commas – 'were strictly limited to late-night viewing and watched in the main by people who either could not sleep or ...'

'Didn't have to get up in the morning and go to work to earn a living for themselves and their family,' interrupted another.

'Exactly right. Still, programmes containing scenes of buttocks engaged in heavy combat of thrusts and counter-thrusts, sighs and moans and all the orgasmic oohs and aahs, were not commonplace. Never once did they come on before news, which, remember, used to be at nine o'clock.'

'I know, I know, nine o'clock used to be the watershed,' the head nearest to him nodded.

'Then, some clever dick, with ratings and what ratings can lead to in terms of money, seized on his chance to push things even further. Surely, he must have pulled the ratings wool over the decision makers' eyes? And so the number and frequency of such programmes went up goodness knows how many folds. Eight o'clock became the watershed to make room for them. Now, I sometimes get the feeling they just wait for children to get back home from schools to put them on.'

'Sex seems to be the only masala film and television producers can think of when they make programmes. And the excuse they put forward, quite shamelessly in my opinion, is that they are offering more choice. More choice, my foot! Is choice between one sex-laden show and six other sex-laden shows really more choice? I don't think they know the meaning of the word.'

'And if they knew it, I tell you, they would have changed it. Easily done, these things,' chipped in a man with a stocky figure and snow in his thatch, who was standing close by.

'One can see it. It's really to peddle sex and pull in ratings. You see, sex is a genie that once out of the bottle is more interested in fulfilling its own wishes than anybody else's.'

'How right you are, brother,' concurred another. 'The speed with which they're ripping the soul out of eroticism on telly, it's only a matter of time we'll wake up to nipples in the face at breakfast, full-frontal sex in full colour and sterophoic sound at lunch, hard porn at prime time on your plasma flatscreen.'

'My friend, you forgot to mention blow jobs at supper,' his listener chipped in hastily, with a laugh.

'Whatever they are. No doubt all this will be done in the name of something fanciful, like "sexual candour" or "erotic honesty". The British are very good at this sort of thing ... hijacking definitions to suit their purpose ... creating new ones where there aren't any? Or maybe they'll find some other cock-and-bull reason.'

'More cock than bull, if you want to know my honest opinion,' chimed in the second one. 'Let's not lose sight of the fact that we now have one of the highest numbers of TV channels in the world and, frankly, it wouldn't surprise me at all if it's the highest, at something like a thousand. Gone, alas, are the days when there were just two or three channels showing good, meaningful shows in black and white. And more channels can only mean one thing: more sex pouring out of the screens, more huffing and puffing, more humping and bumping, moaning and groaning.'

'Too much choice can be as bad as too little choice,' the first man then took over. 'And another thing: have you noticed the level to which language on telly has now sunk?'

'Oh, the less said about that the better,' the man pinched his earlobe in Indian fashion to signify extreme of excess.

'I'll say this: there are so many warnings about sex, violence and strong language before a programme these days that I sometimes feel it would be damn sight better if they warned the viewers about shows that didn't contain these sleazy ingredients.'

Then, doing an excellent parody of a voice-over announcement, he added, 'As the following programme does not contain strong language, extreme violence, mature themes and scenes of an explicit sexual nature, some viewers may find it disturbing.'

Everyone laughed out loud.

Having got the reaction he was looking for, the man continued, 'I'm sure most of you remember that Kenneth Tynan fellow from way back?'

'Kenneth who?'

'Kenneth Tynan, he was a theatre critic and the brain behind the stage play Oh! Calcutta!'

'There was nothing behind in it. Everything was up front.'

'Up, did you say? In front of a house full of audience?' The remark brought a wave of amused laughter.

'Anyway, up or down, he was the one who used the word *fuck* for the first time on British television. It was in a live, late-night TV debate in the mid-sixties. And you can imagine the outrage that sparked. All hell broke loose, I tell you. The newspapers went berserk … front-page stories, editorial comments, letters from enraged readers … the full works. The use of the 'f' word on British television was taken as a national scandal. Believe it or not, even the Parliament condemned it in the strongest terms. The whole thing led to apologies from the BBC. A TV ban was slapped on the theatre critic.'

'Compare that with what is happening now. Just a few years on, programme makers are vying with each other over who can use the 'f' word the highest number of times in their show. I don't know what the latest score is for a one-hour show… thirty two, forty seven, fifty four. They use the word as conjunction to join clauses in a sentence. I'm certain somebody, somewhere in the country is collating and keeping a record.'

'You know, the other day I went to see a film at the local cinema and heard the word fuck and fucking thirty seven times on the screen in the first twenty minutes. Imagine, thirty bloody seven times inside twenty minutes. And that was just the trailers.'

'I heard it more than eighty four times – from one character alone in one film,' said his listener.

'How many characters were in it in total?' inquired one, with a laugh.

'Not even birds and animals, for God sake, are spared so far as showing sex on TV is concerned. For instance, take penguins in North Antarctica or lungoors in the wilds of India. Although these poor creatures live thousands of miles away from major television centres here, even they are not allowed to get on with their monkey business in peace and privacy. Cameras follow them relentlessly wherever they go, recording their every move ... and from every possible angle.'

Another laugh, though not as loud as last time.

'I'll tell you this: the minute they show two animals of the same species but of different gender, you can bet your bottom buck before you can say the *sex* their mating rituals will be in full swing to titillate those who enjoy watching the sexual activity in animals. The way these things are portrayed to the general public one would think that bonking is the only activity animals get up to all the time.'

'All right, let's assume, purely for argument sake, that that's what they do morning, noon and night, day in, day out, all the year round. Then how come the human population has shot through the seven billion mark and is racing ahead like sex is going out of fashion while several animal species are staring extinction in the face. Many of these poor creatures have already been reduced to dangerously low levels and continue to decline at an alarmingly rate. Surely not because lack of their urge to merge? Sex is supposed to lead to an increase in number, isn't it? Multiplication is the name of the game, as the words of the song tell us.'

His like-minded listener reacted, 'With so much pre-marital sex and extra-marital sex in books, magazines and on show in television programmes, you tell me, is it any wonder that nearly every other marriage ends up in divorce court, argued over by lawyers who are divorced themselves and before a judge who is, quite possibly, divorced twice over?'

'Nah, nah, doesn't surprise me at all,' joined in another, obviously with an enduring marriage under his belt. 'It seems these days every Jack is at it … not necessarily with his own Jill. I'm a pukka believer in the old saying that there's a place for everything and everything in its place, however old-fashioned it may make me appear in some eyes. The place for sex is in the bedroom and not the lounge or living room or kitchen table. In most households, these places are shared by all members of the family.'

'True,' nodded a head, emphatically.

'I suspect there's a secret link between sex and TV,' returned the first one. 'I don't know how it works but work it certainly does. You know, whenever I glance at my television aerial, there is invariably a pair of birds having it happily off on it. Hardly surprising then that what the antenna on the roof witnesses, it passes on to the viewers in the living room below. You can only transmit what you receive. No?'

'To tell you the honest truth, in my view, television has all but become the exclusive preserve of murderers, terrorists, sexual predators, paedophiles, rapists, drug dealers, human traffickers, fraudsters, schemers, scammers and other low-life characters. The spotlight is more or less always on them permanently. And yes, one mustn't forget prostitutes and self-seeking politicians. They want and get their fair share of the small screen. In fact, much more than their fair share. Seriously, just tell me when was the last time you saw a world-renowned scientist, an original writer or a genuinely remarkable person, male or female, in their field being interviewed on the box?' His gaze was fixed unblinkingly on the man closest to him. 'Three weeks ago? Six months? A year?'

'The spotlight moves to the good and the great only when they die. And it happens fleetingly to inform the viewers that they are no longer with us. Usually it's done in the form of a brief obituary item lasting twenty three seconds at the end of a news bulletin,' replied the man, with the sour expression of a person who has just licked the back side of a postal stamp.

'How right you are! Good people have to die to get a mention on the telly while villains are there noon, night and day, monopolising the screen. And the more nastiness they have to their name, the higher their profile goes up. Turn on the box any time and you can be sure of being greeted by the face of one of them. With so much wickedness and depravity on open display, you tell me, is it any wonder that the screen of some of the TV sets has gone crooked?'

'And when these obnoxious charters are not there, it's either game show or quiz show, chat show or cooking going on in the kitchen, the beach and everywhere else, trinkets being auctioned for pennies, dirty toilets and bathrooms thrust into your face ... in high definition, for God's sake,' put in one of his audience.

'To tell you the truth, I never watch TV with my family, especially the children. Sometimes it happens that I'm on my own with eyes on the screen and they wander in and place themselves on the settee with me. I stay with them for a few minutes in order not to seem rude. But then, to save each other embarrassment, I make an excuse as if I suddenly remembered something urgent to do, and leave the room.'

'Same here,' declared his listener. 'Frankly, I don't think many, or any, people gather around the television set in the evening and watch programmes as a family these days. Quite often it's so embarrassing watching it with family members, especially the young ones. Naked couple grinding their pelvises with total abandon, all that freestyle bonking-shonking going on in front of your eyes and theirs. Of course they try to pretend they're not watching by shifting their gazes away from the screen. Now I don't mean to sound prude but, frankly, it's quite possible I may even feel embarrassed watching all that huffing and puffing with you,' he added, eyes on the person closest to him

'Surely not us ... oh, come, come now. We're all grown up people ... men of the world, as they say.'

'True, but what kind of world?' he asked. 'I'm not the sort of person to swear at what's being shown but telly's gone so trashy lately that not only do I find myself feel like doing just that but also throwing the bloody thing out of the window. Don't you?'

'I'm not surprised at all. Mind you, I'd rather do the huffing and puffing myself than passively watch others at it.'

'I think India cannot claim to be blameless for the present state the world is in as far as sex is concerned. Surely, part of the blame lies with us. Don't forget it was our ancestors who gave Koka Shashtra and Kama Sutra to the world hundreds of years ago, didn't they?'

'Yes, but they gave these manuals to enhance knowledge ... to bring some spice to the love lives of people who lived all those centuries ago and not for putting swear words and scenes of nudity on display in your living room hundreds of years later, thousands of miles away. Talk of giving choice! Well, go ahead and fill your boots there. How many positions on offer in the Kama Sutra?' the man asked, flashing an enormous smile.

'If India is the spiritual capital of the world, it shows how low the rest of the world has sunk,' Jaggi heard someone express his view as he encountered the next bunch of people. The man then shrugged his shoulders with a theatrical gesture, grinned broadly and added, 'But having said that let me make it clear that I am willing to do anything for India ... except live in it.' This brought a wave of low-key laughter from his listeners.

'Say what you like about India, you can't deny that your roots are Indian. You were born there, grew up an Indian, got your education in Indian schools and colleges and look every bit as Indian as the next Indian. I think, to all intents and purposes, you are still an Indian and will remain so,' observed a man from the group in a patriotic, put-down tone and touched one of the two tufts of grey hair on either side of his head.

'But of course, of course. I have never denied that in the past, not even once, and I will never deny it in the future. Let's put it this way: invented in the East, patented in the West,' and he gave a weird tinny kind of laugh, part blowing it out, part taking it in.

With great fanfare and a blast of music, Sagar made his grand entrance into the hall, wreathed in an ear-to-ear grin. He was oozing charm from every pore as he welcomed the guests by joining the palms of his hands together in front of his chest in the traditional Indian greeting of *namaste*. His face glowed with "mission accomplished" satisfaction as he nodded sagely to the gathered guests and muttered a few words which were drowned out by the loudness of the applause that greeted him.

The guests, urged on by the master of ceremonies to be even more enthusiastic in greeting the host, dutifully obliged, clapping with greater gusto and giving Sagar looks that were full of admiration, tinged with envy and, in the odd case, even jealousy.

Flashguns blazed in a dazzling salvo from the cameras of the press and free-lance photographers covering the occasion as Sagar kept acknowledging his guests with a series of nods and bows punctuated by hearty hand-waving, endlessly pleading, "Thank you, gentlemen, thank you, thank you very much."

He accomplished all this with remarkable ease as his eyes scanned the faces of the visitors with quick, shifting glances.

Sagar was suave, middle-aged, of medium height and had a body with levels of fat that age and a surfeit of wealth bring in their wake. Immaculately dressed, he cut a fine dash in a bespoke Indian outfit – black, collarless Jodhpur jacket with light trousers and a string of eye-wateringly expensive pearls round his neck, as often worn by rajahs and maharajahs in Rajasthan during India's pre-independence days.

Neat, triangular folds of a silk handkerchief peeked out of his top coat pocket. All this was, no doubt, intended to impress upon his fellow countrymen that, despite the long march of time, his bonds with the old country were strong and he was every bit as Indian as he was the day he treaded the gangplank of the Europe-bound Italian ocean liner in Bombay. His well-groomed salt-and-pepper hair was parted on the left and his face had a benign, rather paternal look.

As the din of the welcome subsided, the master of ceremonies, resplendent in dark orange-red regalia studded with glinting silver buttons, stepped forward to take the microphone. Gently tapping it to make sure it was turned on, he began, 'Gentlemen, it is a great pleasure to welcome you all on board The Indian Princess for a very special and, if I may take the liberty to say, somewhat unusual reunion.'

Many heads nodded their agreement with him.

'Reunions come in many shapes and forms. There are school reunions and there are college reunions. Then you have reunions specific to certain professions, doctors, lawyers, architects and so forth. There are also reunions, thanks to the amazing advancements in medicine, of heart, liver and kidney transplant patients. But this reunion beats them all by a long chalk in its uniqueness – a reunion of people who were once fellow-passengers on a ship for a fortnight and then never set eyes on each other for over thirty years.'

Even more heads nodded, accompanied by a light laughter.

'The credit for thinking up the idea, needless to say, goes to your host, Mr Ravi Sagar. Not only that, because it was on an ocean liner that you had first come together, he was determined that sailing should be the theme of the get-together. And he wanted the scenes of long ago to be recreated against the backdrop of water. So, to bring that special magic to the occasion, he decided that the reunion should take place on his personal yacht, The Indian Princess. A truly remarkable and generous gesture by all accounts, I'm sure you will agree with me.'

Without exception, heads nodded and a chorus of "yeah, yeah" went up in the air.

'It's good of you to have responded so stupendously and found time to attend. I have no doubt that most of you lead extremely busy lives in whatever your field of activity is – from managing hospitals, dental surgeries and medical practices to operating your own business empires and generally playing significant roles in the smooth running of the commercial and industrial machinery of this, your adopted, country.

'No doubt, like Mr Sagar, all of you are playing an important role in the entrepreneurial culture of Britain and have become leaders in whatever field of enterprise you've chosen to follow.'

This time there were fewer nods, just a good-natured acceptance of the compliment.

'Apart from revisiting old times, the evening here will give you an excellent opportunity to renew your personal ties and let each other know what you have been doing with yourself and how you've gone up in the world since coming to this country from India which, as we all know, was once the brightest jewel in the British crown.

'Indians, we are told, form the biggest single group among immigrants and they make a significant contribution to the economic life of Britain. You are – and you all know it very well – part of a great success story. And what has made that story so successful? It is, among other things, your vision, self-reliance, commitment to the job in hand and the spirit of enterprise. For the class of nineteen sixty four achievement was cool. The class of sixty four truly has class.'

With a series of nods, Sagar gave the flattering observation his full and whole-hearted support.

'May I take this opportunity to thank you once again for coming here tonight and making this occasion what can only be described as a resounding success. I shall now hand you over to your host who, no doubt, has a few words to say to you. So, gentlemen, please put your hands together for Mr Ravi Sagar.'

As the clapping by guests got under way, with extreme caution and an economy of movement, the master of ceremonies retreated a yard or two, making way for Sagar to take over the microphone, which he did with the biggest smile in his armoury and deftly pulled out from his pocket a set of index cards on which he had jotted down the salient points of his speech. But his confident demeanour made it clear that he would need only limited help from them, if at all.

'Friends,' Sagar began in a voice bristling with self-assurance, 'it's indeed a great pleasure to see so many of you again and to welcome you aboard my yacht. A lot of water has flowed under the bridge since we set sail from Ballard Pier in Bombay. That life-changing journey, that great adventure of ours, for a new beginning took us first to mainland Europe and then brought us to the shores of British Isles.

'I remember vividly that our final day in Bombay was sunny but blisteringly hot. The afternoon, especially, was also terribly humid as I prepared to head for my maiden trip abroad. It was my first passage from India, as probably it was for most of you, if not all. The memory of the fortnight I spent with you on the Italian passenger liner is so fresh in my mind it feels as if the whole thing had taken place only a week or two back, even though, you know it as well as I do, it was over thirty four years … well, umpteen and umpteen years ago.'

A flashbulb from a photographer's camera blazed and Sagar turned his head momentarily in the direction of the light, producing a smile of extreme geniality, albeit a little late for it to be captured by the lens.

'After a gap of so many years, some of you may not recognise each other or me for that matter, and, frankly, who can blame you? Isn't it amazing how the years have flown by? When did we get where we are today, hey, I ask you in wonderment? Nothing ever stays the same. We all change with time. Or, to put it another way, time changes and we change with it. This change is both outward as well as inward. I mean the way we look and also the way we look at life and all that it has to offer.

'In other words, attitude, outlook and thinking … that kind of stuff, you know. When we first set foot on the SS Roma in Bombay we were a lot younger and a lot thinner. We were also full of heart and hope. The more idealistic amongst us also had on their minds the additional purpose to act as unofficial ambassadors of our country in the world at large, where they were going to light a beacon with their hard work, spirit of enterprise and exemplary behaviour.

'Tonight, some thirty four years after we first set foot in this country, here on this yacht, we look a lot older wiser, or should I say wider,' Sagar laughed and his listeners quickly followed. 'Time has played thick and thin with us. It has made us thick around the waist and thin on top. The geography of everybody's appearance has changed.

'But I trust most sincerely that inside we are still the same – full of heart and bursting with hope. Change, you see, is the key to progress. It is also something inevitable in life. Change is the law of nature. Nature never stands still. It's my firm belief that, in today's world, he who does not change is lost. Someone once said so wisely that the only constant in life is change.'

'Hear, hear,' one of his guests, pot-bellied and bald, concurred, a trifle loudly, head nodding like a wound-up mechanical toy's. Sagar winced at the interruption, as if he did not care for endorsement of his own view by someone else.

After a momentary pause he resumed, 'In fact, it was the desire for change that put us on the Italian boat and brought us to this country in the first place. But, while change should remain an important part of our mindset and also our actions, it's good, once in a while, to cast a glance over our shoulder and take account of what we have changed from. And that's why we're gathered here this evening – to take a trip down memory lane, hand in hand like good friends, and relive collectively those hours, those days that we spent in each other's company sailing on the ocean waves.'

He paused to study the reaction of his audience, looked around brightly and what he saw was what he wanted to see. Everyone's attention was focussed totally and utterly on him as they hung on to his every word, in complete silence. Nobody moved, nobody stirred, nobody coughed or cleared the throat. If there were any restless feet in the gathering, they had, for a moment, forgotten to shuffle. All eyes were glued to him, all ears waited eagerly for him to resume. Everything was going swimmingly his way and it turned his face into a billboard for happiness.

'From time to time we read reports in newspapers and see on television screens about the plight of the boat people who battle against high seas, mountainous waves and nature's other awesome odds in search of their promised land, their Shangri-la. Tonight, we have gathered together on this yacht as the boat people of a completely different kind – as different as the boat we used for our journey.

'It was quite a luxurious vessel and free from most hazards, except those of the forces of nature and, let's face it, who can argue with them? We are the boat people for whom the gates of the new country were wide open. We are the boat people who used those wide-open gates to make our entrance. We are the boat people who have notched up success after success since landing on these shores.'

Again, he put a pause in his speech but the brief silence was shattered by the applause from his audience.

'In the sixties we made a conscious decision to come to Britain. The aim was to seek opportunities to take our careers forward as well as bring a little adventure into our lives. We were self-reliant and industrious. We believed in making things happen. When we left India all we had in our back pockets was a princely sum of three pounds. Just three pounds in three one pound notes! We were what is now popularly known – certainly amongst Indian migrants of that era – as the three-pound generation.'

At this point he suddenly broke off and, with all the seriousness of a stage thespian, slipped his right hand into his trouser pocket, rummaged for a moment or two and fished out some coins, which he then pretended to count carefully, muttering some figures in a voice that was loud enough to be heard by everyone, and then declared with a huge, triumphant smile, 'And I still have seventy-eight pence in my pocket.'

The audience let out a ripping laugh. Some clapped to show their appreciation for his sense of humour while others exchanged approving looks and nodded to each other without saying anything.

'On that trip, the money in our pockets may have been in short supply but what we had in superabundance was that rare commodity known as the will to succeed … to storm ahead in life. We wanted to achieve. We wanted to be successful. We wanted to learn. In order to reach those goals we worked hard – of course, each in their own way and everyone at their own pace. However the objective was the same – to improve ourselves, build new and solid foundations for our future.

'We were the can-do generation and it is as a result of that mental state not only have we survived but we have thrived. We can today be proud of notching up stellar successes in our careers, having enduring marriages, family unity and motivated offspring pursuing prestigious professions. I have no hesitation in declaring that we have done proud to both countries – the country we came from and the country we came to. And this is something that should make us hold up our head high.'

Everyone clapped and cheered enthusiastically, exchanged more appreciative looks, nodded and, this time, said a few words to each other. Their host had hit all the right notes. In many ways, he was mirroring their own feelings. They were thrilled with what they were hearing and thirsted for more of it.

'I know for a fact that, on our journey to these shores, many of us fell victims of seasickness shortly after the SS Roma set sail from Bombay and hit the choppy waters of the Arabian Sea. For a few hours, I have no hesitation in admitting, I was one of them. Tonight, let me assure you, dear friends, that sickness tablets are in plentiful supply on this boat. No problem whatsoever, should you feel the need for them. But, to put your mind at ease let me also assure you that the sailing tonight will be a very smooth affair. As smooth as it can possibly be. For this I have my captain's reassuring words and so far in my experience he has never been wrong.'

Sagar chortled at his own light-hearted observation and after a while all the guests joined him.

'I am pleased to say that we are no longer in choppy waters. Left them miles behind. It's time, therefore, for us to savour the fruitfulness of our hard work, our industry and our spirit of enterprise. After this short speech – and I give you my word the rest of it will be short – I shall be coming round to meet each one of you individually and find out how you have fared in this country. So be prepared with your feel-good stories.'

With approving glances the assembled guests made their feelings known to the host as well as to each other.

'We shall be on the yacht for the next few hours. I cannot give you the precise time because we are meeting after a long time and so we need a fair bit of time to talk about our experiences on the boat all those years ago plus the many directions in which our lives have taken us since we got off it in Italy.

'After our cruise is over tonight, arrangements have been made to take you back to your hotels for a good night's sleep. Some of you have come from far-flung corners of the country and, of course, overseas and you fully deserve a good rest. We shall meet again, God willing, for lunch tomorrow afternoon to take up where we leave off tonight. But let's not think about tomorrow. Instead, concentrate on the here and now because, as they say, the night is still young and we have only just begun.

'Please, please feel free to take a look around the yacht if you so wish and should you need any help or guidance about anything, do not hesitate to ask a member of the staff. They are an extremely friendly lot and I'm sure they will be only too pleased to assist you. So, friends, it's time once again to recite our jolly mantra and focus our energies on what we have gathered here for – to celebrate our reunion and to have a great time.'

With the smallest of bows, Sagar slipped back neatly into his pocket the cards he had brought with him but had not needed to consult. Not even once. Neither were there any erms and ums during the entire speech. Then, with another bow, he smartly moved away from the microphone but remained in full view of his audience.

As he did so, there was an explosion of flashbulbs and a huge burst of applause from the guests. They cheered him to the rafters, everyone screamed in excitement, clapped wildly, whistled loudly, turning the applause into a truly tumultuous affair. The cheering followed a set rhythm and went on and on and got louder with every passing moment.

A point came when it seemed the high-decibel applause would go on and on and never end, because no one wanted to be seen as the first to stop. Sagar was glowing with pride as he stood as the centre of attention, revelling in it – in fact joyfully milking it – smiling effusively, making little bows in acknowledgement. His hands were gesturing thanks to the guests and pleading with them to bring it all to a close.

A few moments later, he snapped his fingers to one of his liveried staff, who, fast as lightning, conjured up a double scotch on the rocks in an exquisite crystal tumbler planted in the middle of a silver tray.

Coolly, the big shot picked it up, had a quick sniff, swirled it round a couple of times and took a generous mouthful from the glass. Very briefly, he held it in his mouth, savouring it as if it was his first in a long time and he needed it ever so desperately. Gripping the tumbler in his right hand and casting a casual glance around him to survey the happy scene, he strode forward to begin his social round.

With polite formality, Sagar extended his hand to the first guest, who accepted it smartly, with a somewhat nervous smile at being the first to exchange pleasantries with the man of the moment.

'Krishan Mehra,' stammered the man, tall, with a full head of silver hair, a good-humoured face and effortlessly elegant in a bespoke, pinstriped suit and a tie with small karma elephant figures on it.

'A pleasure to meet you, Mehra Sahib, a real pleasure indeed,' offered Sagar, smiling while he appraised the man with polite concentration. 'I'm really very pleased you could find time to come tonight.'

'Wouldn't have missed it for the world,' exclaimed Mehra, in a strong north Indian inflection.

'Nice of you to say so,' said Sagar, smiling with satisfaction.

'A friend telephoned me in my office and told me about the advertisement in the newspaper. At first I didn't believe him. My initial reaction was that he was having me on and the whole thing was some sort of joke. You see, he is a bit of a joker by temperament and therefore I, well, most of our friends, do not take him seriously. But when later that day we met and he actually produced the newspaper cutting and I saw it with my own two eyes I was really astounded. It was like getting eight crosses in a line on the football pools coupon on Saturday evening.'

'Oh, come, come, Mehra Sahib, surely it's nothing on the scale of a pools win? No not quite like that? It's just an excuse for a little knees-up ... you know, to get together and have a good, old-fashioned chit-chat – some gup-shup, some peena-peelana, as we used to say back home in the old days. Nothing more than that.'

'Well, you know what I mean. After that I read the date of the newspaper and made sure it was not April fool's day prank. Once it was established that everything was kosher, I made up my mind that this was a function I had to attend, come rain, shine or whatever else it is that nature sends. And, well, as you can see, here I am on this beautiful yacht of yours having a super time. Thank you very much for everything. It was indeed an honour to receive your invitation.'

'To see you happy makes me happy, believe me. The response has been staggeringly good ... quite phenomenal, thanks to people like you who took the trouble to come tonight. I can't help feeling that whoever read the advertisement or heard about it from relatives, friends or any other source is here with us. And, frankly, for me that makes the effort of organising the party really worth the trouble. I'm thrilled to see that so many could come. Time for socialising is frightfully in short supply in our busy lives and finding it, I feel, is not always easy.'

'Obviously, I can't speak for others, but I can tell you this that once I had decided to attend, time was least of my problems. Tell me, did you have any doubts in your mind when you first thought of this getting together thing?' inquired the guest.

'You bet your blue cotton socks I did,' Sagar declared with an enormous grin. 'Doubts by the bucket loads. My goodness me, yeah. In the beginning, for a few days, I questioned my own sanity for thinking of such a batty plan. Well, it is outrageous in a sense, isn't it?'

The guest agreed with a nod.

'Let me tell you something I haven't told anyone so far. Whenever I am under pressure, I start to talk to myself. Nothing loud or agitated, you understand. Just a few words uttered here and a few words muttered there to myself while I have a little walk in the room or wherever I am.'

The guest gave a hearty chuckle.

'I don't know the reason for this but that's what I do. I suppose it is a part of my personality. So a few days before the whole organising bit was put into motion, I found myself soliloquizing – if that is the right word – on more than one occasion. Not sweaty panic attacks, more like moments of anxiety. But once the wheels started to turn, I knew there was no going back. And, as you can see, the result is right before your eyes.'

A suave, scholarly-looking Bengali, with a thoughtful face, iron-grey hair, a hearing aid concealed in the left ear and back slightly humped in an intellectual stoop, joined them. Once again the air turned thick with compliments. Speaking with a subliminal stutter, he thanked Sagar for inviting him. The host, in turn, stretched out a hand in his direction, warmly thanked him for accepting the invitation.

The jaw-dropping awe of being on a luxury yacht was slowly beginning to thaw and the cheerful guests, their minds uncorked and bubbling, were mixing like running water amid all the fun, fizz and witty banter.

The party mood had infected everyone and the atmosphere was getting quite noisy and chummy. The visitors to the yacht indulged in powerful embraces, hearty high-fives and whispered confidences. The word "yaar" – buddy – had found its way into the conversation and was being used with increasing frequency. Many showed each other photographs of the members of their family in their wallets and smart phones.

Music, laughter and happy talk were the soundtrack of the yacht. The visitors engaged in non-stop chatter, often spoke over each other. Without any reservation, they revealed details of their lives and made impassioned promises to swap addresses and telephone numbers before the party was over so they could visit each other whenever and wherever they could, or at least remain in touch and attend another get-together of this nature if there was one organised by the current host or anybody else for that matter.

Everywhere one turned faces were wreathed in big smiles and the guests were talking animatedly about what went well and what didn't with them in Britain. In the ebb and flow of life they had notched up far more highs than lows. They also traded their early memories in this country, information about their relatives in India, their profession in Britain and their thoughts on politics, cricket and other sporting events.

From time to time a hysteric burst of laughter would break out and bounce against the walls. Drinking, too, was picking up pace as barra pegs of twelve-year-old scotch were going down thirsty gullets at a fast and furious rate. The visitors were having a blisteringly good time as their host had suggested in his welcome address.

To bring perfection to the party, music being played on the yacht was a blast from the past. The mood-making songs brought a touch of nostalgia to the proceedings. Oozing softly out of Bose speakers, the songs were from both British pop charts of the sixties and old films produced in Bombay. Especially notable were hits from two musical blockbusters of the era, *Sangam* and *Mughal-e-Azam*. They were immensely popular with almost everyone on board the vessel. The voices of Lata Mangeshkar, Asha Bhosle, Mukesh and Mohammed Rafi, remained in the background, at times struggling to get heard amid the buzz of conversation, which was putting on decibels by the minute.

The host, with oodles of charm, was on top form. His modus operandi was to flash a toothy grin here, a hearty chuckle there and a ready smile wherever he turned his head. A hand enthusiastically extended to one person in greeting followed by a chummy pat on the back of another. Bonhomie misted out of every pore of his body and his face looked bathed in warm glow of satisfaction. Clearly he was lapping up every celebratory moment. His actions added sparkle and energy to the goings-on.

While all this was proceeding at a merry pace, he grabbed every opportunity to pose for the cameras with guests, hand resting on someone's shoulder in friendly intimacy one minute, exchanging chummy words with another the next, all the time making cheerful quips of his own on whatever the subject of conversation he walked into.

Wherever the business baron turned he was greeted by his status-obsessed guests with fawning looks, unbridled adulation and handshakes that never seemed to end. And while all this went on, one of a team of photographers commissioned to document the function was always within snapping distance, finger poised to record the moment in a blaze of light.

The modus operandi of his social manoeuvres was pretty simple and straightforward. He spent a couple of minutes with each guest and a little more with those who were clustered together in a group. For those who were to his liking, he found extra time without any problem.

Generally, he inquired about their health, while telling them that good health was the life's greatest gift, what profession they were following, which part of the country they were from back in India and where they were settled in Britain. This was usually followed by questions about the family – how everyone was doing and what kind of progress the offspring were making in their education. If, as in most cases, they were grown up, what careers they had chosen to follow.

Then he traded an anecdote or two, swapped the odd memory about the fortnight aboard the Italian ocean liner. Occasionally, he would touch on the property boom in Britain and make witty observations on how bland the food was when they first arrived in the country all those years ago.

Britain, he would stress, owed a huge debt of culinary gratitude to Indian businessmen because it was their entrepreneurial spirit that, combined with the expertise of top chefs from the sub-continent, liberated the country from the tyranny of one meat and two vegetables.

'By introducing a whole range of dishes with lip-smacking flavours, they had transformed the eating-out scene from a culinary wilderness to a paradise for true-born foodies.' In his view this change in the nation's relationship with food could only be described as a "gastronomic revolution."

'You know, not so long ago, Indian restaurants were found only in India. Here in Britain, Curry was only a surname. But now Indian eateries are around every other street corner right across the country. Pubs may once have acted as landmarks for giving road directions to someone new to the area, that role has now fallen to Indian restaurants. That's how popular curry has become now.'

He would then go back in time to illustrate his point. 'You remember the time when pubs were used as landmarks while giving directions to travellers. Now, it's Indian restaurants.' He would have a big laugh and continue, 'Time was when natural yoghurt was unheard of here. We had to travel from one end of the town to the other to buy a carton of it from some grubby, run-down Asian shop. The amazing thing was that even in those long-ago days, thanks to our spirit of enterprise, there were a number of Indian stores dotted around most towns and cities that sold Asian groceries. Obviously, not many but a fair few. Well, enough to meet the needs of the newly arrived migrants.'

'When we arrived on these shores the local population believed that rice was meant for use in only milk pudding. Look how things have changed now. It has become almost a staple. Let me tell you about an incident that happened to me. We had been in the country no more than six months, give or take, when I went out shopping one day. In a greengrocer's I tentatively asked a woman shop assistant if they sold bhindis. Thinking that she wouldn't know what bhindi was I offered the English word for it, *ladies fingers*. And do you know what? She stared at me in utter amazement and then began to examine the fingers on her hands.'

True or not, the story never failed to raise a laugh.

Occasionally someone would offer an identical tale of their own on the taste and quality of food in the sixties. In one conversation, a guest told him, 'In those distant days, chillies were virtually unknown here. I don't think they used chillies in even chilli con carne then. Now, due to changes brought about in taste by Indian eateries, some customers demand the hottest curry available on the menu, the sort of spicy stuff that would put curls in their hair. Not only that, many towns and cities have started to organise chilli festivals. Regular competitions are held in which contestants show their firepower by eating the hottest chillies available on the market.'

Most of the guests were in awe of Sagar. They greeted him deferentially and the attention they gave him as he progressed around the hall was never less than one hundred per cent. Like everyone else, Jaggi was impressed by the host's immense wealth, success and matching lifestyle. But, unlike many, he was not overwhelmed by all this and decided to meet him after the initial clamour to hobnob with him was over.

He knew sooner or later his turn would come. So there was no need to rush. Until then, he chose to play the silent observer, nosing about the yacht, letting the ambience of the vessel wash over him, keenly studying the surroundings, observing everything, missing nothing and generally listening to other people rather than let his own tongue do the talking.

Lighting up the walls in broad frames were what looked like originals. There were also many other expensive pieces of decorations, like silver figures and hand-painted heads of Kathakali dancers. Black walnut fittings, ferociously pricey in appearance, could be seen everywhere. The brass was gleaming and flowers exploded from crystal vases. One or two people greeted him with a tentative hello and he answered back in similar fashion. A portly gentleman with a receding hairline and glasses exchanged a few perfunctory words with him.

There was also a nod here and a nod there. A couple of individuals rolled their eyes to show their amazement at the opulence of the vessel.

At last, when Sagar was nearing the end of his social ramble, he came to Jaggi, who was alone and had a big, open smile on his face. The businessman reached out, grabbed Jaggi's hand with great enthusiasm shook it three or four times.

He kept Jaggi's right hand into his own long after the formality of greeting was over and patted it with the other before pulling his guest closer to reward him with a friendly half-embrace, his chest lightly brushing against his guest's.

It was as though he had singled him out for his special attention. The message was clear: strangers they maybe, there existed between them a bond of cordiality and that Jaggi was much more than just an ordinary invitee to the gathering.

Sagar beamed a smile as he ran a cool, appraising eye over Jaggi, who looked bright-eyed with the excitement of it all. A flashgun popped and a photographer captured the moment in two or three snapshots taken with quick-fire rapidity.

The businessman seemed to have a knack of knowing what to do when he felt a photographer's lens trained on him. He would pull out from his armoury of charm a well-rehearsed, made-to-measure smile of extraordinary sweetness. 'For the London edition, I take it?' he joked. The snapper, who grinned politely and waved to him.

Sagar took Jaggi by the arm and took him to one side that was relatively quiet so he could be with him alone and talk without any interruption. 'I must say you look in excellent condition. Slim-line, glowing with health, well-preserved,' he said, a suave wave of his hand gesturing complimentarily. 'You're really doing well. I'm impressed. My true, true feelings,' he added, with emphasis.

'Thank you,' Jaggi replied, with a grin. 'It's awfully nice of you to say so. You seem in pretty good shape yourself, if I may say so.'

'No seriously, I'm not saying it just to cheer you up. I mean it, every word, believe me. You are wearing well. Look superbly fit.' Once again Sagar ran an eye up and down his guest. 'I've told some of them here that good health is the greatest gift at this time of life.'

'Very true, indeed,' said Jaggi.

'I wish I could say the same about a few I've had the chance to meet so far this evening.'

The camera flashed again, momentarily dazzling them. Sagar smiled, looked down and took a well-measured swig of his scotch. Again, he held the drink in his mouth for a while before letting it slide down his throat. 'As I said in my speech, many of them have gone thick and thin in all the wrong places. You, it seems to me, have been living on a planet different from theirs.'

Jaggi gave a small laugh.

'Seriously, you've aged without aging.'

'Thank you, but you should see the portrait in the attic,' exclaimed Jaggi, pleased with the compliment.

'Portrait in the attic?' inquired Sagar, looking somewhat puzzled. Evidently, the reference to Oscar Wilde's Dorian Gray was lost on him.

'What I meant was that I keep the time-ravaged bits of me hidden from public view.'

'If that's your intention, let me say this to you: you're making a damn good job of it. Not an ounce of extra fat anywhere on the body, as far as I can see. How do you do it? Tell us the secret recipe?'

Jaggi's reply was a fleeting, bashful grin that thanked the host.

'The missus, I take it, keeps a close eye on you … I mean the weight, general appearance and things of that nature. Keeps you on your tippy toes, does she?'

'Don't they all?' Jaggi said, with a roll of the eyes.

'You know what I mean, don't you?' and Sagar gave a huge, mischievous wink.

Again, Jaggi gave him a cheery look but said nothing.

'Angrezi or Hindustani?' Sagar kept up the jokey familiarity.

'Well, it's a bit complicated, to tell you the truth.'

'What is simple these days, tell me?'

'A few days before I was due to set off for Britain, my mother said she wanted to have a word with me. Just the two of us ... all private. As it was the first time that I was going away from home into the big wide world, she asked me to promise her two things.'

Sagar smiled a private smile, remembering some similar experience of his own.

'The first was that, being a Brahmin by birth if not by practice, I wouldn't eat beef, the cow being, as we all know, holy and all that. The second was that I wouldn't marry without the parents' consent. Which, I took it as meaning, I wouldn't marry a white girl. It was their belief that marriage was for life and not just for the flaming years of youth. However, in Britain marriage breakdown was so commonplace ... and the rate at which divorces were happening was extremely high. Higher than one in three. Well, I went over her conditions in my mind and did what I thought was best all round. Looking ahead into the future and what direction life might take, I told her that I couldn't promise her anything on either count.'

'Very diplomatic, eh!' Sagar touched Jaggi on the arm to compliment him over the way he dealt with the situation.

'No, I genuinely meant it,' responded Jaggi. 'Honestly, I did. I wasn't being diplomatic or fobbing her off. But, just to show my respect to her – mother being mother – I did give her my word that I'd remember her wishes and do my absolute best to honour them.'

'And did you?' inquired the host.

'Fifty per cent,' smiled Jaggi and then, after a brief pause, added, 'I don't eat beef.'

'That means she's a local lady, from here?' Sagar gave a small laugh and threw a light punch in his guest's direction.

'Very much so. From Lancashire, to be precise.'

'Ah, a red rose,' another smile from Sagar.

Jaggi looked down and gave a nod.

'You know what? Mothers are really a funny breed. My mum, a super woman in every sense of the word and of whom I was very, very fond – God rest her soul in peace, she passed away six years ago – was the most religious person in our family. She wanted me to visit five holy sites before setting foot out of India. And this is in spite of knowing that I'm by no means the world's most religious person.'

'Five?' Jaggi exclaimed aloud in horror and stumbled back a foot.

'That's exactly what my reaction was, too, when she mentioned *panch dham* to me. Just imagine, five holy shrines scattered across the length and breadth of the vast sub-continent to be covered in under a couple of months. And you know what travelling conditions were like in those days.'

'Not much has changed, sorry to say.'

'Quite frankly, if I had agreed, I would have been hopping from one to the other without going home.'

'So what happened? Did you do all five?'

'No way, my dear fellow. It just wasn't possible. A definite no-no idea. So, like you struck a deal with your mother, I did with my mum. We had a long chat, often quite animated, and after a lot of persuasion I managed to convince her that there was not enough time to undertake all that. I had to make preparations for the journey ... you know, getting suits tailored to European standards, acquiring a passport, arranging the ticket with the Italian shipping company, dealing with unyielding bureaucrats and going through the red tape for which government departments in India are famously notorious. All this was going to take time ... a lot and lot of time.'

Jaggi smiled, this time remembering some parallel experiences of his own.

'But I couldn't turn her down outright, now could I? She had brought me into this world, raised me, looked after me. No, not in a thousand years. I needed maternal blessings so I struck a bargain with her,' Sagar said in a whispery tone as though he was taking Jaggi into something highly confidential. 'As a compromise, I suggested that I would go to one of the five places she had in mind. To keep her sweet I said she could name it.'

'You must have been very persuasive to bring your mother down from five shrines to one.'

'Or she was quite understanding of my problem,' shrugged Sagar. 'She said she fully understood that I didn't have enough time and, to make up for the four shrines I was leaving out, she would observe a one-day fast every week while I was still at home in India.'

'What a super lady! So understanding. I tip my cap to mothers all over the world. That meant you could carry out your preparations without any outside interference?'

'Oh, yes. She fasted every Thursday until I left India and, who knows, for many weeks after that. I never asked her and she never told me.'

'And did she name the place for your visit?'

'That she certainly did,' Sagar nodded.'Oh, yes, sir.'

'What did she choose?'

'She chose Vaishno Devi.'

'And, like a dutiful son you went there?'

'Yeah, you're entirely right. I did. You see, having given my word, I couldn't possibly go back on it. A word is a word, you know. I had to deliver on my promise.'

'Apart from the pact with your mum, was it also to thank the deity for giving you the privilege to go abroad?' inquired Jaggi.

'I'm not quite sure about the privilege bit,' replied Sagar, wistfully. 'You see, it may seem like that to you, me and millions of other young sons and daughters, but I don't think parents see their offspring moving halfway across the world from them as a privilege ... more so in the case of mothers than fathers. I went to Vaishno Devi, well, at least partly, because I had heard a lot about it but never been there in my life and I thought to myself that once I was so far away from India, it would be highly unlikely that an opportunity to visit that holiest of holy Hindu places would come my way again.'

'You're so right. A four-hundred-mile round trip is a lot easier to make than a ten-thousand-mile one.'

'Mind you, once I started, I enjoyed the trip immensely, although, I must admit, I do not have a strong religious streak. Not easy getting there, I can tell you that. All that miles and miles of steep, uphill trek from Katra. I was completely whacked by the time we got to the top around two o'clock in the morning. So I had a quick shower and went to have devi's darshan.'

'Must have been quite something, the experience?' asked Jaggi.

'Oh, without a doubt. Highly enjoyable. On the way to the temple, the devotees of the goddess were happy, full of friendliness and singing lustily and chanting her praises at night and in the early-morning cool. After the visit to the shrine, there was another climb for a couple of miles to Bhaironath temple, which I decided to take in now that I was so close to it. That, I tell you, was another experience not to be missed, despite being completely worn out. Listen, are you all right for drink?' demanded the host, eyeing Jaggi's near-empty glass and then looking around for a minion, fingers poised to snap.

'Fine, just fine,' replied Jaggi. 'I'm doing quite well.'

'Are you sure, my dear fellow?' Sagar persisted.

'One hundred per cent sure. I like to pace my drink. Easy does it, as they say.'

'How sensible. You told me about the missus, how about children?' Sagar inquired. 'How many?'

'None now. We had a daughter but unfortunately we lost her in a mountaineering tragedy in Nepal. She had gone there with a group of her university friends.' Jaggi's voice went low and heavy.

'Oh, I'm dreadfully sorry to hear that. What a terrible thing to happen to a young girl with all her life ahead of her, and, of course, the family.' Sagar was full of genuine sympathy. The look on his face was a proof of that. 'Really sorry,' he repeated.

'Barbara, that's my wife, lives with her mother now, in the Cotswolds. Has been for a while now.'

'I see,' Sagar said with a nod, which was a mixture of understanding and sympathy, although he did not quite comprehend what his guest meant by it.

For his part, Jaggi felt no need to talk about how long Barbara had been out of his life and when, if ever, her absence might end.

'You won't believe it but one or two people here tonight had the cheek to suggest that I should have invited the wives as well,' Sagar said in a rather pompous voice and creased his brow disagreeably. 'Now, can you imagine that?'

'Don't tell me! They didn't, did they?' Jaggi asked, partly refusing to believe him.

'They did, oh yes, they certainly did, astonishing as it may sound,' Sagar assured him.

'Are you serious?' Jaggi looked truly incredulous as he rolled his eyes and shook his head.

'I kid you not, my dear fellow. I'm deadly serious. They did, loud and clear. But the people who think that way don't realise what a logistical nightmare it can throw up.'

'I'm sure they don't,' added Jaggi, incredulously. 'But the whole idea is insanely ridiculous.'

'Anyway, I wanted this gathering to be exclusively for those who were on the Italian steamer in nineteen sixty four. The boat people, if you like. The whole point of this get-together is to indulge in a leisurely, head-on-the-pillow drift back to the fortnight we spent on the ship while, at the same time, take stock of how we have done in this country.'

'The boat people theme is a brilliant idea. I'd say a real clincher and the execution is even better. Believe me, everyone I've spoken to so far is highly impressed by the way the whole thing has been put together and is being carried out. Nothing but healthy, wholesome praise from one and all. Well done. It's bold, splendidly bold, I should say. Ten out of ten plus one for good luck, that's my verdict, for what it's worth.'

'It's worth a lot of me. More than you can imagine. Thank you very much for such a resounding vote of confidence. Now frankly, between you and me, if I had also invited the wives, girlfriends and live-in partners, the challenge of marshalling a parade of people, if truth be told, would have been a logistical nightmare of class one variety... and, let's face it, it would not have been the same thing, now would it? What a crazy suggestion, don't you think?'

'It is,' agreed Jaggi. 'Although we are virtual strangers ourselves, we at least have the bonding glue of our journey from India. They wouldn't have had anything in common to talk about.'

'And then, who knows, someone might have suggested that I should have invited the offspring as well. And taken to its logical limit, why not relatives, cousins twice removed, house guests staying with them, neighbours, the neighbours' neighbours, pets? Where do you draw the line? Quite frankly, sometimes I find there's no pleasing some people. Right-on unfair. The world is going crazy, don't you think?'

'Sometimes I think it's not going crazy but has already fully gone. But I'm sure some people say these things conversationally and do not mean them, not really.'

'You're probably right ... well, I certainly hope so. But, as I just told you, I wanted this get-together for only those who were on the SS Roma and not a gathering of the clan of Chopras, Chaddhas and Chawalas. Out of the question.'

Jaggi gave an endorsement nod. 'I'm fully in agreement with you on that. It's a perfectly valid reason. Besides, it's your party, you're hosting it, you're picking up the tab and so you should have complete freedom to choose who goes on your list of invitees and who stays out. It's wrong to suggest anything otherwise.'

'Oh, I'm so pleased you see it that way, too.'

'Completely and utterly.' Jaggi had the feeling that the party host had taken a shine to him and that a special bond was developing between them.

'Good, good,' Sagar enthused.

Jaggi knew for a fact that there were seven Indian women on board the ship but decided to underplay his certitude and tentatively inquired of his host, 'You remember there were a handful of women who boarded the Roma with us in Bombay?'

'Oh, clearly.'

'If my memory serves me right there were seven of them. Have we, by any chance, got any of them here tonight? It would be interesting to find out how our female fellow-passengers have done in life since leaving India.'

'In fact, to my great surprise, four of them responded to the advert. One's a high-flyer at the UN, the second one is a professor of microbiology at British Colombia University in Canada, the third is a doctor in the Bahamas doing general practice and the fourth one is a widow, running a sub-post office in Reading with her daughter. Now, for goodness sake, don't ask me how the first three, who are living so far away from Britain, got to hear about our newspaper advertisement. I can only presume they have strong people connections with this country.'

'Oh, wherever they are, in this country or not, it seems the ladies have done well for themselves in life, haven't they?'

'One has to admit that, when it comes to getting ahead in life, our women are no shrinking violets. They have indeed done well ... yes, remarkably well.'

'Anyone here tonight?' inquired Jaggi.

'As you can well imagine it's not easy for three of them to travel to the United Kingdom from their far-flung corners of the world. But we've received apologies from them and that includes our local postmistress. However, with their apologies they've also sent their good wishes for the success of the reunion. I think I should have mentioned it in my speech.'

'I remember when I was at university a number of girls in our college adored Pandit Nehru's sister, Vijayalakshmi Pandit. They saw her as their heroine, their role model and wanted to be like her.'

'Is that so?' Sagar looked pleasantly surprised.

'Oh yes. Basking in the first flush of independence and full of patriotic fervour, they wanted to see the world and were therefore keen to join the Indian Foreign Service, become ambassadors of the country ... things of that sort.'

'You know something, my dear fellow? Here on this yacht tonight, I honestly wonder what happened to those calendar years. Where has time gone? The past has become the new present. Everything feels as if it happened only a few moments ago.'

'Surprisingly, I feel that way, too. The years have fallen away,' Jaggi agreed.

'This was precisely the main objective behind the meeting. It has well and truly rolled back the years, a bit like one of those lovely, hand-made Kashmiri carpets we used to see in a Connaught Place showroom during our evening stroll in New Delhi. There was always a piece of awe-inspiring beauty coming down from the wall like a wavy waterfall.'

'I know, I know the one you mean,' Jaggi chuckled.

'Looking back, I remember sometimes I used to stand there a long time and admire the exquisite beauty of those pieces. Often tried to imagine the time, the hard work, patience and skill that went into creating those masterpieces. A friend once told me that most of the work was done by highly skilled craftsmen using just their hands and two or three simple instruments. No machines of any kind were used. As soon as the showroom managed to sell one, another took its place without any loss of time. Often it was equally beautiful, equally eye-catching. Often, even more fascinating.'

'It seems your magic carpet has brought back the years that had rolled away from us,' exclaimed Jaggi, eyes looking down in front of him as though one of those beautiful carpets lay there at their feet, tightly rolled up, hiding the vanished years in its folds.

Sagar took another measured swallow of his drink and, shifting the crystal tumbler from his right hand to his left, delicately wiped the corners of his mouth with a finger.

'Just out of interest, or call it idle curiosity if you like, do you sometimes wonder what happened to the SS Roma, God bless the ship and all those who sailed in it, including a lot of us from India?' Jaggi asked him, rather unexpectedly.

Sagar fell into thinking, hand on his chin.

''I mean whether the old girl is still tramping the high seas, taking passengers from Europe to Australia and bringing them back from Australia to Europe, or has she reached its journey's end? You know, taken out of service by its commercial masters?'

Jaggi had to wait a while for a reply from Sagar because his attention was deflected by a man with a huge belly, a thatch of silver hair and large popping eyes who had suddenly broken into a bhangra dance routine and was throwing his arms about in the air with careless abandon to demonstrate some finer point about the Punjabi hip-hop or maybe was just trying to regale those standing close by and howling and hooting with uproarious laughter, a clear indication that a good time was being had by them all.

'There's no doubt in my mind, not even a tiny flicker, that the Roma's days of wine and roses ended years ago. It's a nailed-on certainty that it has been consigned to mothballs,' returned Sagar. There was a total lack of concern in his voice.

'You really think so?' asked Jaggi, his head going back a little.

'You see, in today's globalised world there's a lot of competition from airlines. Air travel has become so commonplace. It's cheap and within easy reach of most people. On top of that more and more new, low-cost operators are springing up everywhere and every year. In fact, I wouldn't be too far out if I said there are more planes in the sky than clouds.'

Jaggi gave an amused nod.

'Then, of course, you have also to take into account the changing habits of the travelling public, the increasingly fast pace of modern life, not to mention the new inventions and innovations aimed at saving people time and money.'

This time a series of silent nods from Jaggi.

'Frankly, I wouldn't be surprised at all if the steamer has been sent to the knackers' yard and dismantled for its metal … tiny pieces sold as scrap to merchants who specialise in buying and selling that kind of material. Old passenger liners usually end up that way when they reach the end of their working life. I know it's not a pleasant thing to say but that's their fate.'

'You surprise me,' said Jaggi disbelievingly, feeling a tinge of sympathy with the ocean liner on which he had spent a fortnight, an important fortnight, of his life. And a real life-changing fortnight it turned out to be, because it was as a result of the time spent on that ship that he was where he was that night, thirty-four years later.

'Not only that, you see, the Roma must have put on a fair few knots on its clock and become something of a financial liability. Old ships, like old people, I'm sure, need a lot of care and looking after.'

'Do you seriously believe that?' A shadow of disappointment passed over Jaggi's face.

'Oh, absolutely. I'm in no doubt at all on that score, my dear fellow,' Sagar declared confidently. 'The sort of busy lives we lead these days, who has the time to spend over a fortnight at sea travelling from India to Europe and double that from Australia and New Zealand when you can cover that distance by air in a day, or even under?'

'I suppose you are right. It's really a long time since we walked the planks of the Italian liner in Bombay … and, frankly, quite a lot can and does happen in that time.'

'You see, these days whatever field of enterprise you choose to follow, commerce, politics, sport, or whatever, competition is inevitable. It especially applies to business. Competition comes not from one or two sources. Oh no, from all directions and it can be, well usually is, hellishly intense. Brutal, I should day. In today's business world, as soon as the starter's gun is fired you start to hit your top speed and keep going, absolutely determined that it will be your chest that will break the tape at the finish line. You get the point I'm trying to make, my dear fellow?'

'Oh, yeah,' Jaggi nodded. 'Crystal clear.'

'You have to be the absolute best,' Sagar pressed on. 'That's a very important requirement. There is no other way. Being second-best is no good because, whichever way you look, it is not the best. It is second. And as for also-ran, well, it's pointless, really. If you want to know my honest opinion, whatever the nature of your enterprise, victory is an absolute must. And I'm not talking here of victory for victory's sake, or for the sake of glory, but for sheer survival. Only total success counts. It's a big wide, carnivorous world out there ... believe me ... dog eat dog, big fish swallow the little fish.'

'Pity really. Because, when all is said and done, the Roma, in my opinion, was a good ship ... an excellent ship,' Jaggi shook his head, regretfully, having decided in his mind that the ship was no longer in existence.

'Oh, on that I couldn't agree more with you. Remember the spectacular V-sign it used to make as it sliced through the shining water? I was so fascinated by it when I first caught sight of it. Watched it for hours the first couple of days. Back then on the boat, I used to think it was an auspicious omen for me. Y'know, luck-wise. V for victory and all that. A bit superstitious, I must admit, but there it is.'

'And the ship was manned by some very fine young men. One or two of them, I have to confess, had a keen eye for the female of the species on board but then sailors the world over are known for that, aren't they? And to be Italian on top of that!'

'Oh, they surely were,' Sagar smiled and gave a naughty wink.

'Looking back, I can't help feeling that the Roma deserved a better fate than what you say it got in the end. It should have been put to pasture off the Neapolitan Riviera, under blue skies, in lemony sunshine. Better still, converted into a seat of learning for marine biologists or turned into some sort of floating institution, such as a water sports centre, imparting knowledge and skills on surfing, snorkelling, scuba diving, etcetera. There are plenty of other kind of things, like deep-sea activities.'

'Why not a casino?' suggested Sagar, light-heartedly.

'Why not, indeed. Or a school for teaching opera – the Italians are well known for that sort of thing, aren't they?'

'Oh, they are. A prison, maybe?'

'Perhaps a floating hotel or hospital … a museum of sailing boats, perhaps. I mean something of value … something worthwhile, of integrity. And if it's still battling the high seas, heaven protect its stern and prow as well as its starboard and port sides. It had brought you, me and the rest of the cast present here from India to Europe … and, it has to be said, in fairly good style.'

'Oh, I agree with you there. In think that journey must rank as a high point in its history.'

'High, did you say? In my opinion it was the highest point in its sea-faring days. Easily, man, easily. Let's admit it, in all modesty, once it had successfully done that, what else was there left for it to do? So, well ...' and he gave a happy chuckle.

'Mmm, with that, I suppose, it had achieved its moksha. Buddha attained his nirvana under a tree and the Roma attained its when it docked in Genoa and disembarked us at its journey's end.'

There was a short pause as they gave each other a warm, friends-for-life smile and wondered what to touch on next. Both were enjoying each other's company and the conversation was going swimmingly well.

'This yacht of yours,' Jaggi resumed, after coughing as discreetly as one does in a library or theatre, 'is really something, a beauty.' He made a hand gesture to indicate the décor, the valuable paintings and the eruption of flowers in crystal vases on every table. 'Following the suggestion you made in your speech, I decided to treat myself to a quick tour, aided and abetted, of course, by one of the members of your staff, a thoroughly helpful fellow. I put all sorts of idiotic questions to him and he answered each and every one patiently and in some detail.'

'That's his duty. That's what he gets paid for,' Sagar said, somewhat brashly.

'Still, I would say he went beyond the call of duty in dealing with me.'

'Anyway, I'm glad to know that someone took up the offer,' Sagar added, smiling with pleasure as well as pride. 'Yes, she's not bad at all, the yacht, seen from any angle.' He drew himself to full height as he glanced about him.

'Very impressive. Looks a recent acquisition to me, judging by its excellent condition. Am I right in thinking so?'

'You could say that,' replied Sagar. 'Three years next August. Of course it was new when I took possession of it. Always fancied one of these for myself after watching those beautiful things bobbing about on the river or sailing, majestically on the high seas in the Hollywood movies of the fifties and sixties. I'm sure you would remember them if you were a fan of English films of that era?'

'Oh, all too vividly. Bogart, Gable, Peck, Brando, Holden either at the helm or as love-struck passengers, engaged in courtship rituals with their female co-stars.'

'I used to see those films in Connaught Place cinemas. I'm sure you do remember the picture houses that showed Hollywood and British films, Regal, Plaza, Odeon and Rivoli? There were also one or two others that screened them.'

'Yes. The Race Course cinema was one of them. Quite often I used to cycle there to catch the early morning show on Sundays. There, English pictures were shown at reduced rates. I think it was something like ten annas at full price and five annas at cut-price. Must confess, with more copper coins than paper money in the pocket it suited very well.'

'Ah, yes, looking back now, I do remember the Race Course cinema, although I must admit I went there no more than two or three times in total. I was absolutely mad about English films in those days. It was almost like an addiction, really.'

'It's the same with me. Many of the films seen back then are still blu-tacked on my mind. You see, there was no TV in those days and, like most people of our generation, I needed my fix of entertainment. So it was first day, first show, first row, right at the front. My proud boast was that I was the first to see the film before those who were sitting comfortably in their box seats or up on the balcony.' Jaggi had a nostalgic grin as he recalled the time of his young days.

'So, as it happened, after the boat journey from India, I made myself a promise. Well, several in fact ... a sort of wish list, if you like. And there, right at the top, it was that I would treat myself to a yacht if I came into money. Not ordinary money. No, can't buy yachts with it. But serious money.'

'And you have,' Jaggi said, affably.

Sagar offered no reply but a long and lazy, satisfied grin that spread across his face said it all for him.

'Being a boat lover, you must have thoroughly enjoyed every minute of the trip from India?' asked Jaggi.

'Why, didn't you, my dear fellow?' A quizzical furrow cut across Sagar's forehead.

'You bet I did ... for the most part,' returned Jaggi. 'Although, I must admit, for the first couple of days I was suffering from an emotional hangover. You know, the wrench of separation from the nearest and dearest. I'm sure I wasn't the only one feeling that way.'

'You're so damned right,' added the host.

'Emotionally, it was a busy and difficult time. You know, all those heavy-hearted farewells to parents, close and distant relatives, plus goodbyes to friends from school and university days. On top of that, there was a stream of visitors, those who lived in the neighbourhood or further afield, to meet and greet.

Oh, the goodbyes had no end. Went on and on and on.'

Sagar smiled, understandingly, as if he had a parallel experience of his own to recount.

'Everyone went misty-eyed over your leaving and emotions ran high. Some eyes even had tears. Well-wishers doled out their last-minute advice and other gems of wisdom. Seeing them in their melancholy state had its effect on you and you, in turn, got melancholy. They brought personal mementoes and other tokens to remember them by and you reciprocated by giving them your own keepsakes. They put their hand on your shoulder and asked you to stay in touch and you put your hand on their shoulder and promised to stay in touch with them. And as if all that wasn't enough, there were also fancy females who came to wish you all the best for the journey ahead and life generally after that, you know, that kind of stuff. And finally, bidding adieu to the land of your birth, Mother India!'

'Oh, I know, the emotional mill ground on and on and all we could do was to put up with it, each of us in our own way, some with a smile on the face, others a little wet in the eye.'

'Again, towards the end of the voyage, reality parachuted in with a bump. Not only that, it brought with it a whole gymnasium of apprehensions, doubts and uncertainties. These background worries were there in everyone's case but towards the end they came to the fore. Every migrant group, I suppose, has to face a few hurdles going round the track first time, I know that, but in our case there were additional obstacles because we were from the new Commonwealth, which was not the same thing as the old Commonwealth.'

'You're right. Absolutely right,' Sagar agreed.

'It was natural, therefore, for the nerves to jangle a little even if yours were made of steel. You know, things like finding a job, a roof over the head and coping with isolation, homesickness. These things were bound to affect us more because we were stepping out of the family fold for the first time. Well, in the beginning at least. Britain of the sixties was very different from Britain of the nineties, wasn't it?'

'Oh, absolutely. Chalk and cheese, I'd like to think,' Sagar said, emphatically.

'Reality has a nasty habit of sticking its nose into everybody's dreams, doesn't it?'

'And, if I may add, its sense of timing is also very poor.'

'But the big fat middle between the beginning and the end of the trip was fantastic, full of fun and frolics. Brilliant, absolutely brilliant. I had a thoroughly good time and enjoyed every minute. Just loved everything happening on the boat. Don't know about others but in my case, for the first time, I had wine with every meal for a fortnight. One day it was red, the next day I chose white.'

'Didn't they have the third variety?' Sagar beamed a humorous grin. 'Looking back years later, though, I must say the quality of wine was nothing to write home about. Reasonable house stuff and that's all.'

'Mind you, we were hardly wine connoisseurs in those days. Besides wine, there were many other things going ... all those fancy dress parties, floor shows, late-night movies, not to mention the simpler pleasures of life, such as music of the sea in your ears, taking in the ocean breeze on the upper deck or leaning on the rails to watch the sun go down in a blaze of the most spectacular colours that you ever saw. The flying fish jumping in the water, the smell of salt in the nostrils, the occasional, sea-spray on the face. These were a favourite pastime of mine on the ship. Also, as you just mentioned, there was the majestic V-sign the steamer left behind as it sailed relentlessly on. You must really like the sea?'

Sagar smiled and rubbed his chin as he mulled over his reply. But before he could collect his thoughts, Jaggi put in, 'If not the sea then the things that sail in it?'

This time he chortled.

'I think most inhabitants of Planet Earth have a fascination for the sea. Some have a lot, others to a lesser degree. I must confess, I am no exception to that rule.'

'Among Indians, it's especially true of those who live in the north of India. Maybe because they are so far inland, hundreds of miles from the nearest sea coast. People living close to the sea have an altogether different relationship with it. It's on their doorstep and this gives them a special affinity with the sea. They swim in it, pedal in it, dip their toes in it. On its beaches they go for their morning and evening stroll, especially those with love on their minds. Sometimes they're hand in hand, other times with a supportive hand behind each other's back. They know the sea is there – always has been and always will be, like the sun, moon, stars and other natural phenomena.'

'You're so right, Mr …'

'Bali. Jagmohan Bali,' Jaggi briskly supplied.

'Well, well, well, what do you know!' Sagar's eyes widened with interest mixed with surprise. 'You're not going to believe it when I tell you that my association with this name goes back a long time. To my early school days, in fact. I had a friend who had the same forename. His surname was different, though ... Luthra. Yes, that's right, Jagmohan Luthra. For years we were close friends and bosom buddies. Langotia yaars, as we often say back home in India.'

'Really?' Jaggi said, sharing his surprise, as his face lit up with a huge smile.

'This chum of mine lived a long way from the school. His father was a high ranking government official, like Deputy Secretary or Under Secretary, because the family house where they lived was a massive, ivy-draped place, more like a mansion, if you ask me.'

'Really?'

'It had a walled garden full of fruit trees, mangoes, guavas, pears, you name it. Then there were flower trees, low-hanging vegetable trees and ornamental trees, lovely to look at. Sometimes, mostly on Sundays, I used to go to Jagmohan's house to play badminton with him on his lawn. Also football, occasionally. You know, the sort of football schoolboys play. Tell you what? On that turf I must've scored more goals than any football player at Old Trafford.' And he laughed out loud at his own observation.

'Mind you, Jagmohan was quite a popular name in the forties and fifties ... like Neil and Rohan are in Britain these days,' Jaggi went on to explain. 'I mean, in our school alone, oh, there were no less than a dozen Jagmohans. One or two in each class. Even three in the odd class where, to avoid confusion, they were known by their surname. Mehta, Gupta, Malhotra and so on.'

'It was a pity that when our school days came to an end our education took different directions. He chose to study science for his first degree while my mind was set on accountancy and I opted for that. So we went our separate ways like most kids do and with that our school friendship ended. And as time went on, it was a case of out of sight, out of mind. We lost touch with each other.'

'The story of everyday school friends,' Jaggi heaved a sigh.

'Super chap, this Jagmohan fellow. Very studious and exceedingly bright. Passed every exam first time, and always with grades that would make any parent feel proud. Seldom came first in the class but, I must say this of him, he was never out of the top five. That's consistency, I would say.'

'Certainly is,' agreed Jaggi.

'Pretty good in the sports department, too. Wherever he is at this moment in time and whatever he's doing in life my good wishes are with him. In our circle of close friends we used to call him Jaggi. Strictly outside school boundaries, I mean. School rules forbade pupils to use nicknames, pet names and other shortened versions on the premises.'

'You know what? Most of my friends also call me Jaggi,' offered Jaggi.

'Now is that so?' asked Sagar, even more surprised.

'And they can call me Jaggi anywhere they like. No rules, no limits, no boundaries of areas. Jaggi, I think, is the most popular diminution of Jagmohan.'

'I suppose it is, come to think of it.'

'Some of my English friends and a number of colleagues at work have shortened it even further … Jag.'

'You know why? Because Jag is something they're familiar with … in an altogether different context, needless to say. And Jag is a lot easier for the English to get their tongue around.'

'Anyway, what does it matter? As they say, what's in a name, it's the quality that matters.'

'Absolutely,' and he produced one of his biggest smiles. 'By the way, while you were having a nosey around the place you didn't, by any chance, meet anyone you knew well, or even vaguely, on the Roma?' Sagar inquired and began to study his guest's face for reaction as well as clues.

There was a sizeable pause as Jaggi seemed to dig deep into his memory. Then, a note of disappointment in his voice, offered, 'I'm sorry to have to tell you, no one.'

'Not even a single individual, for goodness sake?' exclaimed Sagar, with a sardonic, low-key laugh, unable to contain his incredulity. 'Surely ... the odd one or two, if not more.'

'Not even a single bod, I'm afraid. Sorry,' replied Jaggi. 'Everyone seems to have changed beyond recognition. And, frankly, who can blame them? It's a long, long time ... nearly half a lifetime. But tell you what, I haven't given up completely ... at least not yet. There are a fair few people I'm still to meet, so there's always a chance ... you see, it's hard to take your mind so far back in time.'

'I know, I know,' agreed Sagar, without any hesitation at all. 'And, as I said, people do change in their appearance as well as in their outlook. Sometimes so dramatically that even they're surprised at the pace and scale of change. I bet you didn't recognise me either, did you?'

'And you didn't recognise me, did you?' Jaggi demanded good-naturedly in return.

Both laughed out loud simultaneously and half-extended a friendly hand in each other's direction for a touch.

'So what have you been up to all these years and what are you doing at present?' Sagar asked.

'I take it you mean professionaly?'

'Of course, my dear fellow.'

'At the moment, like most of your other guests, I'm doing the thankless job of making a living.'

'And what thankless job is that?' smiled Sagar, jovially.

'I'm a chemical engineer by profession and presently I'm working as an analytical chemist. What about yourself?'

A smile spread across Sagar's face lazily as he looked over at Jaggi. It was the first time that evening this question had been put to him by a guest. Everyone else was aware that their host was wealthy. In fact, colossally wealthy. Collectively, they were so dazzled by his success plus the champagne party he had laid on for them that they took it for granted that he was a businessman of one sort or another and forget to ask him how he had made his millions ... or billions.

With a discreet cough, Sagar began, 'I belong to the breed commonly known as entrepreneurs. I mean, basically buying and selling things.'

'Oil, commodities, real estate, metals, currencies, anything in particular or a combination of them all?' inquired Jaggi.

'Companies,' came the laconic reply.

'Companies?' Jaggi was taken aback by the word. In his world of science and scientific research he had not come across anyone who bought and sold companies as a way of making a living. He gazed at his host with his mouth open.

'Why are you looking me like that for, my dear fellow?' chortled Sagar. 'We're living in an age where anything is possible and everything is up for sale. Of course, at a price.'

Jaggi took an enormous gulp, 'Mmm.'

'In today's global market, the east is never east, the west is never west and the twain are at total liberty to meet. Often do. I'm talking here purely from a commercial point of view, you understand,' Sagar explained.

'I do,' offered Jaggi, hesitantly.

'You see, as I often say, from Mussoorie to Missouri … South China to North Carolina, the world is one big marketplace where every day people buy and sell all manner of things – arms, aircraft, cars, clothes, chocolates, newspapers, insurance … you name it. Almost everything, really. I buy companies and I sell companies. As simple as that. The product, I admit, one could argue, is a little unusual. That's all. But then, I don't see it that way.'

'Forgive my ignorance, but I thought that, in view of the millions and billions involved, buying and selling companies was the exclusive preserve of large institutions with banknotes in boxes the size of shipping containers … I mean the larger companies buying smaller ones.'

'You know better now, my dear fellow,' Sagar smiled even more broadly, pleased to have enriched his guest's knowledge in the field of high finance. 'If you want to sell something and I want to buy that thing, well, there's a marketplace. And this marketplace has virtually no boundaries and it's not restricted to companies with budgets running into millions of pounds and dollars. No, nothing of the kind.'

'Really?'

'Yes. Any ordinary mortal can take part in the process of acquisition and disposal, like any big conglomerate. There is, however, one stipulation and that is, in order to buy and sell, they must have the necessary wherewithal. I mean money. After all, as you very well know, to play roulette you have to have your chips.'

'Or to have with your fish,' Jaggi said, light-heartedly.

'Yes, that's another interesting way of looking at things,' Sagar said, with a grin.

'Well, well, in this fast-moving age of ours there's always something new to learn every day, if one is willing?' laughed Jaggi. 'We live and learn, as they say.'

'Indeed there is,' nodded Sagar. 'Of course I'm talking here purely from a business point of view.'

Jaggi gave an understanding nod, then, 'I'm not trying to pry or anything of the kind, just out of curiosity, how many companies have you bought and sold since you ventured into this field of enterprise?'

A pause followed in which Sagar seemed to mull over something in his mind. Then, scratching his chin thoughtfully, he said, 'Quite a few in my time, I must say. Don't lose sight of the fact that I'm a bit of a johnny-come-lately in this game.'

'You mean to say you went into this … whatever you call this business … only after coming to this country from India?' There was a hint of surprise in Jaggi's tone.

'You're absolutely right,' answered Sagar. 'I had no experience of this business in India. Like a number of young men on the boat I had just come out of university. Yes, I earned my stripes here in this country. It was after coming here that I decided to explore this field. Not straightaway, you understand, but a lot later.'

'The British went to four corners of the world to build their empire, you came from one of those corners to build yours in Britain,' Jaggi said with a hugely amused smile.

'Umm ... something like that, you could say,' Sagar said, his face beaming over his achievement.

'It must have been quite an eventful journey, from nothing to everything?'

Sagar gave a nod. 'The first thing I had to do after arriving here was to get the local qualification under my belt so I could practise in my field, which, I think I've already told you, is accountancy.'

'A lot of us had to get the local qualifications. That was the first requisite. We were all in the same boat, as it were.'

'And none of us had the magic bullet or family connections. Hard work was our weapon.'

'We are all agreed on that,' Jaggi acquiesced, readily.

'So once I was over that hurdle, I needed to gain some experience,' Sagar continued with his explanation. 'As it was, that proved to be something of a half-marathon than a sprint. You see, I didn't know anyone who could guide me or smooth things over for me. Neither did I have a family fortune or illustrious ancestors with strong City connections. Also, I didn't possess any fancy title ... Lord Sagar of Moneypur or some other Sir blah, blah.'

'Your spirit of enterprise surely deserves one now ... or more than one, in fact.'

'Oh, I don't know about that,' Sagar flashed a self-satisfied grin. 'That's something for the future. Who knows? We shall see.'

'So it's fingers crossed time?'

Sagar gave a huge non-committal shrug and continued, 'Coming back to where we were … for a while I worked in a securities firm in the City. The next step – more like a leap, if you ask me – was to set up on my own and that was, as you can well imagine, a really long and bumpy road. It took a lot of investment in time, effort and, of course, money. I had to raise it myself. For that there was a lot of groundwork as well as homework to do. So, all in all, it took a long slog for years and years to get to the point where I could do what I always wanted to do.'

'I'm sure. It always does. Before everything else, you've got to build a sound economic base for yourself,' said Jaggi, in order to show his understanding of the basic economics. He had done that himself.

'First and foremost, I'd say,' Sagar concurred.

'Each one of us was treading that path in our own way and at our own pace. Some fast, others slow.'

'Going back to your question of the number, I have so far bought more than twenty companies. Twenty-two to be precise. A healthy mix of small, medium and large operations.'

To Jaggi the figure meant nothing, one way or the other. He didn't know what to make of it and repeated the figure twenty-two under his breath, but it was loud enough to reach the attentive ears of his host.

'So, what do you think? In your opinion, is twenty-two too high, too low or just about right, all things considered?' asked Sagar, smilingly.

Jaggi mulled over his reply for a while, scratching the back of his head to coax out an answer. But he failed to come to any positive conclusion and so he replied, 'It's difficult to say what the answer is. To be quite frank with you, I don't know what to make of the number. It's not everyday essentials we're talking here. Of those things I've some idea but of companies? No, I haven't got the vaguest clue.'

Amused. Sagar grinned. 'It's only a guess, for heaven's sake, I'm asking you to make … gut feeling, you know, that sort of thing. So just give a figure. You don't have to hit the bull's eye, man.'

'I know but, you see, it's as difficult as predicting which way a coin will fall in a head-or-tail toss. It will have to be a wild, wild guess. I think that wild guess is that it's a fairly high number, especially since, as you say, you were a late comer to this game. It's not a simple and straightforward business, I take it, buying and selling companies?'

'It's anything but simple and straightforward. Assessing the true worth of a company you want to buy is not exactly an exact science,' Sagar explained in a lecturing tone. 'And that makes thorough preparation absolutely essential. There's a popular saying in business circles that the buyer has need of a hundred eyes, the seller of but one.'

'I can one hundred per cent believe that,' Jaggi nodded.

'This preparation I call home work. A company is not an item of everyday use. There everything is black and white. You hand over whatever you're selling to the customer with one hand and collect its price with the other – in whatever shape or form it's offered. Not so long ago it used to be just cash or credit. Now you have several other methods of payment, debit or credit cards, cheques, hire purchase, postal orders, you name it. A quick "thank you" and the deed is done and dusted. The whole thing is over in a few seconds, minutes at the most. Simplicity itself.'

'I'd suspected from the very beginning that the business of buying and selling companies is far more complex than seems at first glance. Not simple and straightforward,' returned Jaggi.

'Simple or stress-free? Ha! You can forget it. You'll find it hard to believe when I tell you that at times negotiations can become fiendishly complex. In fact, sometimes they can turn ten times more than complex and can drag on for months at a pace that can only be described as balls-achingly slow. One query followed by one reply. Another query brings another explanation. It goes on and on endlessly. You could say it's like playing a game of ping-`pong in ultra-slow motion.'

'I quite believe it,' offered Jaggi.

'In fact, in extreme cases, a tremendous amount of hard work has to be done over years before you get the seller's signature where you want it. Touch wood' – for a fraction of a second Sagar looked around for something wooden to put his hand on but then touched the table nearest to them whether it was made of wood or not – 'so far in my experience, such devilishly difficult cases have been few and far between. Extremely rare, in fact. Believe me – and I'm not exaggerating here one bit – at times the whole acquisition process can get mired in the tedious nitty-gritty of a million details.'

Jaggi winced, then nodded to indicate his acceptance.

'A lot of painstaking work is then needed to plough through the whole process, checking, cross-checking, going through eye-wateringly small print with a fine tooth comb, reading between the lines, making sure there're no nasties left to cause problems later on. Naturally, all this requires extremely painstaking work by top business brains, teams of crack financial and legal experts and sector gurus.'

'Do you still own any of the companies you acquired?' inquired Jaggi, with a degree of interest.

'Of course not. Didn't I say that I buy and *sell*? I don't buy companies for my own amusement, Jagmohan. May I call you Jaggi? It's more personal, less formal. Besides, Jaggi has a friendly ring to it. Takes me right back to my school days. A look-back within a look-back. It's a little like those Russian dolls, full of themselves. Open one and there is another waiting for you.' Sagar laughed happily and threw a small, friendly punch in his guest's direction, barely touching him.

'Two for the price of one ... or buy one and get the other free,' said Jaggi and beamed a smile.

'Jaggi, I don't own any company except, of course, the one that buys and sells these companies, if you follow what I mean. You could say that's my core company, the one I started with. It still retains its original brand name.'

'So you sold all those twenty-two companies that you bought?' Jaggi gave his host a quizzical look.

'Exactly. To firms that were interested in buying them and run them according to their own rules, taste and style.'

'I presume those who bought them are still running them, successfully or otherwise ... the way they fancy?'

'I've absolutely no idea what happened to them once they went out of our control. I handed over the keys and they transferred money into our account. My dear fellow, the minute you sell a company, your interest in it is over and done with. Full stop. Period. End of the story. You move on and focus your intents on the next venture, whatever that is,' Sagar said dismissively and shrugged his shoulders to underline his point.

Jaggi briefly studided his face.

'Let me give you an example,' continued Sagar. 'It's a bit like Mr Jagmohan Bali selling his highly desirable residence to a Mr and Mrs Smith. Once the legal formalities of buying and selling the des. res. are over, papers signed, contracts exchanged and the completion done, it's up to Mr and Mrs Smith to do with the property what they wish. They're its new owners and as such are at full liberty to tear it down and rebuild it anew, or leave the house as it is or, maybe, rent it out to someone or live in it themselves happily ever after. Mr Bali's interest in it is over and he moves on to a new property, possibly a more desirable residence in a leafy, tree-lined avenue. Mind you, when Sagar Associates – that's my core company – buys another firm it's not necessarily sold in the shape and form it was acquired.'

'You mean it's asset-stripped?' asked Jaggi, his tone accusatory as he gave his host another quizzical look of deep intensity.

Sagar squirmed at Jaggi's blunt observation. He gulped as he shot his guest the kind of hard look that is often reserved for a person who utters a swear word in polite company. In a flash his tone changed and he sniffed with indignation, real or pretended, and remarked, 'That's a term newspaper headline writers vulgarly use when they can't think of anything better to squeeze into their single or double column space. What I mean is that the company is divided into a number of parts and each part is then disposed of as a separate and independent entity. You get the point?'

Although he had made his position on the issue clear, a frown remained in the middle of Sagar's forehead. It was evident from his disapproving look that he was unlikely to field any more questions on the subject. Jaggi, however, didn't like his question being shrugged off so lightly. Besides, he found Sagar's explanation opinion-based and far from convincing.

A blast of cold wind swept over the impressions the two men had been gathering of each other. From the opening minutes, it had so far been a warm and friendly encounter.

As a period of uncomfortable silence ensued, Sagar scratched the underside of his jaw to give himself time to turn something over in his mind. At the same time it also gave him and his guest an opportunity to reassess each other in their eyes. Finally Sagar broke the silence by turning from general to specific. He asked Jaggi where in Britain he was living.

'Stockport, up North. It's near Manchester, that way,' Jaggi's finger pointed upwards.

'Oh, I know where Stockport is,' Sagar declared like a proud boast and smiled at Jaggi with thin, compressed lips. 'Mind you, if somebody had put the question of Stockport's geographical location to me ten minutes before I boarded the Roma in Bombay or during the whole fortnight I was on it, I would have been completely at a loss for an answer. The chances are I would have scratched my head and said it was a northern suburb of Sydney or a southern district of New York. But among the many things that life has taught me in this country are the whereabouts of Stockport.' This time Sagar raised a finger pointing upwards.

Jaggi gave an amused laugh.

'As a matter of fact, I've been to Stockport quite a few times, the most recent being, oh, believe it or not, only six or so weeks ago, two months at the outside. We have an interest in the area, you see,' Sagar said with a wink as though he were teasing his guest over some secret that he had no intention of divulging to him.

'Aye, I've got a bottom of our stairs!' said Jaggi, in an impeccably registered Lancashire accent. 'Wish I had known that. I would've met up with thee on me home turf, me own territory.'

'My dear fellow, it's my territory, too,' replied a bemused Sagar. 'But purely from a commercial point of view.'

'Well, well, well, talk of the world getting smaller. Both of us from the north of India and we wind up five thousand miles away in the north of England. Now wouldn't you call that an amazing coincidence?'

Sagar gave an indication of a nod.

'How did you find the town?'

'What do you mean *find the town*?' Sagar asked, giving his guest a look of part surprise, part inquiry.

'The place, I mean, the weather and, more importantly, the people who inhabit that town.'

'Oh all that kind of stuff, I see what you mean.' The look the tycoon gave Jaggi seemed to suggest that for him these things had little or no interest.

'You know, in the South people help you cross the road, in the North they cross the road to help you.'

'Unfortunately, my dear fellow, I wasn't there long enough to cross many roads. Or any road. But is that the reason you chose to put down anchor there ... and, of course, marry a local lass?' asked Sagar, his brow lightly furrowed.

'I dare say it was a contributory factor, yes. Anyway, why live somewhere else when you can be among friends in the North?'

'As a matter of fact I was in Stockport because my core company is in the process of extending its operations in that neck of the wood.'

'Really? In Stockport?' Jaggi's eyes got jammed on Sagar in total disbelief.

'Don't look so surprised, for goodness sake,' answered Sagar, his friendly tone now restored, almost to the level it was before. 'If there is a business opportunity in an area, no matter how small and how far, no self-respecting businessman will turn it down without checking it out. One has to feel the pulse, you know. That's the most basic requirement. We are forever looking for fresh opportunities wherever they may be. It was in this connection we were there. To have a nosey about.'

'Which part of Stockport?' asked Jaggi, full of curiosity.

'Frankly, I can't remember the exact location, Jaggi,' replied Sagar, 'but we're in the process of acquiring a chemical operation in that area.'

'A chemical operation, did you say?' This time surprise was writ large on Jaggi's face.

'Yeah, yeah. Nothing on a scale that would make one run to the nearest telephone kiosk and tell mum about it, if you see what I mean?'

'Didn't know you were into chemicals as well. I'm an analytical chemist by profession as, I think, I told you earlier.' Jaggi said, looking pleased with himself.

'It's just a small operation. Frankly, between you and me, at times I wonder why I bother with outfits that size.'

'And where does this operation fit into your business strategy?' inquired Jaggi, with casual interest.

'Strategy? I'm sorry, I don't get you.'

'I mean, what you plan to do with it when you've acquired it?' demanded Jaggi, with a bright shrug.

'At the moment I have no idea,' replied Sagar.

'Oh, I see.'

'Jaggi, my dear fellow,' replied Sagar patiently, looking at his guest with a sweet, tolerant smile, 'the industrial sector in this country is a shadow of what it used to be once. It has been on a downward slide for years and years. There's no need for me to spell that out to you as, I'm sure, you are well aware of that yourself. In fact you have been a witness to a large part of it.'

Jaggi narrowed his eyes, thinking.

'All the bellwether industries that put the "Great" into Britain are no longer to be seen. Coal, shipbuilding, locomotives, where are they now? Finished. Gone. More or less consigned to the dustbin of history. Gone, too, with them are things like training, innovation, ideas. Blue-collar manufacturing has been completely hollowed out.'

Jaggi gave a thoughtful nod.

'Like, for instance, how many cars made for British companies do we see on our roads now? Other productive industries, such as iron and steel, are limping along, stumbling from one crisis to another. A finanacial sneeze anywhere in the global market and we catch pneumonia.'

'I'm aware of all that. Tales of decline in these industries were commonplace twenty, thirty years ago. The situation, as you say, must have gone worse since then. A plant shutting down with the loss of six hundred jobs here, another closing with three hundred there is an everyday newspaper headline these days.'

'Frankly, I won't be surprised if manufacturing of any meaningful kind comes to a complete stop. And, mind, I'm not looking far, far away in the distance.now.'

Jaggi attempted a sardonic snort to indicate that he found the whole idea preposterous.

'No, I'm serious, my dear fellow,' Sagar assured his guest, with a restrained smile. Then he stroked and scratched his chin and continued, 'Things that bore the stamp of *Made in England* are no longer made in England. In fact, it wouldn't surprise me one bit if that stamp is made in some other country, like China, Japan or Hong Kong. So it's not a question of if, but when.'

'I know we are not a major producing nation any more but to say …' Jaggi left the sentence incomplete to indicate that he was unwilling to entertain the idea any more in his mind.

'On the contrary, my dear fellow, we're a passively consuming society of products that are made thousands of miles away from Birmingham, Bradford, Sheffield and Leeds. The Industrial Revolution may have started in these parts and turned Britain into the workshop of the world for more than two hundred years with its goods sold in every corner of the globe. But, I'm sorry to say, that era is over. The centre of gravity has shifted from these shores, probably never to return. Don't get me wrong, it doesn't give me any pleasure to say these things to you or anyone else but that's the reality. I'm sure many others share with me this pessimistic view of things.'

'If what you're saying is true, I find the whole thing terribly, terribly sad,' Jaggi went on in a preoccupied voice. 'I remember when I was a wee lad in India we had a gramophone in our house ... one of those huge, wind-up music machines. His Master's Voice or something like that. A little metal plate on one side of it gave notice of its origin. It was made in Middlesex. As kids, we used to have a giggle over that place name.'

'Oh really? How droll,' Sagar exclaimed, with something of a giggle himself.

'Yes, I remember it clearly. The gramophone used to take needles that were placed in the groves of the records once the machine had been fully wound up. It was the needles that produced the sound. Tiny needles, the size of pine kernels, perhaps a bit shorter. They came in little tin boxes, about a hundred of so in one box. After three or four plays they were discarded. It seemed such a waste to me. They were so cute. I always had one or two stuck in a corner of my school bag. Quite pretty to look at, really.'

Sagar flicked a quick glance at Jaggi's glass and thought it needed replenishing. Glancing around for service, he caught the eye of a waiter and signalled with his fingers for two drinks ... in fresh glasses.

'You on scotch, I take it?' he asked Jaggi after he had ordered, without inquiring into his preferences.

'Oh, yes. But, I think, I'm all right at the moment,' Jaggi reassured the host.

'Nonsense. We've been chatting for quite a while and in all that time I haven't seen you touch your drink once. You can't nurse one drink all night, my dear fellow. You're not driving tonight, for goodness sake, so relax. Take it easy. In any case, on this yacht I may not be the captain but I'm in charge. What I say goes. We're having a party here, y' know.'

'That's why I'm here, all the way from ... you know,' and once again he pointed a finger upwards.

'Good. Good. That's the spirit. I like it. I like it. Now where were we? Yes, Jaggi, when we acquire a company the objective is to make it profitable if, for whatever reason, it's not. If, on the other hand, it's making money, then our aim is to increase its profitability, maximise it, before it's disposed of. Well, as a matter of fact, we do keep an acquired company for a time but only until it's absolutely necessary. Not a day under, not a week over.'

'In other words, until you can make some money out of it,' demanded Jaggi.

'You're right. Entirely right. Look, let's be honest about it, you don't go into business to sharpen your intellect or broaden your outlook. Do you, my dear fellow? You go into business to make money. Pure and simple. That's your principal objective.'

'Generate bucks?' Jaggi grinned.

'The more the merrier,' Sagar smiled profusely.

'I suppose if money is your sole objective, everything else is of secondary importance.'

Nodding, Sagar went on, 'When a company is being disposed of, it is in the best interest of everyone involved that it's sold in one piece, as a single entity, if you like. That way, there's less aggro all round. But, unfortunately, sometimes, whether we like it or not, one is forced to break it up.'

Thinking, Jaggi just stared at him.

'Look at it this way: an organisation is the sum total of its parts, some of which, as a purchaser, I want, such as the core business, the brand name and the premises. There are other bits and pieces that do not interest me and I want to get rid of them, even if, at times, it means I need to incur a loss. Now, there are people out there in the market interested in the parts that I do not want to keep. So we get together and start negotiating about the price, terms, conditions and so forth.'

'Which means the company is chopped up? Surely, that can't be in the interests of the people who work there ... the employees, I mean?' Jaggi uncomfortably shifted his weight from one leg to the other.

'I wasn't talking about the employees here,' Sagar replied swiftly, staring at his guest penetratingly.

'Why, who is this *everyone* then that you've just referred to? Are the employees not in the buying-and-selling equation? Are they not people?' Jaggi demanded, a trifle stiffly.

'Of course they are. Undoubtedly they are,' Sagar replied. 'A talented and motivated workforce is a highly valuable asset to a company. An organisation should be truly proud of it. I accept that without any argument at all. But, sorry to say, when it comes to buying and selling a company, the role that employees play is strictly limited. It is high finance that calls the shots at that stage. That, my dear fellow, is the hard reality of the situation, if you see what I mean.'

'But it's also their future we're talking about here, is it not?' Jaggi looked challengingly at his host, his eyes a little stoked up.

'That may well be the case,' Sagar squirmed, with a touch of indignation. 'I don't deny it at all. Like other assets and liabilities, the employees move over to the new owner. Organisations, companies and businesses, no matter how large and successful, are just commodities to be bought and sold on the open market at market price. Isn't that what capitalism is all about? Bid the right price and you get what you are bidding for, bid the wrong price and someone else takes it.'

The drinks arrived and Sagar picked up one and with his eyes urged Jaggi to take the other.

'Good health,' Sagar raised his glass to Jaggi.

'And yours,' responded his guest.

It was clear to Jaggi that there was something very hard-headed about his seemingly pleasant and genial host. What shone on the surface had been put there and was not part of the original package. Nonetheless, he pressed on, 'What you are saying may be okay in theory, yes, I've no issue with that. I also accept that that's what capitalism is about. That's what it preaches and that's what it practices.'

'Good. I thought you'd see it that way,' Sagar gave a tiny crack of a smile and took a sip of his drink.

'But don't you think somewhere in this narrative there's also a human dimension? People who work for the company day after day, year after year, slowly building it from the ground up, brick on brick, layer by layer, with their industry, their experience, their application ... taking it forward, adding to its value with their labour, making it competitive, successful, in a sense, making it what it is.'

'Look, let's be clear here, there are plenty of rules and regulations to safeguard the employees' interests,' Sagar flicked up his eyebrow rather crossly and began to study Jaggi's face as one studies a jigsaw puzzle, trying to understand it, work out which piece will fit where. Then, after a pause, he resumed, 'Pension, superannuation, holidays, sickness benefits, severance packages and all that ... a whole raft of measures to ensure their financial security. They are protected from all sides.'

Jaggi found the argument far from convincing. Despite all these provisions what he was experiencing at his workplace did not come anywhere near that and it was preying on his mind. Employees, who had given their one hundred per cent to the company for years – in many cases their whole working life – were living in fear of being declared surplus to requirement and shown the exit door.

And the story did not end there. They had fresh nerve-racking pressures, both spoken and unspoken, put on them each day. There was a growing feeling among them that they were being treated as no more than a necessary nuisance, to be tolerated while they had utility for the company and then thrown on the jobless scrapheap at the first opportunity if it made the bottom line attractive.

'The safeguards you just mentioned and other compensatory measures are all right in their place but they are a poor substitute for well-appreciated, appropriately rewarded full-time work,' Jaggi added.

'Again, I'll be the first to admit that,' replied Sagar. 'A job is a job. Of course it's all-important, especially if you've trained and worked for years and not known anything different. But let's not lose sight of the fact that, just as an employee has his interest close to his heart, the employer has his to look after. I hope you understand the point I'm trying to make.' Sagar gave his guest a cold, somewhat harsh look.

'Clearly. Of course, each side has.'

'In a vast majority of cases, these interests do not come into conflict with each other,' Sagar went on. 'If the company's doing well, notching up successes, one after another, the employees duly reap the reward from that. They get their share of the benefits in the form of pay increments, promotions to higher paid positions, annual bonuses, improvements in working conditions and so forth. You see, it's good all round if the relationship between the employees and the employers is a happy, harmonious one ... there's total engagement on both sides and profit levels are high.'

'But when the interests come into conflict with each other, which side is the winner then?' demanded Jaggi, looking Sagar in the face.

'Well, we all know the answer to that, don't we?' Sagar said, almost instinctively. 'Obviously the one that has the money muscle.'

'That means the employer?' persisted Jaggi.

'Naturally,' Sagar scoffed, with a wry shrug.

'I'm sorry, you'll have to forgive me for asking these questions. They affect me personally,' Jaggi added, pursing his lips as if the admission had a bitter taste to it.

'Ask away as many questions as you like, my dear fellow, I'm all ears.' The tone of Sagar's assurance brought a pleasant change in the conversation. 'If I can in any way be helpful to you, what greater pleasure could there be for me? After all ...'

'Thank you so much,' Jaggi said, eyes looking down.

'Not at all. Go right ahead.'

'It's a bit like this: just recently, the place where I work has been savaged by a thousand job cutbacks, forced early retirements and, in a number of cases, compulsory redundancies. Hardly a day goes by without one thing or another of that nature cropping up. And it's all being done in the name of restructuring, modernising, improving efficiency and what have you. So, you can see, it is causing a lot of distress and …'

'Judging by what you've just told me, your organisation is presently going through a bad patch. It's nothing new. This sort of thing happens from time to time to the best-run companies in the world, take it from me. Bad patches, occasional trips and little stumbles are all too common. After all, you can't go all the way in shining armour, as the saying goes.'

Jaggi gave a small nod.

'One thing is certain and it is that somebody somewhere in your organisation has not been doing his or her job properly. You see, it is lack of good management that nearly always plays a role in a company's fading fortunes, its decline. You have to keep an eye on the ball all the time. Twenty four hours a day. And by that I mean on the bottom line.' Sagar shook his head, partly in sympathy with his guest and partly as his own general observation.

'Maybe you're right, someone hasn't. But surely the bottom line isn't the only line in the world?' Jaggi felt irritation rising again inside him but tried to keep a lid on it, forcing a smile in order to conceal his true feelings. But the change had made itself clear on his face.

'Not in the world, certainly, I agree with you. But in the business world that's the only line that counts at the end of the day. People may say what they like against making money and, believe me, a lot of them do – especially those who have not been successful at doing it themselves – but there's no getting away from the fact that ultimately it is profitability that determines everything. Success, expansion, modernisation, stability and what have you, they all have their roots in profits, don't they? Anyway, these are topics you can think about till you have a thumping headache and talk about till you are blue in the face and still not reach any definite ...'

Sagar broke off at this point to attend to a tub-guts. A large man with a big paunch and a shambling gait, he had made great efforts to conceal balding patches in his head with an artful comb-over. The man had materialised out of nowhere, merrily swaying on his feet, a big, lop-sided grin plastered across his face. He had been lapping up the hospitality, especially the liquid variety, like he had never heard of the word *hangover* in his life. He staggered up to Sagar to shower on the host his own brand of gold-plated praise on the success of the party.

The host, in turn, thanked him and patted him on the shoulder softly, smiling in acknowledgement.

'On that Italian ship, I remember, it took us a fortnight ... or something like that, to get from there to here. Now, what do'ya think, ha'many days it will take if I went to your captain and told him to poosh the yacht out and take us all, each one of us on this pleasure boat, from here to there?' he asked, releasing a booming, boozy laughter.

'I don't know,' Sagar answered, with a brief, hollow laugh. 'I have no idea whatsoever. You see ...'

'But, aah, it's your yacht, isn't it, and he's your captain, isn't he?' interrupted the tipsy tippler.

'Yes, absolutely true. I do plead guilty to that charge. It is my yacht, you're my guest and he's my captain,' Sagar answered, jovially.

'Seeee there,' he looked mightily pleased.

'But, you're not going to believe it when I tell you that I've never been able to spend enough time on it to figure out such things. Besides, thing is, we may have enough beds, toothbrushes and face towels for all the guests but I am not sure about the position in the piano bar. I get this feeling that in the drinks department we may be a bit short on supplies. Certainly for a five thousand mile trip.'

The fellow stumbled back a little, horrified.

'For return journey, undoubtedly, we can pick up supplies from Bombay. I'm sure you'll agree with me that a cruise without booze is no cruise at all. Wouldn't be much fun, would it, without our beloved old *lalpari*?'

'Corse not ... corse not,' the man went on, his tongue heavily marinated in twelve-year-old scotch and slurring words that came out of his mouth. 'What's a crooze without booze?' he pressed his drink tightly close to his chest. 'You are absolutely right ... one hundred per cent right. And what do you think our chances are of meeting a supply ship on the way?'

Sagar chuckled. 'Sorry to say, not very bright,' he said, making an exaggerated gesture of apology to his guest. 'Scientists may have invented many things, including techniques for refuelling planes in mid-air. But, sorry to say, they haven't come up with ways to supply ships with twelve-year scotch in mid-ocean.'

'And ... and what about pirate shippps?' the guest slurred.

'Pirates never give, dear man. They take, especially old rum and old scotch,' offered Sagar, looking at the drunken guest like he was talking to a dumb child.

'And then there is the question of ice to cool the firewater sherbet,' the man clapped his left hand over his eyes and chuckled.

'Yes, ice may also prove to be a problem if you are a scotch-on-the-rocks person,' Sagar grinned brightly, now fully enjoying the interaction with the boozy guest.

'In that case, shall we scup ... scupper the whole idea of a return trip to India? Throw it overboard into the river ... whoosh! Whoosh! There it goes to the bottom of the water,' the man made a motion of chucking something heavy with his hands and then broke into the sort of high-decibel, discordant laugh that makes the furniture vibrate. 'Cold and shivery outside, cosy and warm inside, isn't it? Drinks, friends, music ... just like the times when songs were songs and music was music.'

'Well, if you ask me, although we have moved a long, long way from vinyl to the download era, songs are still songs and music is still music. The tastes, one has to admit, have changed,' Sagar patted the guest softly again. 'But that's something happening in all fields, all over the world.'

'You think so?' the guest gave the host a quizzical look. 'You seriously think so?'

'I do. Believe me.'

'Now let me tell you something,' he leaned towards Sagar and brought his mouth close to his ear, 'you don't know this because no one has told you. I am a music buff ... of Indian film music. Take it seriously. Very seriously, I do,' he stressed.

'I've no reason to doubt that for a second, let me assure you,' replied Sagar, politely.

'No, no, I am not kidding you. I'm seriously serious. If I was to go on Mastermind programme –

not that I'm thinking of putting myself into that black leather chair any time in the near future – that would be my favourite subject, my specialist subject, you understand?'

'Now is that so? You take your music that seriously?' Sagar said grinningly, as if love of Indian film music was a kind of medical condition and the man was suffering from it.

'Oh, yes, sir, Imagine me in that chair. The spotlight shining on me. Watched by millions of people on television in their homes, answering questions about songs sung by Lata, Mohammed Rafi, Mukesh, Manna Dey, Asha Bhosle, Kishore Kumar, and, yes, also the poets who gave the words to the songs, not to mention the music directors who directed the music. I have said it before and I'll say it again to let you gentlemen know that the heyday of Bollywood film music was the fifties and sixties and no one is going to tell you or me otherwise.'

'If you feel that strongly about it, well, who am I to argue with that? You are the Mastermind material. Obviously you know more than me,' Sagar conceded readily, partly because his interest – and therefore his knowledge – of film music was very limited and also he wanted to avoid getting into any argument with his merrily high guest.

'Ah, the good old days!' he sighed weightily. 'In my view it was the golden age of Indian film music. No question about that. It was music to satisfy the soul.

'You mean music had charms to soothe the savage breast, as the saying goes?' Jaggi asked.

'You've hit it right on the head. Absolutely right... a real balm for the soul even if it was not wounded and needed no treatment. The tunes had all the good qualities that first rate music should have. There was melody and there was harmony ... and rhythm, of course. Sometimes two out of these three things and ...'

'Sometimes all three,' Sagar supplied.

'You are right. Absolutely right, I tell you. The lyrics were also superb. Words and music came together like perfect partners. I tell you ghazals were like the cries of wounded gazelles and touched you right in the heart. And you know why? Because they came from the head and hearts of poets who thinked before they inked. Now that's what good poetry is all about, no? Full of feelings, meaning, subtlety, and ...and...'

'Oh, I agree with you there,' Sagar consented, as his interest in poetry, like his interest in film music, was minimal.

'What they came up with were songs that made you listen to them ... sometimes even forced you to sing or hum along with them, whistle at the minimum. Tell you what? I do miss that era. Music in Bollywood now is shockingly bad. There's no other way to describe it. So bad as to make you lose all interest in it for ever. A silly tune going on and on endlessly and hundreds of people jumping up and down to it like they had ants in their pants and were biting them you know where. Now you tell me would you call that music? More like a Niagara Falls of noise ... crashing drums and soulless synthesisers,' and he began to laugh in a guttural gargle.

Sagar grinned humorously and Jaggi laughed out too.

'Seriously, it is musical vandalism ... if you want to know my honest opinion. No imagination, not a scrap of it. Worst of all, there's no sound of Indian instruments in the tunes. Just imagine, Indian music without Indian instruments. No sitars, no sarods, no sarangi, no shenai … no nothing. Only synthesisers, drums and guitars and ... and…'

'You're probably right. I'd say give me Madan Mohan any day of the week.'

'Or Anil Biswas, S D Burman, Roshan, Salil, Naushad any day of the year. They were real maestros of their craft. Great, just bloody great. If these maestros were to come back and hear today's so-called music, they would drop dead,' the man said, 'drop dead straight away … bless their musical souls.'

Jaggi nodded.

'You know, sometimes it makes me want to cry over the state of today's film music. But then I think to myself the tunes are not worth sobbing over. So why waste my precious tears.'

The man looked a trifle puzzled over something as he pursed his lips and hiccupped loudly. Shaking his head one moment and nodding it the next, he seemed between two minds whether to agree with his host or reinforce further his own point of view. Both were, in essence, expressing the same sentiment, only in different words.

In the end, the jolly good fellow muttered and mumbled something incoherently in his mouth, waved to Sagar, mangled Jaggi's hand in a crushing shake and, grinning like a Cheshire cat, trotted off in the direction of a group of men who were rocking with laughter over something funny, waddling unsteadily as if he had one leg shorter than the other.

'What an interesting chap,' Sagar exclaimed as soon as the man was out of earshot. 'Amazingly sure of his music.'

Sagar flicked a glance at his wrist-watch, looking as though he had a time plan in his mind for the party and was checking to make sure that everything was going according to it. However, time plan or no time plan, he was also aware that his raison d'être that evening was to play the perfect host to the scores of people he had gathered on his yacht, including the one who was standing in front of him, eager to ask questions, keen to say his piece.

Another photographer skidded to a halt near them, focused his lens on them and waited for their conversation to get going again, a hand to move a little this way or slightly that way, a neck to tilt or a smile to break out on the face, anything to make the moment "live" and worth recording.

Both Sagar and Jaggi were conscious of his presence and that had broken their chain of conversation. Each was thinking of making a fresh start. In the end, it came from Jaggi.

'So when do you reckon you're likely to visit Stockport again?' he asked quite politely.

'Soon, I hope. It all depends on when the formalities of taking over the plant are finalised. This time I shall have to find out in a more detailed way what Northern Chemicals is like. Whether it's …'

'Northern Chemicals did you say?' Jaggi was blown over by the shock of it and moved a step back. 'You … you mean to say …' he couldn't complete the sentence. His eyes lit up with the news. His hand itched to congratulate Sagar.

'Why, yes, what's so strange about Northern Chemicals?' inquired Sagar, reading the sudden change that had come over his guest.

'That's where I work. Given the place the best years of my life, twenty three of them, coming up to twenty four next June, with an attendance record that would make anyone scream with envy.' Jaggi's voice shot up a couple of decibels. One or two heads turned in the direction of the two to see what the excitement was about. 'Well, well, well, I never! Northern Chemicals, fancy that! You its new owner. It certainly feels beyond belief. The businessman I've met and known personally ... who even entertained me on his luxurious yacht,' he pressed on excitedly.

'New owner if all goes well ... and only for a while.' The coincidence was not without its surprise on Sagar.

'Oh, I'm sure it'll all go swimmingly well for you,' Jaggi assured Sagar. 'You'll do splendidly, just splendidly.'

'Oh, it's so nice of you to show such confidence in me. As a matter of fact, I'm pretty sure myself that we will do all right in this case. The negotiations are at an advanced stage now. So, all being well, any time now ... really.'

'I'm thrilled to bits to hear that,' returned Jaggi. 'A fellow Indian and also a fellow-traveller on the ocean liner that brought us to GB, the new owner of Northern Chemicals! A wonder of wonders! Can't wait to see the look on the faces of my colleagues when I tell them about you first thing on Monday morning.'

'Some time ago we sought clarification on a number of points. While the management of the plant has cleared up most of them, I think one or two still remain.'

'Is that so?' Jaggi looked somewhat confused.

'We also asked for certain changes to be carried out which, I'm sure, they have either already completed or are in the process of carrying out. You see, having the right chemistry between the buyer and the seller is very important. In the case of Northern Chemicals, I must say, we've been really lucky. So, now it's crossed fingers and hope for the best.'

The word *changes* coming from Sagar immediately struck a chord with Jaggi. As he absorbed the knowledge, his jaw dropped. It went down as far as it could. His expression became wintry, like the weather outside the yacht. The gloss of pleasant surprise evaporated and the high spirits in which he was floating a few minutes ago plummeted like a lead balloon.

So, thought Jaggi, this was the man who had been inflicting the recent upheaval on the company where he worked. He made it sweat in a way it had never done before. Also, he was the one responsible for giving the workers sleepless nights.

The finger pointed firmly at him for the turmoil, the brain-bending stress and the jangling nerves of the employees. The suspense whether they would have a job when they turned up for work at the plant for the morning shift. The most conscientious of employees reporting sick when they would have liked to come to work. Colleagues eyeing each other suspiciously, talking in hushed tones, exchanging little bits of information or trying to hide if they had any, well-founded or rumoured. Secret conferences held in locker rooms. People undervalued and alienated and their morale right down in their boots.

All this was in preparation for his takeover of the plant. So he could breeze in, take over the operation and sell it at the first opportunity, either as a single unit or piecemeal. But whichever method he chose to dispose it of, he was certain to make a whooping big profit for himself.

'You know all those things you told me about buying and selling, you're not going to do that to Northern Chemicals, are you?' Jaggi inquired, with undisguised anxiety on his face, after he had digested the takeover information and its implications.

There was an awkward silence during which the business baron's eyes remained firmly focused on Jaggi's face as if he had started speaking a foreign language that he did not understand a word of.

Then, instead of answering his guest's question, Sagar arched his brow and demanded, 'What's so special …?' but he abandoned the sentence midway and embarked on another one. 'Say that again … I'm not sure I understand what you mean.'

He had understood every word all right, Jaggi was sure, but he was trying to evade giving him a straight, truthful answer. Jaggi attempted to force a smile but his lips rebelled against him, as did his mind. So, with a short intake of breath, he pressed on, 'You are not going to break up the company and dispose of each part separately?'

For a moment, Sagar looked to be deep in thought as he considered his response, then added, 'Let me assure you that at the moment all our energies are concentrated on one and only one thing and that is acquiring the operation. So, as you can well imagine, we haven't given much thought or, in fact, any thought, to what we are going to do with it. All I can tell you this evening is – and, I think, I have made this point clear earlier on – that I do not buy companies to win hearts and minds of other people … or to get my name into the record books. It is my way of making a living, you understand?'

It was amply clear to Jaggi that his chemical works would go the way the other twenty-two companies had gone that the buyout baron had so far acquired. 'In other words it means that one of these days, in the not too distant future, the "For Sale" sign will go up outside the factory entrance? That will be the general direction of travel, am I right in assuming that?' an urgent inquiry hung in Jaggi's eyes.

Sagar heard this without listening and let it pass like it hardly mattered to him. His face reflected no emotion.

'It's a simple question,' persisted Jaggi, his voice rising. 'A yes or no is all it needs.'

Again, Sagar did not reply for a while. Then, looking quite uncomfortable, he dredged up a heavily-layered smile and said, 'I know it's a simple question but as I told you, as things stand at the moment we have no plans whatsoever, long-term, short-term, or any term ... about the future of the plant. We haven't even acquired it yet so you can see how can we think of what we are going to do with it? Once it's ours and we have complete control over it then, and only then, can we be sure about what we are going to do with it. I hope I've made myself sufficiently clear to you.'

'We?' Jaggi screwed up his face in an impatient inquiry. 'Are there other people also involved in it?'

'Of course, there are ... members of my team. You don't think I operate in isolation, do you?' Sagar gave Jaggi a glaring look. 'I have teams of experts working for me. They advise and guide me at every step of the way in negotiations, from the first tentative inquiry to the finalisation of the deal ... I mean until it is signed, sealed and delivered.'

'But as the head of the parent company the final decision rests with you, doesn't it? So, whichever way you decide, it'll be sold off in the end, won't it?'

demanded Jaggi, his voice quivering and serious to the point of being solemn.

'That, I must say, is a fair assumption.' Sagar gave the tiniest of nods, his eyes matching the hardness of Jaggi's look.

'I work there,' explained Jaggi, his right hand tapping his chest. 'Not only me but scores of others … one hundred and fifty five of them. That's where we earn our livelihood. It's our world. Please don't do it … please, please, I beg of you.' His voice was charged and heavy with emotion. All sorts of thoughts were going through his mind, conjuring up images that were disturbing, upsetting and sad. It looked certain that his career was no more than a handful of wage slips away.

But it cut no ice with him and a stony silence was all Jaggi got in response to his passionate appeal. Sagar seemed totally unconcerned if the man facing him and one hundred and fifty five of his colleagues would lose their jobs because what he was bound to do sooner or later.

A distance of two hundred miles from his company's headquarters in London made them look no more than a number, a figure of 156. Sagar did not know any of them, except the one standing opposite him. He had never seen them, or met them. Nor had he spoken to any of them. So what did it matter if they were in work or not?

'Please, please, don't do it. I urge you,' Jaggi begged again, desperation beginning to creep into his tone. For him these were painful words to utter. They made him feel diminished in his own eyes for he had never thought he would say them in a million years. But at the same time he was aware that if he did not do so himself now and convincingly, no one else would do it for him.

The time at his disposal was short, no more than a few minutes, to try to appeal to the better side of the man's nature, if he had one. Once the party was over and he was off the yacht, the opportunity would be lost for ever.

'A good businessman never allows sentiments to interfere with his commercial interests,' the buyout baron said flatly, not a hint of concern in his voice. 'The two, I'm very sorry to say, are entirely separate issues. If a horse makes friends with grass, tell me, what is he going to live on, eh?'

'Please don't do it ... I implore you from the bottom of my heart, please, please ...' Jaggi pleaded again, as his eyes searched the money mogul's face for the slightest sign of understanding. But he found none. Jaggi's words had clearly failed to have any effect on him.

'I understand your position,' Sagar assured him, with a smile. But for Jaggi that smile had a black border around it. Whatever it was in that smile, arrogance, pity, ridicule, it told him that the business baron had little interest in other people, especially those pleading a cause.

'If, as you say, you understand my position then your decision over the future of the plant should reflect that understanding, shouldn't it? The livelihood of a lot of families depends on your decision ... on what you are planning to do,' said Jaggi passionately. He could hear his own voice and once again it did not please him at all. It was an awful feeling.

In response, a brittle laugh and a shrug with a suggestion of helplessness was what he received from his host. A few moments passed and Sagar added, somewhat coldly, 'Let me be quite frank with you, Mr Jagmohan Bali' – formality that had gone out of the window just a few minutes ago was back with a bang and had brought with it a huge change in his tone. 'Quite frankly this is neither the time nor the place to talk about things connected with work routine. That would be talking shop, don't you think?'

'That may be so, yes, but ... but it's also about the future of the place where I've worked for years,' Jaggi said, with an emotional stammer in voice. 'Its closure would mean a future without work ... without anything to look forward to, without hope. You ... you're the one who can do something about it. Your decision is important ... all-important. It means a lot to a lot of working people.'

But, unmoved, Sagar continued, 'Look, after an absence of years and years a chance has come our way to get together again. Quite luckily, I'd say. So let's make the most of this opportunity. Let our hair down ... enjoy ourselves ... have a great time. Talk about our experiences in this country ... you know, the big and small things of life, and find out about the progress we have made here. Most of us have done well, of that there is not the slightest doubt in my mind, or anybody else's mind present here. It is an ideal opportunity to toast the successes we have notched up. I think we'd be quite justifiable making a good, old-fashioned song and dance about it. To be frank with you, that was the intention behind organising this bash.'

Insensitively, he raised his glass while his guest was in a state of palpable unease.

'You see, it's a celebration of our achievements here ... a tribute to ourselves, if you see what I mean.

It's high time we got ourselves noticed in the corridors of power, wherever they may be. At the moment we have no presence, no voice, no say there. Against many odds we've generated prosperity for ourselves and, of course, the country. Don't you think we have something to shout and shriek about? I do. Oh, yes. We deserve a pat on our back ... and a real, hefty one. If you think someone else will do it for us, you're gravely mistaken. We have to do it ourselves. We have to make ourselves visible. Raise our profile, do our own PR ... stand up and get ourselves counted, individually as well as collectively as a group. Let's, therefore, beat our drum, loudly and proudly. There's no shame in it. No shame at all.'

Everything in Sagar's demeanour suggested inflexibility. He appeared to regard the subject of his upcoming takeover of the chemical plant as closed. There was no more to be said, no more to be heard.

He looked about the place casually to indicate that he had given Jaggi enough time and attention and so he was going to move on to other matters he had on his mind, such as meeting other guests, especially those he had not said hello to and shaken hands with so far. In his estimation there were still a few left.

'You ... you want me to have a good time on your yacht knowing full well you're going to take over the company where I work and break it up. You ... you want to end my working career ... take away my livelihood.' Jaggi shot back as his voice got bitter and his eyes gave Sagar a hard, accusing look. 'Not only from me but also from those with whom I share my working life?'

He wanted to say more, much more ... that if the businessman was following a course of action that he thought was best for him, others, too, had a right to carry on with what they thought was best for them. He should not play God with their lives and snatch that right from them.

'One hundred and fifty six people,' wailed Jaggi, struggling to keep his emotions in check, 'who, come rain or shine, get up early every morning, make themselves presentable to go to work so they can give their families a decent standard of living and send their kids to good schools for their education ... the sort of everyday, honest, hard-working men and women that any country would be proud of ... all unaware that, hundreds of miles away from them, somebody is hatching plans that will turn their world upside down.' The words were more spat out than spoken.

Sagar was visibly shocked by what sounded to him an outburst. And all this taking place on his own yacht, his own territory, struck him like a whiplash. For a time he stood rooted to the spot, without moving a muscle in his body, his mouth coiled, holding back words he had on the edge of his tongue. Tension between them rose and they stared at each other intensely, their looks bordering on the hostile.

'You should keep the people who work there ... harness their skills, use their talent and experience. You just can't throw them on the scrapheap,' Jaggi said, with an emotional charge in his voice. His hand reached for Sagar's coat sleeve and took hold of it in one final gesture of desperate pleading. 'You can't ...you ... I beg of you, beseech you, appeal to your inner kindness to please think of those who work there. It is ... it is ...'

Three men standing in a group a couple of yards away broke off their conversation and turned their attention to the two. It was apparent from the expression on their faces that they were concerned about what was going on between Sagar and his guest and wanted to know if they could be helpful in any way. Jaggi flashed a reassuring smile and gestured to tell them that everything was fine, just fine.

When Jaggi's eyes returned to his host, he found his face thunderous. His lips were curled in a sneer and his unblinking eyes were fixed on him and flashing cold steel. Taking all the time in the world, he calmly brought his gaze to where Jaggi's hand was touching him. It lingered there for a time and then, equally slowly, moved back to his guest's face. The message was clear: remove the offending hand off my coat sleeve forthwith.

Realisation also hit Jaggi that, although he had screamed his primal scream as forcefully as he could, it was all in vain. He had been banging his head against a steel door that was closed and firmly locked. A little nervously, he obeyed Sagar's unspoken command and withdrew his hand from the host's coat sleeve.

Jaggi stepped back, regretful of the indiscretion – if indiscretion it could be called – to plead with Sagar. But his eyes did not give up their search in Sagar's face for an answer, maybe a word of assurance of some kind. After all, it was only a matter of time that the tycoon's signatures would be on his pay cheque, if only for a short time because, in keeping with his past practice, he was bound to offload the operation on to someone else after giving it his own brand of treatment.

Sagar flicked his finger at the spot on his coat where Jaggi's hand had come into contact with it as if the touch had soiled it, left a dirty mark there. Briefly, they looked each other in the eye, Jaggi's making one last desperate, desperate appeal while Sagar's were turning it down with a mixture of pity and contempt for overstepping the mark on his own yacht.

All Jaggi's entreaties to Sagar had failed. The tycoon's tightly coiled face was making a clear statement. It was saying to the visitor to the yacht, 'Tough luck, fellow, you and your colleagues at the chemical factory for whom you are so fervently pleading do not figure in my plan for the works ... or any other plan for that matter.'

With a sharp jerk that seemed to say to Jaggi he did not belong there, he wheeled round and strode off without any more words. It left Jaggi feeling crushed.

Some thirty four years ago the two had set off together on their great adventure but ended up so far apart from each other. One had chosen to remain in the south of the country and amassed untold wealth. The other had headed north and life had turned its back on him.

Jaggi stood there alone, a maelstrom of emotions churning inside him. The bitter taste of the meeting with the businessman was in his mouth. From the innermost core of his heart, he wished he had not heard of Sagar or set eyes on him. He resolved never to see him again, even if it meant crossing a busy multi-lane highway to avoid him.

The party was in full flow but Jaggi had lost all interest in the jolly goings-on. It mattered not a jot to him what festivities were planned for later that evening and the next day. Any further participation by him was simply unthinkable. What he had witnessed was more than enough. It was a revelation and a half. His first regret was to accept the invitation to attend the swanky shindig. The second was not having a change of heart later. But holding an investigation into the whole thing was a pointless exercise.

He resolved not to take any further part in the celebrations the minute the yacht's cruise was over and the guests had disembarked. He would, he decided, hop into the first taxi that came along and head straight to his hotel. There, he would gather his belongings and go as far and as fast as he could to sever all links with Sagar. Goodbye to the boat people! Goodbye to their reunion. Goodbye to its organiser!

He did not want to be on the yacht any longer. His emotions were running high in all directions and he was struggling to keep a grip on them. The blood in his body was in ferment. He felt at times that a vein in his forehead was throbbing at a rate he had not experienced in a long time. He seriously regretted that the world he inhabited was also home to Sagar and others of his ilk.

Jaggi knew that the mega-millionaire was driven by his own agenda. His inner eye could see large, five-column photographs of Sagar surrounded by his fawning guests splashed across newspapers with captions written by pun-prone sub-editors, like,: "Long time no sea ... Indian high-flyers celebrate their success in Britain aboard millionaire yacht" or maybe, under a photograph of Sagar along with some of the invitees with raised glasses, "Cheers! India's boat people toast their success on business tycoon's luxury yacht."

In his incensed state, Jaggi began to dissect the no-expense-spared shindig that the businessman had thrown. He thought it to be no more than an exercise in concealing, quite cleverly no doubt, the real motive behind the bash. If you peeled back the layers of the onion, his seedy self-interest became quite clear.

While he took centre-stage at the party he hosted, winning hearts and minds of his countrymen with open-handed hospitality, cosy informality and friendly chatter, and, in turn, earned heaps of praise and adulation from them, the real rewards for his investment would possibly come in a different setting and at a different time.

Jaggi argued in his mind that the tycoon's whole demeanour, the way he dressed, greeted his guests and generally conversed with them showed that the main objective behind the party was to bang the drum of his *own* stratospheric rise in the money league than the modest achievements of his countrymen.

He had made money in tens of millions in a country where money was the principal yardstick to measure someone's true worth. It was quite possible that a huge chunk of it was sitting in some offshore tax haven. No wonder then that the single-minded pursuit had moved from wealth to status and influence. A natural progression, he supposed. He had described it himself as "raising the profile and getting noticed."

Lavishing hospitality on a handful of people, getting them pleasantly tipsy and bestowing on them benign smiles was a small price to pay for getting his picture in the newspapers and raising his public profile. And the way he kept harping on the phrase *the boat people* wasn't that a masterstroke? It was the stuff of headlines in Helvetica bold letters! The newspapers would swallow it like a boneless kipper.

Time after time, off the yacht as well as on it, Jaggi had been told that it was Sagar who had dreamed up the reunion idea. Therefore there was no doubt that he was the one who had put the whole package together and presented to the world in a really clever way.

The smokescreen of charm and generosity he had thrown around the get-together camouflaged his true motive so well. It had been woven so tightly as to be invisible to the unsuspecting eye.

The businessman's next move, Jaggi theorised, would be to donate an impressive amount of money to whichever political party was in power towards their election fund, followed doubtless by a high-profile gesture like sponsoring an arts project or a sporting event. This would lead, in turn, to an honour of one sort or another – depending on the number of zeroes on the donation cheque – possibly a peerage or a knighthood with an opportunity, for what it was worth, to have a mild flirtation with politics.

Right doors would doubtless open for him and, being well-connected by this time, he would make the fullest use of the chances within his grasp by promoting his commercial interests or whatever other sordid scheme he had in his mind. It had all been done before. Many times over, in fact. Stories about this toxic mix of big business and politics were rarely out of the newspaper headlines.

But as far as Jaggi was concerned, after the death of his daughter and the absence of his wife from his life, work was his only hope. But Sagar was determined to snatch that away from him and leave him on the jobs scrapheap. When Jaggi had distilled these thoughts in his mind, it was easy for him to broach the blame for his undoing on the tycoon.

Whenever and wherever there's a major financial scandal in the world, thought Jaggi in his torn state of mind, it's a near-certainty there is an Indian behind it.

If not, there is bound to be one lurking in the shadows, anxiously waiting for his chance. They have a reputation for that. Not only do they easily get mesmerised by money, they are also overcome by a manic desire to possess it, get rich at the speed of an Olympic sprinter. With some, it is a way of life, turning everything into a piece of commerce.

Plenty of examples flashed past his mind and he thought that Sagar's name would go on that list one day. And that day, he felt, would come sooner rather than later.

The yacht cruised on for another couple of hours, the celebrations got merrier and noisier and the music louder but Jaggi took no part in them. Neither did he see the organiser behind them. It was not difficult for him to stay out of Sagar's sight, because there were many people – nearly everyone in fact – who were so lubricated that they were now ready to engage in a conversation with anyone and talk about anything.

When The Indian Princess docked at Westminster Pier, Jaggi was the first to disembark. However, he did not have to bother about looking for a taxi because the limousine that had brought him to the pier in the evening was there to take him back to his hotel. As soon as the chauffeur saw him get off the yacht and come on to the pavement he nimbly stepped out of his vehicle and opened the door to him.

'Had a good time, sir?' he asked Jaggi, by way of greeting.

'Yes, thank you,' replied Jaggi, nodding as he hurried to get inside the limo from the cold.

'Turned a bit chilly,' the chauffeur continued amiably, getting inside the car himself.

'Yes, it was quite chilly there, too, on that thing, if you ask me,' Jaggi pointed in the direction of the yacht with a finger.

The journey to the hotel was made in silence.

Back in his hotel room a few minutes later, Jaggi gathered his belongings, chucked them willy-nilly into the suitcase and slammed the lock shut on it. Within no time at all he was ready to leave for the trip home.

As he came out of the hotel, a gust of icy wind slammed into him and sent an enormous shiver down his spine. His body felt a tremor and his teeth chattered. The night was dry but bitingly cold.

Jaggi stopped, put the suitcase down and buttoned up his overcoat right up to the top. Next, he pulled out the gloves from his pocket and put them on.

But the bitterly freezing temperature did little to cool his temper. Inside, he was still seething and experienced a strange buzzing sensation in his temples. A choking feeling gripped his throat like a pair of hostile hands and made him slow down a little. Without stopping, he loosened his tie so he could breathe more easily.

Moving to the edge of the pavement, Jaggi looked around for a taxi. Three flew past him in quick succession but they were all carrying passengers. Moving to the kerb, he raised an anxious hand to two others that followed but it was the same story again. So, instead of standing there in subzero temperature, he decided to make his way to Euston station on foot.

He knew it was not all that far. Twenty minutes at a brisk pace, maybe half an hour if he took it leisurely. The walk, he thought, would also warm him up. He would, however, keep an eye for a taxi and if one came along with its meter up he would flag it down.

That settled, Jaggi took a deep, determined breath and, shifting the suitcase from one hand to the other, moved forward.

He pressed on, eyes a little watery, not only because of the freezing gusts that kept tearing into him. Jaggi tried to take his mind off what had happened a few minutes ago on the yacht but could not. The thoughts went round and round in his head as he took account of his life, his marriage, his work. All that brought him firmly back to the yacht, its owner and his planned takeover of the company where he worked. The failure to tear himself away from that added to his torment.

The streets were ablaze with lights and the traffic was flowing smoothly. Here and there a couple walked by on the pavement, clinging to each other with affection. Here and there a couple walked clinging to each other for warmth. A sniffly individual bunged up with a cold came towards Jaggi from the opposite direction, slowed down near him, sneezed explosively and then blew his nose into a paper hanky before continuing with his journey, breathing jerkily.

A young, black miss, twenty-something, with a marvellous head of Afro hair and body tightly squeezed into a black leather coat that came down well below her knees, was bellowing down her mobile phone and zapping around the pavement, working herself into a frenzy under a patch of yellow light. Her shouting was so loud it could be heard three blocks away.

Two men, happy in the face and gaiety in their gait, came striding up the road, talking in loud voices, laughing from time to time. A young fellow with three turrets of painted hair crowning his head, a nose-stud, earrings and several pieces of metal embedded in his face, dragged himself heavy-legged, staggering as if he had just been punched out of a boxing ring. His eyes were at half mast with drink and he was bending his body that was clad only in jeans and a jumper against the needle-sharp wind and the sub-zero temperature

Scores of cars, forced into idleness at red traffic lights at traffic junctions, breathed out the fumes of their impatience. As Jaggi passed by a takeaway, its lights went out and the shutters came down with an ear-splitting bang.

From a nearby street, large parts of which were blocked by yellow tape and plastic barriers because of the extensive repair work going on there, an ambulance came whooping out, missing by inches the warning signs and intermittently sounding its siren. It emerged on to the main road and veered by Jaggi. Seconds later, a fire engine screamed past him, lights flashing and noisy in its hurry. A police siren wailed in the distance for a moment and then went quiet.

In his disturbed state, Jaggi had under-estimated the distance between the hotel and Euston station. It was much longer than he had imagined and it took more time to get there. By the time he arrived it was twenty past one on the station clock and the last train for Stockport had gone long ago. The announcement board displayed the time and platform numbers of trains scheduled to depart next morning.

The concourse was deserted, except for a number of tramps, down-and-outs and other human debris. Their hair was heavily matted and on their bodies they wore scruffy overcoats. Hunched over in a corner, most of them were leaning against the wall.

With faces brutalised by excess of alcohol, humiliation and hopelessness and bodies all burnt out and coked up, these damaged characters had sought refuge there from the bone-chilling cold and the freezing wind that tore into their bodies despite the layers of dirt-encrusted clothes they wore. Three of them had their hands under their arms to keep them warm.

One was engaged in a furious argument with himself in a loud, angry voice. Another, with an unwashed beard appeared asleep in a sitting position, head bowed, chin nearly touching the chest and threads of saliva from his mouth dribbling down on to the floor.

One or two were concussing themselves into stupor, drinking from bottles they hid in the side pockets of their long coats. To them Jaggi seemed a figure of fun, all dressed up but going nowhere.

A scruffy, broken-toothed, rheumy-eyed wreck with deep hollows in his cheeks and loud, forked veins in his nose, took a swig from his bottle and turned his ravaged face to Jaggi. Slowly putting the bottle back into his pocket, he half-raised a hand, waved to Jaggi to come over.

He followed this gesture with a few unintelligible words which he spat out in a rough, pebbly voice. Jaggi turned to him but remained rooted to the spot where he was. A moment or two later the man beckoned him again, patted the ground near him and invited him to doss down there for the night. Jaggi shot another glance at him but did not move.

The man persisted with his invitation, this time accompanied by a toothless grin.

So this is where life had brought him, thought Jaggi and smiled. Jaggi always smiled.

Lightning Source UK Ltd.
Milton Keynes UK
UKHW041147021020
370905UK00002B/56